THE SCAVENGER HUNT

Kill or be Killed

THE
SCAVENGER HUNT

By

C.L. LOWRY

Creedom Publishing Company
Philadelphia, Pennsylvania

The Cataloging-in-Publication Data is on file at the Library of Congress.

Creedom Publishing Company

Visit the website at:
www.CreedomPublishing.com

ISBN-13: 978-1-946897-05-3

Printed in the United States of America
10 9 8 7 6 5 4 3 2 1

For,

CIVILIZATION

THE SCAVENGER

[RECAP]

The mission seemed as if it would be an easy one. Searching for supplies and survivors was much different than creeping around, trying to avoid everything and everyone. Kyle had grown accustomed to having Candice and Marcus by his side; it felt a bit awkward to be out on the streets without them. They stayed behind with Dannie, to figure out what their assignments will be in the organization. Word got back to Micah about how Kyle snapped on Jin and Micah decided to recruit the man for Adina's search team. Riding around with a group of eight people seemed to be a lot more secure than his original group of three. With eight people, they would be able to cover more ground and their searches would be much quicker. Kyle sat back in the seat and checked out the scenery as the group caravanned in three different vehicles. Kyle rode shotgun in a beat-up Ford Explorer, which trailed behind a Chevy Silverado and a Saturn Vue. He was amazed at how much territory The Association was able to claim and clear out. As presentable as the leaders of The Association made their organization seem, Kyle got a bad vibe about them. Something was not sitting right with him, but he couldn't put his finger on it. There were so many questions left unanswered. The Association had no explanation for the innocent lives that were lost at the hands of their men.

After forty-five minutes of driving, the vehicles pulled over onto a deserted block. There wasn't a soul in sight. Kyle carefully scanned each home, and they all appeared to be undisturbed. His main focus was on the windows above, which is the vantage point he had when executing intruders. If someone was perched up in the window, his chances of returning fire would be higher than the other shooters he was accompanied by. All of the vehicle doors flung open, and men began exiting. No one left the Chevy, so only Kyle and four others hit the streets. Being the loner he had always been, Kyle began checking the vehicles on the street while the others began checking homes. "Let us know if any of those vehicles have keys in them. We can take them with us," the driver of the Chevy yelled out. Kyle nodded, confirming he acknowledged the order. He peeked in each vehicle, aiming his rifle and ready to fire on any opposition. If anyone dared to pop up from one of the seats, Kyle was ready to put them down. Each vehicle was mostly cluttered with trash and loose change. Three vehicles had the keys inside, and they would serve as nice additions to The Associations growing collection.

"Please stop. Why are you doing this?"

The desperate begging caught Kyle's attention as he peered over his shoulder to see where it was coming from. A middle-aged man was being dragged from one of the homes. Kyle's brows lowered as he saw how roughly the man was being handled. Being dragged by his legs, the man's back scraped across the uneven cement as the coarse ground ripped his skin. For an organization that was all about growing in numbers, they sure weren't treating the fragile man with much respect. *Who would want to join a group that roughs them up?* Kyle thought, remembering how sincere Micah seemed when discussing the organization's expansion plans.

"Who are —"

CRACK!

The man's statement was interrupted by the force of a baseball bat striking the back of his head.

"What the fuck are you doing?" Kyle raised his gun and aimed it at the bat-wielding man. With the slightest movement, Kyle was going to place a bullet between his eyes.

"Calm down dude. You are the new guy, right?" one of the other members asked, stepping between Kyle and his target.

Kyle didn't entertain the question; he just looked past the man's slim figure and had his rifle locked on his target's head. "Lower your weapon." The order forced Kyle to eye up the man that felt brazen enough to bark orders at him. He had no idea of what Kyle was capable of doing to him, or the skilled marksmanship that would lay him to rest. On the other hand, Kyle didn't realize he was eyeing up Wolff who was one of the organization's most loyal and dangerous members. The ginger male was hardly intimidated by the former vet's grimacing stare. His left hand had a strong grip on the gun he kept close to his hip, as his right hand combed through his orange beard. A cut off denim vest fit loosely on his shoulders, and his skinny Gap jeans fit snug around his slim waist and rested on top his black Vans sneakers. His strong reputation made up for everything he lacked in stature. His persistence and loyalty had gained him a powerful position directly under the current leaders. Tattoos covered both arms, as the colorful sleeves of ink told a story of his life through precise detail. From the sea of skulls on his forearm to the shredded Irish flag that draped his shoulder blades, Wolff was proud to display his heritage as well as his demons.

"Who the fuck are you talking to?" Kyle asked Wolff, his rifle still aimed at his target.

"Listen, you need to lower your weapon. This isn't your fight," Wolff replied to that man. He was taken back a bit because no one ever disrespected him in that manner and got away with it.

"Our job is to look for resources and bring people back when we come in contact with them."

Wolff laughed at the naïve response. "Who told you that?"

"Micah told me that."

As soon as those words left Kyle's lips, the entire group burst out in laughter. Kyle's eyebrows moved closer together, and the wrinkles on his forehead became more visible, as he looked around at the laughing men. For some odd reason, they became amused once he mentioned Micah's name. This type of disrespect did not sit well with the former soldier. In his opinion, there needed to be a level of respect shown to the ranking members of the organization and clearly, there wasn't.

"We don't answer to Micah," Wolff snarled. "And seeing as though you were chosen to roll with us that means you don't answer to him either."

"Well, who the hell gave us the authority to drag an innocent man from his home and beat him like an animal?" Kyle asked as he stepped forward, getting face to face with Wolff. It looked as if the two men were being showcased at a weigh-in for a pay-per-view boxing match. Despite Kyle's stockier frame, Wolff didn't back down. He turned the trucker hat he was wearing around and got eye to eye with Kyle, showing him that he was ready for whatever move that was about to be made. The other members of the group began circling Kyle. The readjustment of their grips on their weapons showed they all had one intention. Kyle felt their presence surrounding him but kept his eyes fixated on the ginger male standing in front of him.

"BACK DOWN." The direct order caused the group members to back away from their newest member. It also made Wolff take a few steps back from Kyle. Turning his hat back around, he acknowledged the powerful figure that exited the Chevrolet Silverado. A pair of boots clicked on the hot ground, as the sound became louder with each step. Kyle felt a hand touch his shoulder softly and turned to see whom it belonged to. His heart skipped a beat when he saw who had approached. The hand slid from Kyle's shoulder and worked its way down to his hands. Chills fluttered up his spine once he felt the warm palm graze the back of his hand. He felt his rifle being pulled away from his hand. His body was frozen due to the shock he was in. The only movement was Kyle's eyes blinking when the sound of the rifle firing traveled in his ears. He watched as the rifle was raised and a bullet was sent through the skull of the battered man that was lying on the hot ground.

"I know what Micah told you, but things are going to be done my way."

Kyle was shocked to hear those words, especially coming from Adina. Although her words were deceiving, her appearance had his attention. The sun blazed down, bouncing off her chocolate skin. Adina was the definition of perfection when it came to her exterior, but inside she carried around demons from the past and present. Adina had taken her braids out, so her hair stood up straight like it was reaching towards the sky. Her large afro was distinguished and allowed her to tower over average-sized men. The Association's second in command had given orders that contradicted the vision of her counterpart. Her vision was of a world that bowed down to their organization in fear. The neighborhoods they caused havoc in were once homes to hardworking, middle-class residents. The same people that looked down upon those who struggled to live a life that barely crossed the line of poverty. The same people would cross the street when they walked by a shelter, to avoid being in the presence of degenerates like Adina. She felt they were the problem with the country and would not allow them or the rich to survive in the new world unless they proved to be beneficial in the enhancement of The Association. The man that was dragged from the house served no purpose to her, so she did what she has done many times before. The sinister grin that spread across her face displayed her willingness to execute the innocent for her evil cause.

"If you are not with The Association, you are against us," she announced. The members of her small group broke out in loud cheers and praise for their leader. Kyle was still stuck as the demonic cheers drowned out his thoughts. Adina basked at the moment, gliding over to Kyle and handing him back his rifle.

CRACK!

Kyle drove the rifle stock straight into Adina's nose, breaking it. Blood poured from her nostrils as he held her in a chokehold. The barrel of the rifle kissed the back of her head, as Kyle backpedaled away from the rest of the group. The warm fluid dripped down his forearm as he tightened his grip. The broken sunglasses Adina wore were completely shattered when she was struck in the face. There were multiple guns pointed at Kyle, and he kept Adina close to prevent a clear shot. He wasn't too worried about anyone except Wolff, who was focused on him.

"What the fuck are you doing?" Adina asked, choking on her blood.

"Central Avenue," Kyle replied.

"What?"

"Central Avenue." He pressed the rifle harder against her head.

"Agh." Adina cringed in pain as the force from the rifle felt as if it was piercing into her head.

"We can't save everybody. That guy wouldn't have done anything for us, so why avenge his death?"

"His death? I'm not worried about him. You really don't remember?"

"Remember what?"

"Central Avenue. Your men attacked my home, and I lost my family."

"I don't know what you're talking about. What does that have to do with me?"

"They were under your orders. You allowed them to do what these men were doing today. Their blood is on you."

The other members of the group looked around at each other, trying to figure out what the next move was going to be. Kyle was continually backpedaling, while they slowly advanced.

"Back the fuck up, or I will blow her brains out."

"If you do that I will kill you myself and you can go visit your family in hell," Wolff shouted. He was a man who stood behind every decision he makes and his sins did not haunt him. Guilt never crossed his mind. He could care less about Kyle's grief; he wanted blood. He aimed his pistol but did not have a good shot. He was confident to take it but didn't want to risk the safety of his leader. Noticing the loyal ginger was not backing down, Kyle was running out of options. He could attempt a shot at the man, but the passive resistance Adina was displaying was an indicator that she would put forth an effort to escape when she had the opportunity to do so. Squeezing tighter on her neck, the tenseness she was displaying began to fade.

"Throw one of those canisters on your hip," Kyle whispered in Adina's ear. Right before she shot the man on the sidewalk, he noticed two canisters on her hip. Adina didn't immediately respond to Kyle's request and began wiggling around trying to free herself from his strong hold. This caused Kyle to squeeze harder, crushing her trachea. "Throw the canister at them and don't try anything else." The strong leader had no more fight left in her. Struggling to breathe, she gasped for air as blood trickled into her mouth. Her adrenaline wasn't pumping as much, and the pain from her wrecked nose was shooting through her entire face. No one had ever violated her in such a way and for the first time in years, she was afraid. Something about the former soldier rubbed her the wrong way. He was strong; too strong to break. Compliance would be the likely key to her survival. She reached down and grabbed one of the canisters. The members of the group were so focused on Kyle; they never saw the gestures made by Adina. Orange smoke began to seep from the canister, as Adina removed the pin from the device. She tossed the canister towards the group of men.

"Move, move, move," Wolff ordered as they began to scatter, avoiding exposure to the gas. His gun was still aimed towards Kyle during his retreat.

The smoke began to spread throughout the air, as the wind blew the particles around. Kyle had no way of reaching for his mask; if he did, it would mean removing his arm from around Adina's neck. It was time to get out of the area. The smoke covered Wolff's silhouette, and Kyle no longer had a visual on his adversary. A sharp sting shot through Kyle's forearm as he felt a strong clamp pinch his skin. Adina's last attempt at freedom was effective. Her bite broke the skin on the arm of her capturer and loosened his grip from around her neck. The rifle was still pressed against her head, but she attempted to run.

BANG!

CHAPTER

1

Adina fell to her knees, then flat on her face. Blood continued pouring out of her nose, and now it was also coming from the back of her head. Wolff heard the shot and rushed toward Kyle and Adina's location. Kyle pulled his shirt up over his nose and mouth and maneuvered his way through the thick smoke. He just put a bullet in one of the leaders of The Association, and now it was time to go to war with the remaining members.

Wolff saw his leader down and immediately went into rescue mode. He held his breath as he sprinted through the orange smoke. He grabbed Adina up by her shirt collar and began dragging her away from the smoke. Adina was just dead weight as the thin man did his best to remove her from more danger. She appeared to be unconscious and in dire need of medical attention. Judging by their current predicament, this was medical attention that Wolff was not able to provide.

More shots rang out, but Wolff could not tell where they were coming from. Kyle shot blindly into the smoke, and shots were fired back at him. It sounded like a war zone. Wolff worked his trigger finger back and forth as rounds blasted out of his gun and through the smoke. Wolff finally cleared Adina from the smoke and watched as Kyle hopped in the unattended Chevy Silverado. The driver of the Chevy had exited the truck in an attempt to assist the rest of the group, but a precise headshot from Kyle put him down quickly. With Adina still in his grip, Wolff gripped his pistol with one hand and continued firing at Kyle.

The shots tore holes into the Chevy as it turned around and sped away. BANG! BANG! BANG! BANG! BANG! BANG! CLICK! CLICK! CLICK! CLICK!

The sound of the empty gun angered Wolff as he did his best to land some precise shots on the fleeing truck. The Chevy maneuvered to the left and right as it sped down the street, striking anything that got into its path. Although the Chevy maneuvers were sharp, Wolff's aim had been sharper. The orange smoke continued spreading throughout the air. Wolff holstered his weapon and picked up Adina. His skinny frame was deceiving because he had the strength to throw her over his shoulder. Wolff made his way over to the remaining two vehicles that the group arrived in. Wolff noticed that the smoke was making its way toward the vehicles and did his best to pick up the pace.

As Wolff approached the Saturn Vue, a large shadowy figure emerged from the smoke. He stopped in his tracks and eyed up a mutated beast that was inching toward him. The beast was still actively mutating, as its teeth formed into fangs, and the hair thickened into fur. Once a member of The Association was now a blood thirsty mutation that had its red eyes on Wolff. The beast sized him up and continued inching.

Wolff held on tight to Adina. His hand grazed the top of his tucked gun. He almost forgot the gun was empty and considered pulling it out to defend himself. Instead, he reached over and pulled out a large hunting knife from a leg holster. With no ammo left in his firearm, Wolff had no other option but to take on the beast with another weapon. As fearless as Wolff was, it did not stop his heart from beating out of his chest. He was panting heavily as he watched the beast's claws dig into the ground. He clenched the knife as the beast inched closer and closer toward him. This was literally going to be the fight of his life.

BANG! BANG! BANG!

Shots rang out, striking the side of the beast, and a few went into the side of the Saturn. Two members of

The Association continued firing at the beast. The beast turned its attention to the gunmen. The shots pierced through the beast, and it let out a loud roar. Another roar was let out, but it was not from the injured creature. A large figure lunged through the smoke and mauled one of the gunmen. The other gunman sprinted toward the vehicles, and the injured beast followed. With the beasts focused on the gunman, Wolff used this opportunity to get Adina to the Saturn.

"Help me," the gunman yelled out to Wolff as he continued sprinting to the vehicles. Wolff was able to go unnoticed as he opened the backdoor and plopped Adina down on the backseat. He climbed over her and slid into the driver's seat. More gunshots rang off.

"Stay with me, boss. I'm going to get you home."

Wolff started the vehicle, when the front passenger door opened, and the gunman hopped in.

"Go, go, go!" he yelled.

The shots he let off finished the injured beast, but the second one was on the trail. The tires screeched as Wolff slammed his foot down on the accelerator. More shots rang off as the gunman leaned out the window and did his best to put the beast down. The beast continued its stride, hopping over parked cars and making itself a difficult target.

Wolff hit several turns but noticed that the beast was still in pursuit.

"Why is that thing still alive?" he asked the gunman.

"I can't hit the damn thing," he replied as he left off another shot that struck the side of a home. "Fuck, I'm out of ammo."

Wolff hit another turn and checked his rear-view mirror again. The beast was gaining on their vehicle. *We aren't going to outrun that thing*, he thought as he continued mashing on the gas pedal. The Saturn was already at its max speed. The steering wheel began shaking. The gunman climbed back into the vehicle. He opened the glove compartment, looking for ammo. He also checked under the seat.

The rear windshield of the Saturn shattered after the beast took a swipe at the back of the vehicle. Its claws ripped through the rear bumper on a second swipe. Wolff took a sharp left turn, hoping to shake the beast, to no avail.

"Here, take my gun. It's loaded!" Wolf shouted, handing his gun over.

The gun man hung out of the window once more and pointed the weapon at the beast. CLICK! "What the fuck. This shit ain't loaded."

Wolff slammed on the brakes and pushed the gunman, causing him to fall out of the window. The beast immediately pounced on the man and sunk its teeth into his shoulder. The man screamed as the beast continued feasting on his flesh. He desperately swung the gun, striking the beast. With one bite, the beast ripped off the man's arm. He let out another scream. Wolff checked the rearview mirror again, seeing the distance he was putting between himself and the beast. It was time to head back to The Association.

CHAPTER

2

Kyle did not want to admit it, but he needed help. Two of the bullets that Wolff fired at him had pierced the Chevy and tore through Kyle's right arm. His teeth clenched down on the nylon strap, and he turned his face away from his arm, tightening the makeshift tourniquet that he applied to his arm. Kyle almost lost control of the Chevy, as he focused on his injured arm. The flow of the warm fluid that dripped down his arm began to slow down. Blood covered the interior of the truck.

I don't have much time before nightfall. I have to find shelter.

The sun began to set, and Kyle slowly drifted down the street. He checked the rearview mirror, ensuring he was not being followed. He did his best to dust off the orange smoke particles that covered his clothing, but with only one good arm, there was only so much he could do. He checked the tightness of the torniquet once more.

"I think you need to get that looked at." Kyle heard Jacqui's voice and smiled.

Hearing her voice made his heart melt. His tough, masculine exterior was temporarily shut down after her words were spoken. Kyle missed his deceased wife so much that he never questioned why he was hearing her voice.

The Chevy sideswiped a few parked cars before Kyle straightened up the damaged vehicle on the narrow street.

"Honey, I think you should pull over."

There was a bright glow coming from the front passenger seat in the truck. Kyle looked over and saw Jacqui's stunning face.

"What are you doing here? This isn't real."

"Are you not happy to see me?"

"Of course, I am. The only problem is that if I'm seeing you, that must mean—"

"Don't say it. It doesn't mean anything. I'm just here to visit you."

"Why? Why are you here?"

"I'm here because you need me to be. I know what you just did. I just want to know why you did it."

"I had to do it. That woman was the reason why you and Chloe aren't with me. If it weren't for her, I wouldn't be in this mess. She had to die."

"Honey, she didn't have to die. You wanted her to die. You can't keep going like this. Look at you. You're a bloody mess."

Kyle began breathing heavily. "I just . . ." He had trouble catching his breath. "I just have to get inside somewhere, and I'll be alright. I can patch myself up."

"You have to stop this, Kyle. You can't do everything on your own. You need help."

"I don't need help. I need you."

"You have me. I'm not going anywhere. I will always be with you."

"How is it?"

"How is what?"

"Heaven. How is it there?"

Jacqui laughed. "What type of question is that?"

"I think I'm ready to go. I need to be with you," he added, reaching his hand out toward her.

"I can't let you do that."

"You can't let me do what?"

"I can't let you come with me. You have to wake up."

"What?"

"Wake up, Kyle. Wake up."

The blaring horn grabbed Kyle's attention. He regained consciousness and grimaced in pain as he felt the discomfort travel through his body. He was pinned down inside the vehicle. Flipped over on its side, the truck was wrecked. Kyle did not even know he crashed and flipped the pickup truck. The last thing he remembered was seeing Jacqui's face.

Kyle did his best to gather himself. He was covered in blood and shattered glass. He sat up, looking at the damaged interior and brushing the glass off his clothing. Everything in the truck was crushed and thrown around. The engine had been pushed through the dashboard and was pressed up against the driver's seat. *How the fuck am I going to get out of here?* He looked up at the driver's door, which he was not sure how he would get open. He would have to somehow get around the engine that was now in the way. Kyle slowly looked around. He needed to find a way out of the truck.

Kyle mustered up the energy to crawl in the back seat of the truck. With the torniquet wrapped around one of his arms, he only had one good arm to work with. He grabbed the headrest of the backseat and pulled himself up with one arm. He was now standing up and attempting to get the back door open. With the vehicle on its side, gravity was naturally working against him. Kyle could not get the door to budge.

Kyle let out a loud scream and slammed his hand against the headrest. He needed a way out. The pain shooting through his body began worsening. It would not be long before Wolff and the other members of The Association pulled up. "Jacqui, I need a sign," Kyle muttered as he did his best to fight off the feeling of defeat.

Kyle hung his head as he tried to plan his next move. Sun rays shined into the vehicle and were caught in the peripheral of Kyle's eye. He looked over and noticed the rays were shining through the truck's sunroof. Just outside was a church that sat on the northwest corner of the intersection. "Thanks, Jacqui."

Kyle struggled to crawl back into the front seat area of the truck. His battered body was giving up on him. With the little bit of energy he had, he delivered a front kick to the sunroof. It did not budge. He tried again with the same result. Kyle stopped and stared at the church on the corner. Something about the building was grabbing his attention. The sunrays suddenly stopped shining into the vehicle. Thick clouds began covering the sky. Kyle's eyes scanned the interior of the Chevy, looking for something that would help him break the window. With the engine pushing in the dashboard, he could not spot anything useful in the vehicle.

Kyle sat back up and looked at the church again. It seemed as if the dark clouds were moving in around the church but not directly over it. The little bit of sunrays that peeked through the clouds were shining down over the sanctuary.

Suddenly, a figure appeared from the dark alley way that separated the buildings. The thin, wiry figure headed directly toward the Chevy. Kyle tried to crawl into the back seating area as the figure was getting closer. He was able to make it into the back of the truck, however, before the glass on the sunroof shattered, and he felt someone grab him by the ankle.

CHAPTER

3

For Levi, the end of the world started in the church. His parents ran the church and did a lot of beneficial work in the community. His father is Pastor Lewis, a beloved figure in Philadelphia. Paster Lewis was one of the few pastors in the city who put themselves on the frontline when it came to protesting social injustice and police brutality. Although many praised the pastor for his work, others despised him for being on the frontline. They felt that the pastor's new views and actions conflicted with that of the church. Members of his congregation were not happy that the pastor was spending more time in the community than in the sanctuary.

When many of the protests turned into riots, anarchists took that opportunity to launch attacks on the church. They shattered windows, spray painted the building, attacked members, and threatened to kill Pastor Lewis and his family. Ironically, when Pastor Lewis tried to report these incidents to the police department, he was often left with inadequate service because they also did not approve of his role in the protests.

Pastor Lewis was left to protect his family and church on his own. Not even the members of the church knew what he was going through. Unfortunately, Levi witnessed it all. He often faced backlash in school from other students who took opportunities to terrorize him because of the media attention his father was getting. There was nothing worse than showing up at a private school that was majority white when you were the son of a man who was shouting "Black Lives Matter" every day on the news. Levi felt lost in the world for quite some time. Luckily for him, his father enrolled him in boxing classes at an early age. This led to Levi being able to not only defend himself against bullies at school and in the neighborhood but to also become more confident and willing to defend his family.

Once the riots became violent, several of the church members wanted to escape the chaos, so Pastor Lewis opened the doors of the church to anyone needing a safe space during those times. He even stayed behind when the evacuations took place so that he could keep the church doors open for those in need. The pastor held services twice a day, and the church was stocked with food. Some members served as security guards to protect the church and the members due to the recent threats and attacks. Many believed it would be the end of the world, but Pastor Lewis ensured them that the chaos would pass, and brighter days were ahead of them. The pastor never lost his faith.

Unbeknownst to Pastor Lewis, the chemical gas was released, and the mutations began happening all across the city. Levi still remembered the day the gas was released. He had gone to the hardware store to pick up a few items needed to board up the church. Pastor Lewis was caring, but he was not naïve. He knew there was evil outside that would eventually work its way inside the church. As Levi made his way back to the church from the hardware store, he noticed that the sky appeared to be turning orange, and people began dropping like flies in the streets. The warnings about mutations had already been put out, but it seemed like something out of a horror story. In a full sprint, he made his way back to the church in minutes. Once he warned his father about his observations, they hastily began boarding up the church. All the members of the church were called inside, and wooden planks were nailed across the front, rear, and side doors.

Once the church was secured, Levi worked his way up to his favorite place, which was one of the production rooms that overlooked the main level of the church. This was the room that controlled the audio and visual aspects of the church services. There were three rooms on the upper level, but the middle room was significantly larger than the other two. Levi and a few other teenagers often hung out in this room. Levi's best friend, Noah, had left the city with his parents during the evacuation. The rest of his crew was right by his side, however, in the production room. Two brothers, Cameron and Jayven, were a couple years younger than Levi, and Sade was a year older than him.

The group of four teenagers were kidding around with the equipment when they heard screams coming from the main level of the church. They looked and saw the church members scrambling to cover the doors and broken windows. The orange chemical gas began seeping into the church. The teens began panicking and attempted to help get people into the upstairs rooms, but Pastor Lewis ordered them to get back into the room. The last thing the children remembered was watching the mutations. They remembered seeing human fingernails grow into claws and body parts expanding and growing larger. The children also saw facial structures transform from human and turning into a beast. It was horrifying.

That night changed Levi's life. He no longer had his parents by his side. After the release of the gas, he was just left with his friends. They were just four teenagers trying to navigate in a new world. They went through several ups and downs that forced Levi to take on more of a father-figure role, despite Sade being the oldest out of the group.

The crash got all the teens' attention. Levi climbed through one of the church's side windows and crept through the alley. With all the doors still secure, Levi and his friends entered and exited the church through certain windows. This allowed them to keep people and beasts from easily wandering into the church. It was almost dark out, and Levi hated being out at night. *That noise came from this way*, he thought to himself as he tiptoed through the alley, wielding a baseball bat.

It did not take long before he spotted the blood trail in the alley. He followed it to the street, where he noticed the damaged Chevy Silverado flipped over on its side. Levi quickly peeked into the truck. Blood covered the driver's seat and the sunroof. Levi scanned both directions of the street. There was no one in sight, only blood, broken glass, and bullet holes.

Levi tracked the blood trail back into the alley. A smell was in the air. The smell of dampness. Rain was sure to come soon. The wind began picking up, filling the air with the stench of trash and decayed bodies. This was the new norm. Once in a while, a new body would appear, either mauled by one of the creatures or murdered at the hands of another human being. Either way, it did not bother Levi too much.

The young teen's average-sized stature appeared much larger in his shadow that extended down the alley. His boxing training kept him in good shape. Sade had recently braided his sandy brown hair, which was draping down past his shoulders. Levi barely had a mustache, but puberty caused his voice to begin cracking.

Rustling sounds came from the rear of one of the stores. The blood trail continued in the direction of the store, so he followed it. Although curiosity killed the cat, it fueled Levi. He never backed down from a mystery, even if it meant walking through an alley to approach possible danger.

The blood trail began thinning out. Levi turned the corner in the alley and saw a dark figure hovering over a body. The dark figure was thin and hunched over, not much of an opposition for the skilled teen. "Hey, get off of him!" Levi yelled. The dark figure ignored the command. "I said, get off of him!" Levi shouted, running up to the figure and swinging the bat at him. The bat connected on the side of the figure's face, knocking him to the ground. The nails on the bat had ripped through the man's face when the bat struck him. He fell to the ground but quickly popped back up and ran off into the shadows.

Levi turned to the man on the ground, who was a bloody mess. "Are you okay, sir?" Levi asked.

Kyle mustarded up all the energy he had left to sit up straight. "I'm fine," the stubborn man replied.

"You're far from fine. Come on, let me get you inside because that guy might come back."

Levi helped Kyle to his feet and assisted him back to the church. The young teen was so focused on helping Kyle that he never noticed the man watching him from the shadows. Blood trickled down the man's face, and he wanted revenge. Levi thought he left, but he was right behind him, and he had company with him.

CHAPTER

4

"**How the fuck did this happen?**"

"Micah, it was that military dude you sent with us. He did this to Adina."

"How?"

"He pointed his rifle at—"

"I don't mean literally, you idiot," Micah barked at Wolff. "I'm asking how he was able to get to my queen when there were six of you to go through to even get to her."

"The chemical gas. He had her release the gas, and none of us had masks on. Half of our men turned into those things, and the other half had to try to fight them off. We failed because we ran out of ammo."

Micah flipped a table over. "Ammo? Are we really talking about ammo right now? We have stockpiles of ammo, and you motherfuckers are going to come in here and tell me that you ran out." Micah paced back and forth. He swiped at a set of candles that were on another table, sending them flying across the room. "I just don't understand why he did this. Why did he go after Adina?"

"He said something about us killing his family or some shit like that."

"His family?" Micah paced the room as he tried to wrap his brain around the entire incident. "What is he talking about?" Micah asked Dannie.

Dannie was sitting by Adina's side, practically in tears. He was holding her cold hand. He looked up at Micah. "I don't know anything about that man's family, nor do I care to know. He tried to kill my sister, and I'll die before I give him another opportunity to get close to her."

Wolff side-eyed Dannie. He was not buying the innocent act and did not trust the young man who was parked by Adina's side. "Boss, how do we know that they aren't all in this together. This fuckin' fairy and the other two came in here with that punk. For all we know, they planned this attack."

Dannie jumped up and punched Wolff in his face. He just blacked out. The quick blow caused the thin man to stagger back. Adina was Dannie's family, and to be accused of setting her up was the worst form of disrespect he ever faced. Wolff countered with an elbow strike to Dannie's face, knocking him to the ground. Dannie immediately tasted the blood in his mouth. Dannie kicked Wolff's leg, forcing it to buckle. Wolff threw a flurry of punches at Dannie. He was able to block a few of them, but most of them landed. Dannie scratched Wolff across the side of his face, drawing blood.

Wolff hit Dannie with another elbow and slipped a knife from his waistline, sticking it in Dannie's side. Dannie screamed in pain. "Break this shit up," Micah ordered, seeing Wolff cock his arm back for another strike. Two of Micah's henchman grabbed Wolff and pulled him off Dannie. Dannie held his side, attempting to stop the bleeding.

"Get the fuck off of me!" Wolff yelled.

"You need to calm down."

"Micah, you better get these men off of me, or you'll pay."

"Or I'll what?" Micah asked, holding a Desert Eagle pistol to Wolff's head.

Micah frowned. He was not in the mood for the disrespect. He was still emotional about the dilemma he and the organization were just put in. Wolff didn't say a word. "I asked you a question. Or I'll what?"

"Nothing."

"Nothing, who?"

"Nothing, sir."

Micha lowered the Desert Eagle. "You need to get one thing clear. You work for me. The next time you decide you want to threaten me, I promise you that you're going to eat a bullet."

Wolff raised his head and looked Micah in his eyes. Wolff wasn't the least bit intimidated by Micah, but he knew that without Adina, there was not much he could do. He was going to have to conform to Micah's orders if he knew what was best for him. He still tried to escape the grip of the henchman but was unsuccessful once more.

"Now, go fetch us a few cars to take out. We have a new mission."

The henchman drug Wolff out of the room. Micah sat down beside Adina. He never knew seeing the strongest woman lying there helpless would fill him with rage. His people had brought first-aid supplies up, and their medical staff was scurrying around, preparing to treat Adina.

Micah looked around at the staff. "Where the hell is Doctor Jin?" he asked angrily.

"We don't know. He wasn't in the lab with us," one of the medical staff members replied.

"Somebody go and find him and let him know what just happened. I need the best of the best tending to Adina."

"Yes, sir."

Micah grabbed one of the cloths and began wiping the blood from Adina's face. It did not take long for the cloth to get covered and for him to grab another one. Micah really did not want to leave Adina's side, but catching Kyle was more important to him. Leaving the mission up to Wolff was not an option. Micah wanted to be hands-on with this mission to ensure that it would be carried out properly. He also planned to take his best men along for the ride.

"Baby, I promise you that I will end this. We are going to hunt him down."

CHAPTER

5

Hours had passed since the sound of the crash. Sade gazed out the broken stained-glass window and stared at the full moon. Dark storm clouds were beginning to cover the sky, so she enjoyed the sight of the moon before it was blocked. Below her, the beasts were howling, which were followed up by more howls coming from outside. The night breeze was soothing as it cooled her skin. Sade imagined being in a different world. She imagined a world in which she didn't have to hide all day behind silence and fear. She missed her parents. Unexpected tears fell from the corners of her eyes and fell into the dark pit below her.

Sade inched over. A part of her wanted to fall with those tears. She longed to put an end to her misery.

She attempted to run her fingers through her tangled hair, but it was no use. Her fingers got snagged on every attempt. It had been so long since she had combed or done anything with her hair. Soon, it would start to lock. Giving up on the knots in her hair, she shut her eyes.

All was quiet in the church. The beasts were no longer howling, and Sade was sound asleep. Rain began to fall, trickling down the side of the church and into every broken window and cracked siding. Hearing the rain was soothing. The other teens were also sound asleep.

There was a bang at one of the side windows of the church. Then, there were two more. The board on one of the windows was being kicked in. One of the culprits was holding a shirt up to his bloody face, while the other was making his way into the church. He broke out the glass window and donkey-kicked the wooden panel that Levi had nailed up.

"I'm going to fuckin' kill that kid with the bat," Worm said while holding the shirt up to his face.

"You should have done that when he hit you with that bat," Bucky replied.

Worm and Bucky were two peas in a pod. Both were drug addicts who killed and stole just to feed their addiction. Their main concern was getting their hands on anything that would get them high. They were two of many men and women in the Underling organization with some type of addiction. Some were drug addicts, some were alcoholics, and others had sick sexual addictions. Before, the addicts used to run around scavenging houses to see what they could find. For the most part, they stayed out of the way.

Things changed when The Reaper took over. He empowered them all, even though they were flawed. He gathered up societal rejects and brought them all together. He united the criminals, addicts, and survivalists. The Reaper helped them build their name and struck fear into the streets. Before, they used to stay in the shadows. But now, they operated from the shadows. They learned to use the darkness to their advantage and that was when they struck.

When it was nightfall, they had to worry about the monsters. Not only the ones who were mutated but also the ones who lurked in the shadows. The Reaper took pride in this. His group travelled in packs, and they raided any building they could. He let the addicts have free range in the pharmacies, and the alcoholics were let loose in the markets and bars. The Reaper encouraged this type of reckless behavior, and because he did, they all followed him without question. Those who did not want to follow were killed, and if they were not killed, it was because they were only following so that they would not be killed.

Worm and Bucky were two of the worst in the group. They did not care who they stole from, which was why Worm was running through Kyle's pockets despite the man being so close to death. Worm carried around an ice pick and would have jabbed Kyle with it if he had put up a fight. Bucky was too busy scavenging through a building but ran out once he heard Levi yelling. Now, it was their time to strike back.

"These motherfuckers definitely got something to hide in here," Bucky said as he continued kicking through the window.

"I bet it's fuckin' drugs," Worm replied, licking his chops.

"It's a church, you idiot. They don't have drugs."

"How you know?"

"Because who the hell keeps drugs in a church?"

"The same people that board up a church to keep people out of it."

It was like a lightbulb came on over Bucky's head. Although there was no logic behind Worm's explanation, to a drug addict, it was good enough. Bucky began kicking harder and was able to knock off the nailed up 2X4. Both men were soaking wet.

Bucky climbed through the window and into the church. Worm waited patiently to follow him in.

"I can't see shit in here," Bucky said when he landed into the church. The dark clouds in the night sky prevented the full moon from shining through the window.

Worm climbed halfway through the window and started digging into his pockets. He gripped the small BIC lighter and pulled it out, handing it to Bucky. Bucky took the lighter and stepped forward with it. Bucky attempted to spark the lighter, but it was soaking wet and did not work. He wiped it on his pant leg, hoping to dry it off a bit.

"What's going on, Buck?"

"I'm tryin' to get this stupid lighter to work. Is it empty?"

"Naw, I just used it a couple days ago."

Bucky flicked his thumb on top of the lighter again, hoping to ignite it. The lighter sparked but did not light.

"Come on, Buck. Light the damn thing. I can't see the ground, and I don't want to fall when I come in."

"Man, here. It's your fuckin' lighter, so you get it to work," Bucky said, walking back over to the sound of Worm's voice and handing him the lighter.

Worm wiped the lighter off with his bloody shirt, then shook it. He flicked his thumb on top, and the lighter ignited. The small flame provided enough light for Worm to see in front of him.

"It's about damn time. Now, hand it over."

"Your ugly mug should be left in the dark," Worm joked. He extended his arm out to give Bucky the flame.

The flame from the lighter not only lit up Bucky's face but also a few feet behind him. Worm's mouth hit the floor.

"B-B-B-Buck," Worm tried muttering, but his words would not form.

"What the hell is wrong with you? Give me the damn lighter."

Bucky saw that Worm was not moving or saying a word. His eyes were bulging out of their sockets, and his pale skin turned almost paper white. "What the fuck, Worm. You are acting like you saw a ghost or something."

A growl came from behind Bucky. He froze in place once he heard it. He heard another one, then a few more. He wanted to turn around but was stuck on Worm. Worm still did not move or say a word. The growls were getting louder. Bucky slowly turned his head around and was facing a set of large sharp fangs. He screamed and ran toward the open window. Multiple beasts ran after him.

Worm dropped the lighter and climbed back out the window. He took off running, not even looking back to see if his friend made it out. While running, he could hear Bucky's screams.

CHAPTER

6

BOOM!

The front door being kicked in shook the entire building. Micah and his team of goons stormed inside like a SWAT team. Interior doors were knocked off the hinges, and furniture was sent crashing to the ground as the team thoroughly searched the property.

"Kyle!" Micah yelled out. "If you're in here, come on out."

Micah was different. The usually calm and strategic leader had a demonic grimace on his face. He wanted nothing else but blood. On any other day, he would be up for negotiations and to hear someone out, but in this case, nothing could explain Kyle's actions. In

Micah's opinion, not even the loss of his family at the hands of The Association could justify what Kyle did.

The stock of the Remington® shotgun was digging into Micah's shoulder, and the barrel of the gun entered each room before he stepped foot in them. His finger was just inches away from the trigger. The image of Adina's bloody body was stuck in his head and fueled the fire that burned inside him.

"I'm going to kill this motherfucker," Micah uttered under his breath.

He gestured madly for his team to search each floor. Stepping over the broken doors, Micah was sure to double-check every room in the home, which appeared to be deserted. The stale stench in the air and dust-covered walls confirmed his suspicions.

"Hey, boss. Come look at this," a croaky voice yelled from the master bathroom.

Heavy footsteps swiftly entered the hallway, headed toward Londo's voice. A thrill of a curiosity ran down Micah's spine. Londo was one of Micah's loyal followers and the head of his main security team. Londo shared the same beliefs as Micah, but he was also a survivalist. Although he was born and raised in Philadelphia with his mother, Londo spent the weekends and summers with his grandfather hunting in Karthaus, Pennsylvania. When they weren't hunting, his grandfather took him to the range to perfect their marksmanship. It was not a coincidence that Micah had Londo lead the hunt for Kyle.

"What you got?" Micah asked as he stepped into the bathroom. Curiosity was getting the best of his nerves.

Micah immediately spotted the remains of a body on the bathroom floor, next to a small tub. He bent over to exam it further. The remains appeared to be in some type of nightgown as he slightly lifted it to get a better look.

"This isn't who we're looking for. This body had to at least been here for weeks." The disappointment could he heard in his voice.

"More like months," Londo replied. "By the looks of it, I would say that grandma probably fell and wacked her head on the tub a while ago."

"So, what the fuck does she have to do with our mission?"

"Well, seeing as though this body is all decayed, I'm sure that this blood right here doesn't belong to her."

Micah immediately popped up. It was true. There was blood on the medicine cabinet and sink.

"It looks fresh too," Londo said. "I would say that someone was just here in the past twenty-four hours."

"It had to be the guy we are looking for. If he's bleeding, that means he's injured. Wolff did say he unloaded on the truck, so maybe he hit him."

"Or maybe that's Adina's blood on him," Wolff chimed in as he stepped into the bathroom.

Micah shot Wolff a look that could kill. The image of Adina popped back into his head. "I suggest you watch your mouth before it'll be your blood in that sink."

"Come on, boss. I didn't mean anything by it. I'm just saying it could be a possibility."

"He's right," Londo added. "This could be some type of distraction or set up. You never know what this dude is up to. If he's anything like me, he's a scavenger. If we're going to catch him, we have to be two steps ahead of him. We need to know how he thinks so we can know what moves he's going to make next."

"And how exactly do you suggest we do that?" Wolff asked.

"We ask the people that were closest to him," Micah said.

All three men looked into the hallway. Dannie had just assisted in searching one of the other rooms and entered the hallway. "I'll get this little bitch to tell us everything he knows," Wolff said, marching toward the hallway.

A strong hand wrapped around Wolff's bicep, pulling him back into the room. "Why the fuck are you grabbing me like that?" Wolff scoffed.

"Watch your mouth. You're not going out there. I think you've done enough damage. We don't need you fuckin' this up."

Wolff pushed Londo. Londo pushed Wolff back, knocking him into the wall. "Chill out!" Micah yelled, stepping in between the two men and stopping Wolff from charging at Londo. Both men had their guns locked and loaded, ready to put the other down.

"We don't have time for this shit," Micah stated.

"Step aside, Micah. This will only take a second," Londa said, raising his gun up and pointing it at Wolff.

"Make your move," Wolff replied, pointing his gun back at Londo.

"Are y'all two serious right now? We have a mission, and we need to stick to it." Micah stepped forward, putting himself in between the barrels of the two guns. "Where was this energy when you let the sucker shoot my queen?"

Wolff side-eyed Micah, who was staring him dead in his face. "I think it's best if you went back to the base."

"Are you serious? I should be the one to put a bullet in that son of a bitch."

"You already had the chance to do that," Lonzo added. The tension between the two men was intense.

"Don't make me repeat myself," Micah muttered. "Head back to the base. I'll deal with you when we get back."

Wolff gave Micah a look that could kill. A part of him wanted to stay to stand his ground, but he peeped the energy in the room. Not only did Londo look like he wanted a piece of him, but so did the other members of the team. He was outnumbered. Letting Kyle shoot Adina and get away caused Wollf to be alienated. He tucked the handgun into his waistband and exited the room, staring at Dannie as he continued down the stairs to leave the home.

Londo turned to Micah. "Are you sure it was a good idea to bring him with us?"

"He's one of our best men. It seemed like a good idea to have him on this mission. He's going back now, so let's just focus."

"I wasn't talking about him," Londo said while stepping aside.

Micah glared into the hallway at Dannie. "What other choice did I have? I need to keep him close, and I damn sure wasn't leaving him alone with Adina."

"Just kill him."

"I can't do that."

"Why not?"

"Adina wouldn't want that to happen."

"Well, Adina will understand that it had to be done."

"Naw, I don't think she would. She considers him family and would probably kill us if we killed him."

"Well, that's a risk that I'm willing to take."

Micah looked over at Londo after that response. It was not really what he said – it was more so that Londo was the kind of guy who means what he says. Micah knew he just unleashed a beast. He knew what type of person Londo was, and that was why he kept him close. Londo was not just a hunter, but he enjoyed the thrill of the hunt. He enjoyed killing. The look in Londo's eyes was one that was awfully familiar to Micah. It was the same look that Londo had on his face every time he was planning to kill. If that was his plan, there was nothing Micah could do to stop him.

CHAPTER

7

It was the crack of dawn, and Sade was staring at the collapsed church ceiling. Rainwater was still dripping from the gaping hole. Being a night owl, she hated getting up early. Getting up before noon was an insult to her. She loved sleep and even more so during the current climate. Any chance to get away from her reality was an enjoyable moment, so she enjoyed every minute of sleep that she got. The screams of the intruder during the night did not even wake her.

Whenever there were heavy thoughts on her mind, she climbed up to the ceiling joists and either stared at the ceiling or at the human and beast remains below her. Sade had been coming to the church since she was a little girl. Her father was a deacon and incredibly involved in the week-to-week operations of the church. On that horrific night, he was among the group of members who were exposed to the chemical gas. Sade was not sure if her father died after inhaling the gas or if he mutated, but what she did know was that she could feel his spirit whenever she was on the joists. The feeling calmed her.

The sun rays slowly began creeping into the church through the broken windows. With no electricity in the building, the rays served as the lighting inside the building. Jayven and Cameron were still sound asleep in the production room. Levi was up and keeping watch as usual. He usually patrolled the church at night, but he was occupied last night. He had not told his friends about the new guest who he brought into the church. He knew Sade would not have approved. She hated outsiders and did not want their lives to be put in danger while trying to be hospitable. The group had already been through those trails weeks after the gas was released. So many different groups of people tried to get into the church, hoping to find food and shelter. Luckily, the doors were secure. Several attempts were made to break into through the roof, but that resulted in people plunging to their deaths. If the fall to the main level did not kill the intruders, the beasts below did.

Sade's stomach growled with hunger. She needed to eat something before she withered away to nothing. She carefully stood up on the joist, doing her best not to make a noise and awaken any of the beasts below her. They had the capabilities of jumping high and climbing up walls, so it would be easy for them to make their way up to her. Over time, the teens knew which joists to walk on, and they mastered the art of moving in stealth and silence. The slightest noise in the church caused the beasts to go crazy, looking to hunt. Sade grabbed her lantern off the end of the joist and quietly made her way to the kitchen area in the basement.

I know when I die it's going to be from starvation, Sade thought as she softly opened the new box of meatless jerky that was tucked in the back of one of the kitchen cabinets. Sade and her father were vegans, so it was extremely difficult to maintain that lifestyle when there were no choices when it came to eating. It was hard enough to find food in the new world, let alone attempting to stick to specific dietary restrictions. Luckily, the church's kitchen was stocked with peanuts, meatless jerky, and protein powder. Sade was thankful that the other teens despised the taste of the jerky, so they usually stuffed their faces with cereal and spam.

Sade chewed through the tough jerky as if it were her last meal. She grabbed a dirty coffee mug from a cabinet and dipped it into a bucket of rainwater. She chugged the water, relieving the dryness in her throat. The backroom that she entered in on the lower level of the church was usually unbothered. The other teens did not bother with it because it was used as an old storage area for Bibles, hymn books, fans, and choir gowns. All the rooms on the lower level had about an inch of water on the floor from the rain leaking inside. It took about a week for the water to drain out, but by that time, it would rain again, and the rooms would fill back up.

Sade took a particular liking to the room because it was docile. She was at peace and away from the other teens and the beasts. It was just her, her jerky, and the dripping sound of rainwater dripping into her bucket. Even though the drip only occurred occasionally after storms, she looked forward to it. She used it to help break up the thoughts in her mind during the times she was in the room.

The one thing she never saw in the back room was a bloody bandage that Sade spotted in the corner. *What the heck is this?* She kneeled, looking at the bandage. The blood was fresh. Sade held her lantern up as she scanned the room. Her mouth dropped when she saw the bloody figure slumped over in the corner of the room. She wasted no time exiting the room and making her way to Levi. If it were not for their current circumstances inside the church, she would have been yelling to inform them about what she saw. That type of noise, however, would alert the beasts and would create a bigger problem for the teens.

Levi was perched in the window, monitoring the outside. The streets were quiet. The strong tap on his shoulder gave him an inkling that something was wrong. He turned and saw a panicking Sade with a bloody bandage in her hand.

"There's someone downstairs," she whispered.

Levi grabbed her hand and began to climb out the window. The teens exited through the window and climbed the fire escape. Once they got to the roof of the church, they hopped over to the roof of the neighboring building, which was an abandoned thrift store. This was the usual location the teens chose when they wanted to have conversations and even when they wanted to get fresh air. Being up there allowed them to see if anyone else was one the rooftops but also provided them the opportunity to monitor what was going on down at the street level.

"There is someone in the basement," Sade said at a normal tone.

"I know there is," Levi replied.

"What do you mean you know there is? Who the hell is that?"

"I don't know his name."

"Did you kill him?"

"No, I didn't kill him. I ran into him outside, and he needed help."

"So, you bring him to us? Why would you do that?"

"Sade, we are in times that are going to bring out the worst in people. God wouldn't want his children to turn their back on others that are in need."

"God? You want to talk about God, Levi? God did this. All of this. God is the reason our parents aren't here with us. Where was your God when our parents died and got turned into those monsters? Our parents were good people, but yet God chose not to spare their lives."

"Sade, you can't think like that."

"I can think however I want. We don't even know if our parents died or if they turned into those monsters down there. Don't tell me how I can think. Anyway, you need to get that guy out of our church."

"And put him where? On the street to die?"

"Yes. You don't know who he is or what he is capable of doing. What if he's with the Underlings? He'll tell the rest of them about the church, and then what's going to happen?"

"He's not with the Underlings."

"How do you know that?"

"Because I chased one of them off of him the night, I found him in the alley. That's why they came rolling around that night."

"Wow. You really did all of that and didn't tell any of us about it. Those dudes could have killed us that night if they knew we were in there."

"They won't kill us. I told you, I'll protect you."

"With what, Levi? That stupid bat you have with the nails in it? The Underlings have knives and guns. Your little bat isn't going to scare them away."

"It did the other night."

"Yeah, whatever," Sade said, heading back to the fire escape.

"I'm serious, Sade. I can tell this guy isn't like them. He needed help, and God gave us the ability to help this man."

The teens' conversation was cut short by the blaring sound of emergency sirens. Both teens hit the deck and gave each other frightening looks.

CHAPTER

8

The blaring sound of emergency sirens echoed through the air. Sade and Levi crawled to the corner of the roof and peeked over the ledge. Two ambulances pulled up to the Chevy Silverado that was flipped over in the middle of the street. Both ambulances had been spray-painted black. If it were not for the horrendous spray paint job, they would look more like armored cars than ambulances. The first ambulance pulled up and struck the front of the truck, which knocked it back a few feet. The second ambulance pulled directly next to the first.

The doors of the ambulances flew open, and small groups of men and women poured out of both vehicles. They were all dressed in black militia-style clothing, which included bulletproof vests, gas masks, boots, and gloves. One of the men was an odd figure who everyone seemed to be following around. He was wearing a long black hooded trench coat, black ripped jeans, and black boots. His face was covered by an altered gas mask that appeared to have a bloody skull attached to it.

Fear swept over Levi and Sade. They wanted to make their way back into the church, but they could not risk being seen by this group. It was not hard to spot the Underlings. This was one of the most violent groups that began terrorizing the city after the evacuations. The creepy man who Levi chased away from the alley the night prior was dressed similarly to this group. They were back for revenge.

"Now, what do we have here?" the mysterious man in the skull masked asked, approaching the damaged truck.

The man walked up to the truck and seemed to be examining it. The truck was familiar to him. He had seen it before. He even remembered taking it out on a mission about two months ago. He closed his eyes as he reminisced about that day, then quickly snapped out of the trance. "I need you to bring me whoever was in this truck. Dead or alive. Start off with the alleyway that Worm said he was in. I want the person that was driving this truck, and I also want the boy with the bat."

"What about the church?" a voice asked from the group.

"We'll save it for the end. If Bucky isn't in there, we'll burn it to the ground."

The groups of men and women began cheering and ran off to follow the orders. Many of them headed into the alleyway, and others broke off into small groups and began checking buildings. Levi and Sade carefully peeked over the rooftop ledge, watching the Underlings scatter around like roaches, running into the different buildings. Levi counted twenty-two members in total, all armed with different type of weapons. Some had guns, while others had metal pipes, knives, and wooden boards.

"We have to get out of here," Sade whispered.

"How? They are in the alley."

"We have no other choice. We gotta jump the roof."

"Are you crazy? We can't jump that roof."

"We have no choice. They're going to spot us up here if we don't make a move. If we jump that roof over there, we can just keep going, and they won't catch us from all the way over here."

"What about Cam and Jay? We can't just leave them. You heard what they said. They're going to burn the church down."

"Follow me. We'll go get them and then get out of here."

The teens low-crawled across the rooftop to get back to the window of the church. The Underlings had slipped down the alley, following the blood trail. The teens could hear the other members of the group smashing up the buildings that they had entered.

Glass was shattering, doors were being kicked in, and any other destruction to the buildings that the Underlings could cause was happening.

"We can't let them get into the church," Levi said. The teens stayed low, hoping not to be spotted. They noticed a couple of the Underlings were aiming rifles up toward the high-level windows and rooftops. The mystery man stood by the vehicles with a woman. Those two seemed to be running the show.

Just as the teens were making it to the church window, one of the Underlings began banging on the front door of the church. "Bucky, you in there?" the man yelled. The door banging and yelling got the attention of the beasts that were inside the church. Loud growls could be heard coming from the interior of the church.

The riflemen heard the growls and focused their aim at the church. "There's movement on the roof!" one of the men yelled before firing shots at the teens. The shots barely missing the teens as they knocked out chunks of the church's stone exterior. Levi and Sade stayed as low to the rooftop as possible, but their movements were now limited.

"You gotta make a run for it!" Levi yelled over the gunfire.

"I'm not going to leave you," Sade replied.

"You have to. I'll have them focus on me while you make the run for it."

"No. I'm not going to . . ."

Levi popped up before Sade could finish her statement. The riflemen now had their target. Shots continued going off. Sade quickly crawled to the other end of the roof. She wasted no time popping up and taking the quick leap. The shooters were so focused on Levi they never even noticed Sade popping up and leaping over to the next building.

Levi continued ducking the shots as he descended the fire escape. The shots continue plinking off the metal rails on the fire escape. Levi made it down and dove into the window of the church.

"Jay! Cam! The Underlings are outside."

Shots continued to ring out, and the beasts were going crazy. Suddenly, there was silence. The men outside were regaining positions. Their focus was now on the church. They just knew the occupant of the truck had to be in there. Loud bangs were coming from the back door of the church, then shortly after, a very loud bang came from the front of the church. It almost sounded like an explosion. More gun shots followed.

Sade hopped from one roof and onto another. She did not even look back. She could still hear the commotion coming from the church and wanted to get as far away from it as she could. The young teen was desperate, and the only thing on her mind was getting away from the Underlings. Fatigue was starting to kick in, and she began slowing down. She was about six rooftops away from the church and was now on top of an old laundromat. The laundromat was on a main road, so she had nowhere else to go but down to the road. It was about a twelve-foot jump, and it was dicey. The store sign and an awning stood in the way of Sade and the ground. She did a quick peek over the rooftop edge. There was no sign of the Underlings or anyone else. For the moment, the coast was clear.

Sade noticed that the other buildings alongside the laundromat also had awnings. None of them were in the best condition, but the laundromat seemed to be sturdy. Sade held on to the rooftop ledge and attempted to drop onto the awning. Once she did, the awning gave out, and she fell straight through it, and it collapsed on top of her.

BOOM! Another explosive sound rocked Levi's ears as he went on the search for Jayven and Cam. "Jay, where you at?" the scared teen yelled out. "Cam, where are you?"

Roars and howls echoed through the church, followed by another explosive ram at the front door. The Underlings were determined to open up the church and get to Levi. The teen ran up the stairs and began checking each room. Bullet holes decorated the door and walls, so he crouched down to avoid being on the other end of one of those rifle rounds.

"Get that fuckin' door open."

The driver of the ambulance slammed on the pedal again and smashed through the front door of the church. The first four attempts at the door loosened the boards, and the fifth attempt was successful. Just as the ambulance entered the church, multiple beasts pounced on the vehicle and began digging their claws into the ambulance. With beasts covering the windshield, he was unable to see the large pillar in the center of the room. The crash rocked his body forward. After slamming into the pillar, the driver threw the ambulance in reverse. The power of the beasts was on full display as one's arm broke through the front windshield. The driver of the ambulance ducked but not in time before the claws of the beats ripped through his shoulder. He yelled out in pain. Another swipe missed the driver.

His shirt was covered in blood, and he was stuck. The beast blindly swiped into the ambulance, cutting its arm on the broken windshield. More gunshots rang out as members of the Underlings entered the front door. They did not realize they were walking into a pit of death, but it wouldn't take long for them to find out. The first member to walk into the church was mauled by one of the beasts. The sharp teeth tore through the flesh of the unsuspecting woman. One of her comrades fired their handgun, striking the large, furry figure that was feasting, but his attack was halted when long claws pierced through his back and out of his torso. The man was lifted off the ground and thrown into the wall.

More shots rang out as the Underlings did their best to defend themselves. Outside, the deathly screams of his subordinates caused a knot to form in the masked man's stomach. He was now standing in the back of the ambulance with three other members of the Underlings. He carefully watched as his people entered the church one by one, only to be slaughtered by the beasts. A few of the beasts escaped out of the front of the church, only to be gunned down by the rifle men. The man's stare was intense under the mask. He had plenty of encounters with these beasts and knew that his people did not stand a chance against them.

"Burn it down," he muttered.

Two of the men who stood by his side sprang toward the church. With Molotov cocktails in hand, they lit the incendiary devices and threw them inside the church. The bottle burst, and flames spread out across the floor. Two more bottles were thrown in, aimed at the walls. The two men began lighting more bottles. Just as the first bottle was picked up, a large beast came charging out of the church. The beast lunged at the men, knocking them both to the ground, along with the Molotov cocktails. The improvised incendiary device that fell to the ground ignited and sent flames spreading across the area where the two men fell. The flames also caused the other devices to ignite.

A ball of fire burst into the air, engulfing the men. They screamed and rolled around on the ground, which didn't help as they began covering themselves more in the accelerant and flames. More beasts began pouring out of the church. The riflemen could not shoot fast enough to put them all down, as they began scattering throughout the street. The Underlings were outnumbered and attempted to retreat. The doors to the second ambulance closed as the vehicle sped off. A few of the beasts pursued the ambulance as the others attacked the remaining members. The church was now fully engulfed in flames. It was a true warzone.

CHAPTER

9

The sun had set, and all was quiet in the streets. In the distance, black smoke continued to fill the sky. The fire that was started in the church had spread to the neighboring buildings, leaving nothing behind but shells of buildings that were now charred. Some of the buildings were still smoldering. Soon, there would be nowhere else for the flames to spread. Between the clothing in the thrift shop and the stacks of paper in the print shop at the end of the row, the fire had enough fuel to burn throughout the entire day.

Sade grunted. A sharp pain shot through her left arm. She was underneath a pile of metal and plastic from the broken awning. She gripped one of the metal pieces and pulled herself up. After standing to her feet, she could tell something was wrong with her arm because she could not move it. One of the metal bars was stuck in it. She did not even know how much blood she lost because she was knocked out.

Her head was spinning and throbbing. She held onto anything she could find as she crawled out of the pile of metal and tried to make her way down the street. Stumbling forward, she leaned up against the building to prevent herself from falling over. Everything seemed to be spinning, and Sade struggled to stay focused. The large lump on her head was just one of many injuries she sustained as a result of the fall.

Working with one arm was becoming a battle. Sade needed assistance walking but was unable to use the injured arm to hold herself up. While leaning on the building, she took small steps, attempting to get out of the area. The last thing she needed was the Underlings finishing what they had started.

The head injury she suffered during the fall was taking a toll on her. She felt like she was being stabbed in the head, which made her unable to walk without staggering. Her senses were off too. She never even noticed the van that drove by her.

"Who the hell was that?" Wallace asked, looking out the filthy window of the van.

Brock hesitated to answer, his foot steady on the gas. He knew exactly where Wallace was going with the question. Wallace always did his best to help others in need, but Brock was the complete opposite.

Brock was paranoid. He feared everything about the new world and what it had become. The reports of looting and murders built up a defensive wall that Brock did not want anyone getting behind.

"Brock, stop the car and go back," Wallace ordered.

"No, we have to get back."

"Brock."

"Come on, man. We just got all this gas and supplies. We need to get it back. That was our job."

"I know what our job is. But I think I saw somebody back there."

"Wallace, maybe your mind is playing tricks on you because I didn't see anyone on this road. It's pitch black out here, so how do you even know if you saw someone?"

"Yes, you did. You had to see her. She looked like a kid. Now go back because maybe she was involved in that big fire we saw earlier." Wallace worked his way to the front of the van to get a better look at their surroundings.

"That doesn't help your argument. What if she was involved in that fire? You want to go pull up to a pyromaniac?"

"Just go back."

Brock came off the gas, and his foot hovered over the brake pedal. The girl who Wallace spotted was now just a dark blur in his rearview mirror. Against his better judgment, he made a sharp U-turn and headed back. "If something bad happens, it's on you," he whined.

"Oh, be quiet. Nothing bad is going to happen."

The rusty Chevy Express van cruised back down the road. Brock activated the high beams, which illuminated the street and sidewalk.

"Right there," Wallace announced when he spotted the girl. She was staggering and appeared injured. Moments later, she collapsed. Brock pulled up, and Wallace hopped out of the van. Brock kept watch, knowing that danger could be right around the corner.

"You don't look so good," Wallace said to the girl who was staggering. He wrapped his arms around her to help her keep her balance. As soon as he did, he felt a warm fluid dripping down his arm. "Oh no, you're bleeding."

Wallace hoisted the girl over his shoulder and carried her to the van. With one hand, he slid the gas containers over to make room and laid her down.

"Yo, man, she is jacked up," Brock blurted out when he saw Sade's bloody arm.

"Thanks, Captain Obvious. Just hurry up and get us back."

Sade was out of it. The head injury left her discombobulated. She had no idea she had been placed into a van and definitely did not know where the men were taking her.

"You have to hurry up!" Wallace yelled. "I have to stop the bleeding from her arm."

He removed his belt and placed it on the upper portion of Sade's arm. Wallace pulled the belt as tight as he could, and the makeshift tourniquet seemed to slow down the bleeding. He removed the plaid shirt he was wearing and pressed it firmly against her wound.

"Is she going to make it?" Brock asked.

"Only if you drive fast and get us there. I don't think she's conscious. She needs a doctor."

CHAPTER

10

Standing in the doorway of the home, Londo stared at the twinkling stars in the sky. Hours ago, he had watched as a large fire burned a few blocks away. He wondered who set the fire, but Micah chose not to go and investigate it. Londo thought Micha was just scared, but the leader heard the gunfire and knew it wasn't coming from the man they were currently hunting. Howls could be heard coming from a distance. *Where did this guy go? He can't make it that long out here alone. Maybe he had something to do with that fire.*

These thoughts thumped Londo's awareness, and suddenly, the hairs on the back of his neck stood up. Londo quietly closed the door and ran behind a parked car that was a few houses down. He ducked behind the older model sedan and peeked out.

The heavy paw of one of the beasts dented the front of a newer model Honda Civic that was parked on the corner of the street. It stepped up onto the roof the car. It looked up and let out a shrieking howl.

Londo patiently watched the mutated creature's movements. The cool breeze blew its fur back. Blood and saliva dripped from its mouth. Londo's focus turned to three shadowy figures that were approaching from the intersecting street. From the darkness, three more figures appeared and worked their way up to the beast that was standing on the Honda. Londo clutched the handle of the machete that was strapped to his back. He glared at the furry figures, calculating their next moves.

The beasts on the Honda jumped down and huddled up with the others. The beasts rubbed up against each other, licking their fur and letting out steady growls. Londo noticed that a lot of the attention was focused on one specific beast. It was smaller than the others, and gray streaks of fur lined its back. Its movements were slower than the others. Another howl came from the distance, causing the beasts to perk up. Seconds later, they took off running. All of them sprinted off, except the creature with the black and gray fur. That creature hobbled over to the Honda and leaned up against the damaged vehicle.

Londo noticed the beast's hobble. He crept from behind the vehicle and slowly approached. He carefully took each step, doing his best not to make a sound. Londo stepped in front of a home, his eyes still locked on the beasts. It was odd. From his experience, Londo knew that the mutations caused the beasts to have heightened senses, but this one did not budge for anything.

Picking up a loose brick from the front patio, he threw it across the street and struck a station wagon. The beast slowly turned to the sound of the brick crashing into the driver's door of the vehicle, but it did not move from its current position.

Londo ran over and, with one swipe of the sharp machete, took off one of the beast's back legs. It then let out an ear-shattering squeal. The beast whipped its head around, attempting to take a bite out of Londo. He took another swipe at the injured creature, missing it by inches. It attempted to lunge forward at Londo but could not do so because of its missing leg. Londo gripped the machete with two hands and took another swipe at the creature, slicing it on its side. It fell onto the vehicle.

Londo followed up with several more swipes to the face and body of the creature before taking off. The creature let out a few gut-wrenching howls before becoming silent. It panted heavily, still leaning on the vehicle. Blood smeared down the vehicle as the beast slumped over, taking its last breath.

It took approximately twelve minutes for the other three creatures to return to the area. They returned with four others of different sizes. Londo was crouched down in the window, enjoying the show. A sinister smirk spread across his blood-splattered face. The creatures let out heavy growls and began sniffing the area around the slaughtered creature. A couple of them began tracking the scent they picked up, leading them to a vehicle, then to the front door of a home. Londo looked on. One of the creatures stood on its hind legs and began scratching at the door of the home. The deep scratches tore through the door and ripped the knob off. The creature got back on all fours and charged the door, bursting into the home. The other creatures followed.

Londo sat back and stared at the bedroom door with his machete in hand. Blood trickled down the blade and onto the tan carpet. Dannie looked over at Londo like he was a mad man. Dannie had run to the window when he heard the creature squealing. He watched everything Londo did to it.

"Are you expecting those things to come over here?" Dannie asked.

"You better hope they don't," Londo responded.

"Come on now, handsome, don't get beside yourself. I saw what you did out there but don't for a second think that you're the only one who can draw blood." Dannie held up the AK-47 that he brought with him on the hunt.

"Since we're locked in this room together, there are some things I need to know."

"Like what?"

"I want to know all about your friend, Kyle. What are his mannerisms? Strengths? Weaknesses?"

"I don't know how many times I have to tell y'all this, but I don't know that man. I was all on my own, just me and my dog. This man and his two friends rolled up on me. Obviously, they seemed like nice people, so I tagged along with them, and we ended up at The Association. That's it. I didn't even know them for a week before we got to your place, but for some reason, you guys don't want to accept the truth."

"That truth is very hard to believe."

"Well, I don't know what to tell you."

"You're going to tell me how I can catch him."

"And how exactly am I going to do that?"

"By giving me something that I can use," Londo said, approaching the gun-toting man.

Dannie held up the gun, pointing it directly at Londo's chest. "What are you doing?" Dannie asked. "Back up."

"I wouldn't do that if I were you. If you fire that shot, all seven of those monstrosities out there are going to run right up here. Is that how you want to die?" Lonzo continued walking forward, placing his hand on the gun, and pushing the barrel down toward the ground. "I highly doubt that being ripped to shreds by a bunch of furry beasts was the way you envisioned that you would die."

Dannie licked his lips. "So, I'm guessing you have a suggestion. Let me guess. You sweep me off my feet, and we go on the run and never look back."

"My suggestion is that you tell me how to find your friend, and I promise you will get a chance to start over. Right now, there are a bunch of people that want you dead. I suggest you help me help you."

Dannie rolled his eyes. "This is the last time I'm going to tell you this. I don't know where Kyle is. If I knew, I would put a bullet in him myself."

"Suit yourself. It's your funeral," Londo said before walking out of the room.

"Wait, what is that supposed to mean?" Dannie asked, trying to stop the man from exiting. "And where are you going?"

"I'm leaving. I went through that other house before coming back in here. It's only a matter of time before those things come sniffing over here, following my scent."

"So, what am I supposed to do?"

"Try not to die."

CHAPTER

11

Back at The Association, it was business as usual. Jin stood outside the locked room, waiting for the gas to disseminate. He readjusted the mask that covered his mouth and nose, then looked down at his watch. *It should be about a few more seconds.* He approached the door, accompanied by two armed men, and unlocked it. The three men entered the small, bare room. There were two windows that were partially open. Dry blood stains decorated the walls and floor. Jin kneeled to check the vital signs of a man who was unconscious in the corner of the room. The man was completely naked and made no movements. Jin placed two fingers on the man's wrist, then the side of his neck.

"No pulse," he muttered through the mask.

As soon as Jin made his statement, both gunmen aimed their pistols at the unresponsive male. During previous experiments, the test subjects mutated into creatures within a minute. The gunmen were there to ensure any mutated subjects would be immediately executed. The man's blood would add to the current décor of the room. Jin watched as the minute hand on his watch ticked away. After two cycles went by, he glanced back up at the body. It hadn't mutated. Jin immediately stormed out of the room and removed his gas mask. He used the walkie-talkie to transmit to the rest of his team.

"I need another canister of the gas we just used on Subject 27."

"Really? Did it work, boss?" Sierra asked during the transmission.

"No, it didn't. There was no mutation."

The sound of the front door of the building opening made Jin smile. He watched as Sierra entered his makeshift laboratory and ran up the stairs toward him. She was cradling a gas canister as if it were a football. She handed the canister to Jin who immediately headed toward another room. The two gunmen followed him. Sticking the key into the locking mechanism, Jin unlocked the door. He pulled the mask up on his face and cracked open the canister. Red smoke began seeping out of the top of the canister. One of the gunmen opened the door slightly, with his pistol pointed inside, as Jin tossed the canister into the corner of the room. The door was slammed shut and immediately locked. The men backed away from the door. Each of them ensured that their masks were put on properly. The red smoke began seeping under the door, forcing the three men back even farther. As expected, the smoke rose and disappeared into the air within minutes.

Jin began advancing on the door. Hs stopped in his tracks, noticing one of the gunmen had grabbed him by the back of his lab coat. It was Brody. Brody was one of the troops on the convoy that was attacked by The Association. After the attack, he submitted to the group, knowing it was his only chance of survival. Although some of his brothers in arms joined him, they also had to watch as some were gunned down during the initial attack, and others were imprisoned only to be experimented on by Jin and his research team. Brody often felt like he betrayed his troop by choosing to conform and not be killed. This was a guilt that ate at him daily.

The other guy was a younger man named Mikey. Mikey was one of the stragglers who was brought into The Association early on. He knew how to follow specific orders, so it was not long before Micah assigned him to a security team. Mikey readjusted his mask, which was digging into his nose. He hated putting it on because of this reason.

"Give it another minute," Brody said to the eager doctor. The last thing he wanted to do was rush into the room, knowing what was waiting for them on the other side of the door.

Jin looked at his watch as sixty seconds quickly went by. Brody approached first, putting his ear up to the door. He did not hear anything. He pointed to the doorknob and gave Jin a head nod. Jin slowly unlocked the door, and Brody raised his gun, preparing for a possible attack. The door crept open, and Jin allowed his protection to lead the way. Brody was the first in, hooking to his left upon entry and digging into the deep corner. Mikey crossed to the right. Both men cleared the respective side of the room until they finally had their guns pointed at the subject in the far corner of the room. Just like in the other room, there was no movement, but instead of a man in the corner, it was a beast. It was tied up to an old radiator. The beast was sprawled out on its back.

"See if it's alive," Jin suggested as he tiptoed into the room. Sierra soon followed.

"What's wrong? You don't want to go over there a check its vitals, doc?" Brody laughed.

Jin nodded his head and stayed at the door with Sierra. Brody kept his gun up and grabbed a long metal pipe that was leaning up against the wall. With the pipe in hand, he slowly advanced with Mikey. Sierra and Jin watched intently, as there was still no movement from the beast. Brody jabbed the pole into the side of the beast. There was no reaction. He dug the pipe in once more.

"Nothing," he turned and told Jin.

"Was that supposed to happen?" Mikey asked. "Was the gas supposed to kill it?"

Sierra looked over at Jin. She knew the answer because she worked closely with the determined doctor. Additionally, Brody noticed the disappointed expression on her face.

"Unfortunately, the complete opposite was supposed to occur. The mutation was supposed to reverse, and our friend here was supposed to become human again," Jin replied.

The doctor approached the beast to examine its features. "Sierra, can you log this for me?"

"Yes, sir," she stated, pulling out a small notepad and pen from the pocket of her lab coat.

"The time is 16:35, and there has been no change in Subject 28. Mutated characteristics remain unaltered, and the subject appears to be unresponsive. Vial X was used on both the last four subjects, and we will be moving on to the trials for Vial Y."

Sierra quickly jotted down the notes but paused at Jin's last statement. She knew that there were only two vials left and wondered what they would do if the next two had the same effect. Mikey walked over to the beast and kneeled beside it. He grabbed the beast's hand and held it up, examining the claws. He released the hand, and it fell. "These things sure are ugly," he muttered, looking at the beast's features. Mikey used the tip of his gun to separate its lips. "Look at these teeth. They are sharp as shit."

"Come on, Mikey. Let's get out of here," Brody said.

"What's the hurry?" Mikey turned and asked. "I always wanted to see one of these things up close."

Just as he made the statement, the beast popped up and sunk its teeth into his hand. Mikey screamed and dropped his gun. He threw a flurry of punches, hoping the beast would release its bite from his other hand. Brody raised his gun and aimed at the beast.

"No!" Jin shouted as he jumped in front of the Brody's gun. "Don't shoot it."

"What the hell do you mean? That thing is going to kill him."

"That specimen over there will help us save the world. We have to let this happen."

Brody lowered his gun and watched as Mikey battled with the beast. "Help me," the bloody man yelled as he threw another flurry of punches. The beast bit harder into his hand, snapping it at the wrist. Mikey screamed. The beast clawed into his arm and pinned him to the ground. Mikey fought for his life, but he could not overpower the beast. Pain shot through his entire body until the beast bit into the side of his neck and put him out of his misery. Sierra turned her head, avoiding having to watch the blood bath. However, Brody and Jin looked on. Brody did not care too much for Mikey, but he did not believe the foolish man deserved to die in such a gruesome way. Jin, on the other hand, was intrigued. He wanted to see what kind of effects Vial X would have on the beast. Bite after bite, the beast gnawed away at Mikey's lifeless body. Suddenly, the creature collapsed.

CHAPTER

12

The sound of barking dogs filled the subway tunnels, followed up by a roar of cheers.

"We have hidden in the shadows for far too long. It is time for us to rise up and start a new life. A better life," a man preached, standing on the platform of the tunnel.

The smell of stale urine, trash, and body odor filled the air below. With no power supply, the subway was completely dark. It was even difficult for someone to see their own hand in front of them unless they had a way to illuminate the eerie darkness. Rats crawled around, hoping to find a meal along the subway tracks. Insects crawled through certain sections of the tunnel, seeing what was left over from the rats.

Hundreds of onlookers cheered the man on. The harsh odor did not faze him at all. He was not only used to it, but he preferred it over some of the areas he has been through. What once served as a popular hub for underground transportation was now used as a base for a small militia. Using the subway system to shield themselves from the rampage that was happening on the surface, they were protected from the beasts and other groups of people who feared what was hiding within the darkness. Besides the few creatures that mutated while in the subway stations, the only interactions the militia had were when they sent small groups out to scavenge for food, water, and supplies.

"I have seen what lies on the surface. I have gone toe to toe with those abominations. I will lead you all to the promise land. A place where we can rebuild. A place where we can rule."

Cheers roared again. The subway station was packed with people of all races and ages. Most of them were dressed in black, but those who weren't were still in some type of dark clothing. All eyes were focused on a man standing on the platform of the subway station. He stepped carefully over debris that had fallen from a damaged roof that caved in, ruining the platform.

He stood tall over the crowded platform, ensuring that everyone was able to see and hear him. He ran his fingers through the thick, brown beard that covered his face. The man had an average build, but his presence was enormous. Most of the people who lurked in the world below the surface were those who were not comfortable dealing with the new reality. While others did their best to keep a bit of normalcy in their lives and protect themselves and their property, there were people who just wanted to stay alive. They did not want to deal with the mutations.

Occasionally, the mutated creatures found their way into the subway systems, but they were quickly dealt with. Killing the beasts gave the group courage to begin resurfacing and wreaking havoc on the world above them. They scavenged, bringing back food and supplies. They developed a reputation on the streets. Known for robbing people and burglarizing properties, the group supplied themselves. They were even able to arm themselves after hitting a gun store.

Like with any good thing, nothing lasts forever. The militia's reach was not far, seeing as they only hit areas that were close to the subway stations. It was easier for them to be able to disappear quick, rather than take their chances hiking through the city with supplies. Soon, the amount of supplies that the group was able to collect would slowly deplete.

"We are not going to let time tick by as we sit in these tunnels to rot. We were once America's rejects, but now we will be the rulers of this city. People will bow down to us. We will live like kings and queens." More cheers erupted. He looked on at the cheering crowd. He had big plans for each and every one of them as long as they stayed in line. There would be zero tolerance for treachery. "I came from a group that had the resources to survive for years. The problem we ran into were not being able to separate what we need to be doing versus what we wanted to be doing. Too many people had their own way of doing things. If you are one of those people, leave now because there is no time to waste."

He continued watching the crowd, daring someone to make the wrong choice. In his mind, there was no way out of this scenario. He had an advantage in the war he was about to start, and it was only because he knew the inner workings of his enemy's operation. He would not allow them to have the same opportunity against him.

A smug smirk spread across the man's face as he watched his plan unfold. Just think, he was written off as a dead man, and now he would lead his small militia toward a brighter future. He would lead them toward a future that involved him being the most powerful man in the world. He knew exactly what he had to get his hands on in order to make this dream a reality.

"It is time for The Association to burn, and it is time for the Reaper to return home."

CHAPTER

13

Under the dim lights, beads of sweat trickled down Jin's flat face. Although summer was coming to an end and a cool breeze was flowing through the window, the anticipation of the next experiment caused Jin's body temperature to rise. He looked over at Sierra and the rest of his team, and judging by their moist faces, they felt the pressure as well. The building used as the laboratory was slowly falling apart. The structure was giving away to the elements, and the interior was attracting various types of bugs and rodents. The once unbearable stench no longer affected the occupants of the building. Their own personal body odor and filthy clothes masked any odor that attempted to travel through their nostrils.

The specimens they had caged up did not offer much to them in terms of science.

Until now, they were not able to put a beast down without sending a bullet through its head. Seeing as though Jin's last batch of gas from Vial X seemed to do the job without mutilating the beast, he was eager to dissect the creature that was being strapped to a table. The guards used zip ties, rope, and belts to restrain the deceased creature. Brody looked on, still angry at Mikey's senseless death. Now, Mikey's killer was lifeless and being strapped to the table. Once the guards were finished securing the beast, one of the team members walked up to Jin with a handful of supplies. Jin reached over and grabbed a large scalpel. In the past, he would ensure the supplies had been sterilized, but in the current setting, he was just happy to have the used instruments.

Jin ran his left hand across the chest of the beast. His fingers combed through the thick, black hair that covered the beast's skin. The hair was course. He carefully examined the body. Jin had the guards pour water all over the beast prior to it being brought over because it was covered in Mikey's blood. This was the closest he got to one of the beasts without it trying to devour him or their bodies being covered in blood. The arm of the beast was heavy. "The skin is tight," Jin muttered.

"That's probably because it stretches during the mutation," Abraham muttered through the mask that covered his nose and mouth. Abraham Patel was an associate of Jin and also a medical consultant at the time the government contract was received. Abraham was a surgeon, and like most people, he wanted to stay behind to help others. At the time, Abraham had faith that he could contribute to a cure in some way. Since then, his hope in humanity as a whole had wavered. With no immediate family of his own in Philadelphia, the decision was not hard to stay behind and assist Jin. All of Abraham's family was in India. He had no way of communicating with them to ensure them that he was alive and safe. Mobile communications were still down. He figured he'd fly back to India at the first opportunity that came around once they found a cure for the mutations.

Jin was amazed at the transformation that occurred during the mutations. The beast that was strapped to the table was formerly Corporal Brent Kostowski, who was a young soldier who was passionate about defending his country. The corporal's average-sized body had transformed into a much larger frame. Although the height only slightly increased, the beast's mass was much greater than the former 170-pound body. Jin lifted the hand and examined the large claws that extended past the fingertips. Some of Mikey's flesh and blood was still underneath the nails. They were rough and sharp, explaining why they easily ripped through metal and concrete. The claws on the beast's feet were just as sharp as the ones on its hands. *This is fascinating*, Jin thought as he continued examining the body. Thick knots decorated the beast's body, displaying locations in which the bones had elongated and broken down, only to rebuild. The rebuilt body left the beast with a hunched back, broader shoulders, longer limbs, and bones that were denser than the originals.

Jin stuck his pen in the mouth of the beast, prying the teeth apart. Thick saliva and blood covered the pen. Jagged teeth filled the beast's mouth. There seemed to be an excessive number of teeth that filled the mouth, which Jin knew was a result of the mutation. He remembered Brent's perfect smile that had the potential of being advertised in a Colgate commercial. Now, there were twice as many teeth on both rows.

"Can you clear up a spot for me?" Jin asked, turning to his research team.

Abraham quickly responded to the request, eager to begin the operation. He took a BIC razor and began swiping away at the hairs on the beast. The rusty blade on the old razor barely did the job. Abraham continued swiping away until he was somewhat able to clear a spot on the chest.

"This might be the best I can do. I think this is our last razor too."

"It's ok. This should be fine," Jin replied as he brushed away the shaved hairs from the center of the chest.

He carefully placed the blade on the beast's chest and applied just enough pressure to puncture the skin. Jin slowly slid the blade downward toward the navel.

Jin shot a look at Abraham once he saw the fluid that was escaping the body. *This look is very familiar*. Jin gave the same look during the testing for the martial law operation, when their team was first exposed to the lethal gas. They lost five chemists during that testing, which frightened Jin.

"Is that blood?" Sierra asked. A disgusted expression masked her face.

"I believe so," Abraham replied as he reached over and touched the thick, black fluid. "It looks more like dirty motor oil."

Abraham continued probing the body of the beast as his stomach began to turn. There was not much that could upset his stomach, but for some reason, this examination started taking a toll on him. Staring at the body of what used to be a human being set in the reality that there was no coming back from the destruction he helped cause. Finding an antidote to reverse the mutations would be damn near impossible. "Even if we find a cure, how the hell would we administer it to the entire population?"

There was no immediate answer to his question. There was only silence as Jin made a large, deep, Y-shaped incision that was made from shoulder to shoulder, meeting at his initial incision location and extending all the way down to the pelvis. After the incision was made, the chest flaps were pulled open, exposing the rib cage. Jin worked diligently to carefully remove the rib cage from the skeleton, which appeared to be deformed from the mutation. The task was much harder than expected. Each rib seemed to be thicker, and Jin counted six extra ribs. It was as if the beast's body added an extra layer of protection for the organs.

No one in the group had ever seen anything this extraordinary. The mutations were hideous on the exterior, but the interior was fascinating. The thickening of the bones in the human body would be a remarkable breakthrough. The body would be able to protect itself from breaks and fractures and provide an increase in strength. Jin was heartbroken knowing he would not be able to conduct more research into duplicating these characteristics. Without the luxury of a government-funded research facility and equipment, Jin was limited in what he could do with the corpse, and he was down to his two last vials. If one of them was not the cure, they would be back to square one. If they had to go back to square one, Jin knew that Micah would want blood for all the wasted time. Their leader wanted a cure, and right now, Jin and his team could not provide one.

"I just don't understand any of this," Abraham muttered. "What the hell did they put in that gas that could cause these types of mutations?"

"I have no idea," Jin replied as he continued working on the ribcage. "Don't just stand there. Help me get this thing off!" he yelled at two of the gunmen who were guarding the warehouse.

One of the men grabbed a saw and began working on the ribs. Back and forth, he worked the saw on the thick bone. The repeated motion was exhausting, but he kept trying to no avail. The insignificant cuts in the bones were not going to do the job. They needed more than hand tools to accomplish their goal.

"Let me give it a try," the other gunman suggested. He had a rusty ice pick in one hand and a hammer in the other. His associate moved out the way and watched as he placed the pick on one of the ribs and began hammering away. Using the tool as a chisel, he was sure he would be able to chip away at the thick bone. Strike after strike, the hammer pounded on the top of the ice pick. With each strike, more force was being applied. He continued striking with all his strength. Suddenly, that gunman hammered the ice pick, and the force of the strike caused the pick to slip off the bone. The rusty instrument punctured the liver, and black blood shout out of the organ and into the face of the gunman. He stumbled back and fell over one of the tables.

A canister of the original mutating gas was on the table that was knocked over. The canister opened when it hit the ground, and orange smoke began seeping out. "Run!" Jin yelled as he, Abraham, and the other research team members headed for the door. "Lock the door," he ordered once everyone got out of the room. Everyone was able to make it out except the gunman who had fallen over the table. He was consumed by the orange smoke as everyone was escaping.

CHAPTER

14

"Watch your step," a male voice said.
The group of four stepped over the damaged sign. What was once a florescent sign posted above the front doors that welcomed guests into the 30th Street Train Station was now a damaged pile of metal that blocked the main entrance.

"Are you sure it's safe in here?" Abigail asked Orlando.

"No, I'm not sure, but we don't really have a choice," Orlando responded.

"We did have a choice," Duncan replied. "I told you that we could have checked the other apartments in our building."

"We went up and down the whole floor, Duncan. We got all that we could from the other apartments that were empty. What else was there to do?"

"You know what we could have done," Duncan barked.

"We aren't going to have this discussion again. I already told you that I'm not going to break into other people's apartments and take what's theirs. It's not right."

"Orlando is right. We can't just take from other people," Carol chimed in.

"We can do whatever the hell we want!" Duncan yelled. "There are no laws and no rules anymore. Now let's go."

Th group crawled through the pile of rubble at the front entrance and entered the train station. The abandoned station looked like something out of a horror movie. Every inch of the building told a story of carnage. The damaged signs, broken benches, and caved-in walls did not give the group much hope. What they needed in that moment was food. The 30th Street Train Station was filled with stores and vending machines that could not possibly have been cleaned out.

"It looks like a bomb went off in here," Abigail said.

"It probably did," Duncan uttered. "Look over there."

The group looked in the direction that Duncan was pointing. Bodies were sprawled out all over the floor near a few of the ticket gates. They were all lifeless.

The remains of some were charred, matching the fire and smoke damage that covered that portion of the train station.

"We need to leave right now," Carol said in a terrified voice.

"Leave and do what, Carol? Starve to death? We need to see if there is food in here."

Although she did not want to admit it, Orlando was right. They were out of food and needed to find some quick. Word had gotten out that violent groups had taken over supermarkets, gas stations, and convenience stores, so the group had no choice but to check uncommon locations. Taking the risk and trying to check a supermarket would not have been a good decision. They could not risk running into one of those groups because they had no way to defend themselves. Duncan was a pretty tall guy, standing at six-foot-seven, but he only weighed about 170 pounds. He was more of a marathon runner than a fighter. Orlando was average height and around the same weight. In all honesty, Carol and Abigail had more fight in them than the males who were escorting them in through the train station.

Carol staggered behind the group. Something did not sit right with her. She looked back at the charred corpses that the group spotted when they first walked in. Her intuition was telling her to head back to the apartment building, but she did not want to leave her boyfriend and friends.

"Hey, guys, look," Abigail announced, spotting a vending machine that was illuminated.

"Jackpot!" Duncan shouted as he rushed the machine to get to the contents.

The others ran behind him toward the machine. Everyone hovered over the machine except Carol, who was still lingering in the back. Her head turned back and forth as she continued scanning the environment. The hairs on the back of her neck stood up. "Carol, get your ass over here before Duncan eats all of the chips!" Abigail shouted.

All three of their eyes lit up once they spotted the few snacks that remained behind the cracked glass of the vending machine. Two bags of Cool Ranch© Doritos©, a bag of plain Lay's© chips, a bag of barbeque flavored Lay's chips, and two bags of Cheetos© remained. Pressing his hand against the button pad, Duncan waited a few seconds for the machine to respond. The signal with the price of the item appeared on the vending machine. "You gotta be fuckin' kidding me. I'm not paying for this shit," Duncan barked before cocking his arm back and elbowing the glass. He attempted another strike on the machine, to an avail. The glass still did not shatter. Orlando stood on the side of the machine and began shaking it, hoping the snacks would fall from the slots.

Carol laughed as she watched her friends put in so much effort to get some chips. A sudden movement in the shadows caught her attention. What was that? She stared at the area but did not see anything. The only light that was in the room came from the moon shining through the windows and from the vending machine. Every other light in the station had been broken out.

More movement caught Carol's attention, this time from the area of the charred corpses. Her mouth dropped when she noticed one of the corpses stood up. Then another. She thought her mind was playing tricks on her, but unfortunately, everything she was observing was happening. "Duncan," Carol called out. Her voice cracked out of fear. "Orlando. Abby."

"What?" Abigail responded, still busy trying to shake the vending machine.

"We—we—"

"We what, girl?" Abigail asked, turning around to see what Carol wanted. "Oh, shit," she blurted out.

Dark figures began to emerge from the shadows. Dozens of them. Slowly lurking from the darkness, they surrounded the group. Duncan grabbed Carol's arm and pulled her behind him. "We don't want any trouble," he mumbled.

The dark figures continued pacing back and forth, making it difficult for the group to determine who they should focus on. A deep growl startled them all. Along with the dark figures emerged three pit bulls from the shadows. A hefty man had the dogs secured, using chains as leashes. Each of the pit bulls were ready to be let loose. Their growls turned into repeated barking.

Orlando was sweating. Abigail tried inching behind him but ended up more so behind Duncan with Carol. While Duncan jumped into protector mode, fear left Orlando stuck. Sweat dripped down the scared man's face as he eyed each of the figures who had surrounded them. It was unknown if terror or instincts kicked in, but Orlando was now in a full sprint toward the entrance of the train station. He did not even bother looking back to see if his friends had followed along.

Just as he trampled over the rubble on the ground, he could hear other steps doing the same. However, those steps were not from Duncan, Carol, or Abigail. The steps were from the three pit bulls that were closing in on Orlando. As soon as he took off running, the hefty man let the dogs off their chained leashes. The pursuit was short, as one of the dogs sunk its teeth into Orlando's left calf. On his next step, Orlando's left leg buckled, and he stumbled onto the floor.

The pit bulls wasted no time diving onto the fallen man's back and sinking their teeth into the first portion of his body that became available. Orlando screamed as he felt the pain from the vicious bites to his arm, neck, and side.

"Orlando!" Abigail screamed as she ran toward the injured man.

"Abby, no!" Carol yelled, trying to stop her friend.

Unfortunately, her friend reacted without thinking. Stomping over the debris, she stopped and grabbed a rusted metal pipe. Abigail swung at one of the pit bulls, cracking down on its back. The struck pit bull did not budge. The dogs were locked on to Orlando's limbs as he continued screaming. Blood lined their mouths. He tried to fight them off but was unsuccessful. The force of their bites was excruciating.

Abigail lifted the pipe again to deliver another strike. She was struck on the side of the face and knocked to the ground. "Don't hit my dog again, bitch." The deep voice of the hefty man echoed in the abandoned train station. He stood over Abigail, who had blood dripping from her face from the strike. She never saw him creeping up behind her with the chains and swinging them at her. The metal links split the side of her face wide open.

"Leave her alone!" Carol yelled.

The hefty man picked his head up and looked at Carol and Duncan. A smile spread across his round face, revealing several missing teeth. The ones that did remain were dark and rotted. It did not take long for the smile to turn into a grimace. The man stepped over Abigail and headed toward Carol. His bloody chains were dragged behind him. The dogs continued mauling Orlando as the man approached. The other figures followed suit and closed in on the frightened couple. Duncan and Carol backed up against the vending machine. There was nowhere else to go.

CHAPTER

15

The man let out a low growl. Jin cautiously locked on with the gunmen by his side. The mutation was occurring, but it seemed to be much slower than the usual occurrences. The man was on all fours and began screaming in agony. As he screamed, Jin noticed his teeth began falling out. However, they weren't just falling out, but they were being pushed out. Fangs appeared to be pushing through the bloody man's gums. The only difference seemed to be the color of the blood.

"This is astonishing," Jin uttered under his breath.

"Look at his eyes," one of the gunmen said.

Jin noticed it too. The whites of the man's eyes were changing. They were turning black, matching the color of the blood that was dripping from the mouth of the mutating man. The man began clawing at the floor, trying to get to Jin. He was relentless. The man's hair began falling out. Jin was fascinated at the mutation. Although similar to the beasts that Jin had previously encountered, the mutated man in front of him did not completely transform.

He did not increase in size, which most people did during the previous mutations. Rather than becoming covered in thick fur, his hair fell out. Calluses also began developing all over his skin. It was the gunman who had knocked over the table and released the gas. Being exposed to the gas caused him to mutate, but it was much different than what was expected.

"Doctor Jin, I have the data you asked for," a voice said through the cracked door of the room.

"Doctor Abraham, please come in."

Abraham reluctantly entered the room. Although he was on Jin's research team, he took a backseat when it came to the up close and personal interactions with the live test subjects. He much preferred dealing with subjects who were deceased or knocked out under anesthesia. Even after entering the room, he stood close to the doorway.

"Isn't it remarkable, my friend?" Jin asked as he took the clipboard from his colleague's trembling grasp.

"Are you sure that it's safe to be in here?"

"It's perfectly fine. Our subject is currently restrained." Jin held up the clipboard and began flipping through the handwritten notes. "Now, let's see what we have here."

Abraham kept his eyes on the mutated man. He was scared to death. As a surgeon in his previous life, Dr. Abraham did not have many encounters with anything out of the ordinary. He was used to normal human anatomy. So, dealing with this subject was truly a concern for him. In his position on Jin's research team, Abraham's primary role is to guide Jin through any surgical operation that needed to be conducted on the test subjects. Outside of his role on the research team, Abraham assisted with any and all medical needs of The Association members. When someone came back to the camp injured, Abraham was first in line to treat them. It was sort of his way to stay connected with the outside world without having to leave the camp.

"Why does this one look different than the others?" Abraham asked, noticing the subject's characteristics.

"He looks different because he is different. He is the product of our decisions, both good and bad."

"What does that mean?"

"Well, my friend, it means that I think we found a breakthrough."

"What breakthrough?"

"I've been thinking ever since I came back into this room. The only difference between this one and everyone else that mutated is that he came in contact with the blood of the beast before being exposed."

"What does that mean?"

"That means we may have found the secret ingredient that will allow us to control the formula in the gas."

"If we can control the formula, then we will eventually find a cure, right?"

"I don't think that's important right now. First, I want to experiment more with this new formula."

Abraham nodded solemnly, hiding the look of concern on his face. When he volunteered to join the research team, a part of him did not mind because Micah wanted them to find a cure for the mutations. Despite Micah's violent persuasion, deep down inside, Abraham knew that once they found the cure, they could work toward getting the world back to normal. He considered Jin to have an intelligent mind but could not understand why the cure was not the focal point of the research.

Jin, on the other hand, was in a world of amazement. He was looking at the big picture. He saw the possibility of altering the chemical gas to create different levels of mutations. This would serve as some sort of balance of control when it came to weaponizing the gas. "Bring in the second subject," Jin ordered.

One of the gunmen walked outside and returned briefly. He was dragging a middle-aged man by his leg. The man appeared to be kicking and attempting to scream, but the layers of duct tape that covered his mouth muffled all noise that he attempted to make.

The gunman delivered a swift kick to the stomach of the bounded man, gaining his compliance.

"I suggest you don't fight with us. You're going to need that energy in a minute," Jin whispered in the man's ear. "Your sacrifice will help save the human race."

Looking into the man's tear-filled eyes had no effect on Jin or the decision he had made. He had seen that look so many times. This was the same look he got from the original test subjects that the government volunteered for the first trials and from the troops who were captured and caged at the hands of Micah. Jin had no problem sacrificing a few lives if it meant that he would get a chance to save millions more.

"Untie him," Jin ordered.

The gunmen cut the rope from the man's wrists and ankles. The man instantly tried to bolt for the door but was met with a pistol in his face. On the other side of that pistol was someone who would not hesitate to pull the trigger. Brody was willing and ready to blow the man's brains out all over the floor. A strong front thrust kick sent the man flying backward into the reach of the mutated subject, who wasted no time jumping on the vulnerable prey.

Abraham felt his heart jump in his chest but did his best not to react to the brutality he was witnessing. The mutated subject sunk his claws and fangs into the man, tearing into his flesh. It was a complete massacre. The man did not even try to fight back. He just screamed helplessly as he tried to push way from the mutant. The mutated subject began devouring the man's organs. Abraham could not stomach it any longer and vomited all over the floor before running out of the room. He could not believe what he just saw. It was murder. He recognized the murdered man as being one of the newest members of The Association. *I can't believe they are doing this to our own people,* he thought as he ran back toward his quarters. *Dr. Lee was right. She was right about it all. I have to warn everyone.*

CHAPTER

16

What do you want from us?" Carol yelled. A wool sack covered her head. Tears poured down her face, and snot ran down her nose. The image of Orlando being mauled to death by the pit bulls was stuck in her head.

"Please let us go," Duncan added while squirming to get out of the tight rope that was tied around his wrists. There was a slight tear in the sack that covered his head. He did his best to peek through the tear, but all he saw was darkness. He was kneeling and could feel the debris beneath him stabbing through his flesh.

Blood caused Abigail's sack to stick to her face. Her wound was severe, and blood continued running down her face. She did not even bother putting up a fight because she feared being struck again. A tall figure hovered over the three terrified friends. He remained silent, ignoring their questions and pleas. Their three capturers stood behind them. The chains that were once used as leashes for the pit bulls were now wrapped around their necks. The men on the other end of the chains were chomping at the bit to get a piece of the women. They waited impatiently for the approval to attack.

The tall figure gave a hand signal, and the capturers pulled the sacks from the heads of the captured. Once the sack was off his head, Duncan tried his best to scan the area for the man who was pacing back and forth, but there was nothing but darkness in front of him. He looked back over his shoulder. A strong punch from one of the capturers knocked Duncan to the floor. The pain from the punch throbbed in his jaw.

"Don't fuckin' touch him!" Carol yelled.

Her capturer delivered a front thrust kick to the back of her head, knocking her to the ground. Her capturer yanked on the chain, causing it to tighten around her neck. Carol coughed, the tight chain making it difficult to breathe. Duncan tried to jump up but received the same treatment. The only difference was his capturer was the hefty man who was handling the dogs, so his tight grip began choking Duncan with the chain. Although she remained silent, Abigail suffered the same fate as the others as her capturer pulled on the chain that was around her neck. Abigail fell back as he continued pulling on the chain.

The tall figure stepped forward. Dressed in all black, an oversized hooded coat covered his head. He waved his hand, and the capturers released their grips on the chains. Duncan, Carol, and Abigail were all coughing and attempting to catch their breath. "Do yourselves a favor and shut the fuck up unless I ask you a question. The next time either of you step out of line, I will let you meet your fate. Do I make myself clear?"

Carol nodded her head in agreement. The hooded man looked over at Duncan, who remained silent. Then, he glanced over at Abigail, who was still on the ground. The blood from her wound began to pool around her face.

"You three have a very important decision to make. Currently, we are preparing for war. In order to win this war, I need an army, and that's the only reason you three are still alive. So, the decision that needs to be made is whether or not you will stand with me or against me."

The three remained quiet. The hooded man pulled his jacket back, revealing a sawed-off shotgun that was slung from his belt. He gripped the shotgun and stuck it in Duncan's face. Duncan almost pissed himself as he stared down the barrel of the shotgun. "What's your answer? Do you plan to join my army?"

"Yes," Duncan mumbled.

"What about you?" the man asked Carol, pointing the shotgun toward her.

"Yeah, I'll do it."

The man turned the shotgun from Carol to Abigail. "Last, but certainly not least. What's your answer? Are you with us?"

Still on the ground, Abigail nodded her head.

The hooded man slung the shotgun back on his waist. "Congratulations to you three. You get to live to see another day. Welcome to the Underlings," he announced.

Loud cheers erupted from all over. Torches were suddenly lit, illuminating the dark tunnel. Duncan and Carol looked around in amazement. They were being held on a train platform, and they were surrounded by hundreds of people. They did not know how to feel in that moment. A part of Duncan was grateful that his life was being spared, but the guilt of Orlando's death was a bit overwhelming. If it were not for him and his irrational decision making, the group would still be in the apartment and would have never gone to the train station. He led them all into an ambush.

Abigail was still on the ground in the pool of her own blood. Her physical wound was bad, but the emotional wound was even worse. The loss of Orlando left her numb. She did not know how to feel. A part of her wished she were dead, just so she could be with him. She stared at the sea of people who filled the train tunnel below her. There was no way they would have gotten out of that situation alive.

The hooded man looked down at Abigail. Blood had covered the left side of her face. "Big Rome, take her down into the tunnel and get her patched up." Rome was the hefty man who delivered the brutal blow that split Abigail's face. He released the chain that was wrapped around Duncan's neck and walked over to the thin man who was holding Abigail's chain.

"Why can't I take her, boss?" the scrawny man asked. He knew the answer, but he just wanted to hear it from the boss.

"You know damn well that if I let you take her into that tunnel, she won't make it out."

"So, you just gon' keep hiding the women from me. I got needs, too, boss."

"What you need to do is worry about this move we are about to make and take your mind off these women. Once they become one of us, they are off limits."

"So, what the hell am I supposed to do when I get my cravings?"

"You got two options. You either get those cravings under control, or you give in, and instead of bothering our women, you go stick that dirty dick of yours inside one of those creatures that are out there."

"That's bull shit," he replied before walking away and entering the darkness of the tunnel.

The hooded man turned to Rome and gave him a nod. "Make sure you keep him away from her. You know we need all hands on deck when we head up to the surface."

CHAPTER

17

Abraham ran into his quarters and closed the door. What once was a classroom in the abandoned school now served as the living space for him and two of his peers. Most rooms housed four to five people, but the privileged personnel were given more space and freedom than others. Abraham stumbled onto the old gym mat, which served as the sleeping area in the room. His stomach was still turning. He ripped off his lab coat and threw it against the wall.

"Doctor, is everything okay?" Lori asked. Lori was a nurse in her past life and used to work for Abraham. When the evacuations occurred, she stayed behind with the doctor and a few of their other friends in an effort to care for the wounded who were left behind.

When the group stumbled upon Micah and The Association, they were welcomed with open arms because of their expertise in the medical field. They were seen as an asset to the group and quickly proved to be much more than that.

"No, Lori. They are doing it. They are killing people."

"Who is?"

"Doctor Jin."

"Are you serious?"

"Yes. You need to go get Charlotte and the others. We need to leave."

Lori shared the room with Abraham, along with her teenage daughter, Charlotte. Although she was not a part of the research team, Lori worked with Abraham to help him take notes and stay organized. Often, he would be up late going over formulas and trying to make sense of the changes that occurred in The Association.

When the group first arrived, their biggest concern was treating the wounded and tending to the sick and elderly. Lori also checked on a few of the pregnant members of the organization. When there was a demand for supplies, Micah would send out a team to raid pharmacies and doctors' offices to get Abraham everything he needed. The medical team did not have to worry about working security details or being on search teams, either, which was a benefit to them. The only exception was when Cierra and Amanda went out on the research mission to observe the beasts in the area of the strip mall. That mission ultimately took the lives of several members of The Association, including Amanda's brother. That was also the mission that brought Kyle and his crew back to The Association.

It seemed that once Micah's focus shifted from pure survival to experimentation with the beasts, things changed. Abraham remembered the day that Jin and the soldiers were brought into the building. Abraham and his staff patched up the soldiers just to watch Micah and Adina throw them all in cages and experiment on them.

When these events occurred, Micah's behavior changed too. He became more demanding and began threatening the doctors and researchers when he wanted immediate results. The doctors also noticed that they were treating less people and were soon stuck in the building with the caged beasts all day. A few associates of Abraham did not feel safe under the new dictatorship of Micah and Adina, so they left The Association. This was a decision that Abraham wished he made at the time, but he was still in disbelief. He still saw the potential in The Association and what they could have meant for the survival of Philadelphia and the rest of the country.

"Tell me exactly what happened."

"I just left the room with Doctor Jin. Inside of the room was a mutated subject, and they brought in an innocent man and let that mutant kill that man. This is a part of Doctor Jin's experiments."

"Are you telling me that they are keeping some of those things in this building?"

"Yes and no. It's not the same mutations. This one wasn't that big and didn't look anything like the other ones, but it was just as dangerous. They have it over on the medical ward. It's in a room at the end of the hallway."

"Do you think Micah knows about this? He said he wanted a cure for this disease."

"They don't want a cure, Lori. They want to start a war. Doctor Lee was right. They don't care who they kill to get what they want. Who will be next? Me? You? Charlotte?"

"Don't say that!" Lori could not imagine anything bad happening to her daughter. She vowed to protect her only child, and if Abraham was telling the truth, they all would be at risk.

"Lori, we have to warn the others before it's too late." Abraham popped up and began gathering his notes and other paperwork that was scattered around the room.

"What if you're wrong?"

Abraham stopped in his tracks and looked back at Lori.

"What if they won't harm us? What if we are safe?"

"Lori, don't be naïve. We are not safe here. You saw how Micah reacted during the last research meeting. He threatened to kill one of us because we didn't have the cure. Guess what? We still don't have a cure."

"But he didn't, Doctor Abraham. Those are just scare tactics that he's using to make us work harder."

"So, what about the man I just watched die? Was that a scare tactic too?"

"I don't know what that was, but we can't just overreact and leave. You know they won't just let us walk away from this place."

"I know how we can get out. We just have to find the right time. Just like Doctor Lee and the others."

"And where would we go? Do you have that factored into your little plan? Or do you expect me to take my daughter from a place that we feel safe and walk her through these streets of uncertainty?"

"Safe? You feel safe here? Like you said, we can't leave. We are prisoners in here. What will happen when we are no longer useful to them, Lori?"

"Let's hope we never find out, Doctor Abraham. But as of this moment, I think it's best that we think rationally and do what we have to do to survive."

"I am doing that, Lori. I'm trying to survive."

"Am I interrupting something?"

The third voice in the room startled Abraham and Lori. They both turned to find Jin standing in the doorway. "Doctor Abraham, I came to check up on you. How are you feeling, my friend?"

"He needs rest," Lori chimed in. "Isn't that right, Doctor?"

Abraham looked nervously at Lori. He did not know how much of their conversation Jin had heard. He put down the papers he had gathered, not to draw suspicion. "Yes, Lori, I think I need to get some rest. Is there something you needed, Doctor Jin?"

"Yes, I need a hand with something very important."

"I can help you," Lori insisted.

"Thank you, Lori. Can you do me a favor? Wait for me in the hallway. I'd like to have a quick word with Doctor Abraham."

Lori grabbed her lab coat and clipboard. She gave a brief look to Abraham before walking out. Abraham was unquestionably brilliant, but Lori knew that emotions could get the best of him. After walking out, Lori slowly shut the door but did not close it, hoping to eavesdrop on the conversation.

"Mom!" a voice yelled, coming toward Lori.

"Charlotte, I was just about to check on you."

"Have you seen Tyler?" the teen asked while gasping for air. She had sprinted to the quarters from the supply room.

"No, I haven't seen him. Is something wrong?" Lori asked, seeing the concern on her daughter's face.

"I don't know what's going on. One minute we were doing an inventory in the supply room, and the next, two men with guns came and got him. They told him that they needed him in medical, but they didn't say what they wanted."

"Well, I'm headed over there now. If I see him over there, I'll tell him that you asked about him."

"Okay, thanks, Mom."

"Now, you go back to the supply room and finish up. I'll see you when I get back."

The two hugged, and Charlotte headed back to the supply room. Tyler was Charlotte's best friend, and Lori knew that she would be interrogated by her daughter if she did not relay the message. Charlotte looked after Tyler like a little brother. They grew up in the same neighborhood and went to the same schools since first grade. When he was younger, Tyler was diagnosed with epilepsy. Tyler had the disease under control when he was medicated, but that medicine was rare to come by during the supply runs, so his conditioned worsened. This prevented Tyler from being able to join the security teams and search teams like other young men. Instead, he was placed in the supply room. During one epileptic episode, Tyler had a seizure and dropped a carton of eggs on the floor. The security guards were livid that the food was wasted, and they took it out on Tyler. They beat him down and forced him not to eat for a week to make up for the broken eggs.

Charlotte felt bad for Tyler and snuck him half of her rations during this time. She noticed that his condition was worsening, so she helped him out in the supply room and watched over him when he had episodes. Lori knew that without Charlotte, Tyler would not be able to manage his day-to-day responsibilities. Lori waited for Jin to exit the room, then the two headed toward the medical ward.

CHAPTER

18

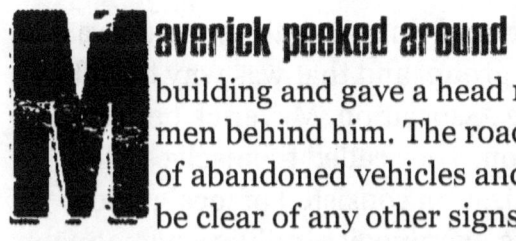averick peeked around the edge of the building and gave a head nod to the three men behind him. The road, a filthy stretch of abandoned vehicles and trash, seemed to be clear of any other signs of life.

"Let's move," he ordered, leading with his rifle. The former Army vet and Philadelphia police sergeant was very comfortable with the weapon he toted. Any sudden movements would result in him putting his marksmanship skills to use. Maverick was fortunate enough to have a couple of his officers rolling with him on the mission. Once the evacuations were announced, almost all the officers he knew took their families and headed out of the city. This would become a decision that Maverick wondered if he should have made too. The group moved stealthy toward their target, which was a crappy hospital that sat catty-corner from their current position. Even before the world changed, the hospital was one of the worst in the city.

It was known for poor service, angry employees, and being in dire need of remodeling. Despite a reputation that would make anyone with common sense turn away from the building, it was still a medical facility, and Maverick 's team needed to restock on the supplies that could be inside.

"I don't know why we just don't take the building," Dalton uttered quietly.

"Because it's too far from our safe zone," Maverick replied. "We can't take any unnecessary chances right now."

Dalton was a forward thinker, but Maverick was the most logical in the group, and that was why he led them. Just like The Association, Maverick belonged to his own organization. They called themselves The Saviors. The organization consisted of local police officers, firefighters, paramedics, military personnel, and civilians who wanted to take part in the new battle between good and evil.

The Saviors were on a mission to protect innocent civilians who were still in the city and to also take down any criminal organizations that existed to cause terror. The Underlings were at the top of their list. Although there were brutal attacks on officers and their police stations during the end of times, The

Saviors managed to preserve their station, which was also on the same block as the fire department, grocery stores, a used car dealership, and two small pharmacies. There were also similar groups like them operating in other parts of the city. Using radio communication to update each other, there was a common goal to take back the city and to restore humanity. They cordoned off a five-block radius in this neighborhood, planning to continue to spread their reach throughout northeast Philly. The Saviors would have to spread out to approximately eighteen blocks if they wanted the hospital to be in their safe zone. This was a task that would take them a few months and would stretch them thin.

"I'm not going to give up an entire neighborhood for this shitty ass hospital," Maverick said to his team. "Plus, we don't know who or what is in this place."

This was the first time The Saviors branched out to the hospital. Most of the medication and supplies they obtained were from the small pharmacies that were in their safe zone and a few that were just outside of the zone. They, along with others, had cleaned those places out, and it was time to find a new source.

"I hope this place isn't booby-trapped like the Walgreens was last week," Jace said as he swiveled his head backward to ensure no one attempted to ambush his team.

"Well, if there is, Darren and the Bravo team can roll up and give us a hand," Maverick replied.

After almost losing a member of his team due to someone setting up a homemade explosive device at the Walgreens, Maverick made sure a second team came along with them. That team was led by Darren Gardner, a former bomb squad technician with the Philadelphia Police Department. Darren's team conducted an initial sweep of the exterior of the hospital for any suspicious devices, but none were located. They were now going to secure the exterior of the hospital while Maverick and the Alpha team carried out their mission.

"Dalton, hit the door," Maverick ordered.

Dalton was breathing heavily, awaiting the order. He nodded, then headed straight to the front doors. He looked back at Maverick after tugging on each handle. "They're locked."

"Get them open."

Dalton pulled out his Glock 17 handgun and screwed on a suppressor on the end of the barrel. He sent four shots through the large glass on the door, shattering it. He then pulled out an expandable baton and knocked out the remaining glass before sticking his hand through the new opening and unlocking one of the doors from inside. Dalton opened the door, allowing his team to move in.

The glass cracked under their boots as they crept in. Maverick's rifle was locked and loaded. He was the point man in the diamond formation as they entered. This was a position he had been in often, leading

SWAT teams on some of the most dangerous situations throughout Philadelphia.

Sunlight shone through the windows, providing ample lighting for the team as they moved through the building. Any other areas would be lit by the flashlights on the end each man's weapon of choice. The bright LED light on Maverick's rifle hit the dark corners and lit them up.

"Look at this place. It's a mess," Maverick muttered under his breath.

"It was already a mess. The apocalypse just gave it an upgrade," Dalton chimed in while chuckling.

"You got a point."

"Hey, look on the bright side. Maybe the poor reputation of this place was enough to keep the scavengers out."

Other members of the group laughed at Dalton's statement. He could not help himself. Dalton found humor in every situation, no matter how serious or dangerous it was.

Maverick raised his fist, stopping the group in their tracks. "Give me two left," he ordered. His eyes were focused down the hallway, ready for any type of threat to pop out. Two of his men broke the formation and stacked up on the doorway of a room on the left side of the hallway.

Dalton and Erik tactically entered the room. It only took the two men seconds to clear the small triage room. Dalton hooked, and Erik crossed, both digging deep into the corners of the room. Dalton noticed that the cabinets and drawers in the room were all ransacked.

"The room is clear," Dalton announced.

"Come on out," Maverick ordered.

"Someone already cleaned out that room, Mav."

"Figures. What kind of room was it?"

"Triage."

"Copy. Let's keep moving and try to find the supply closet."

Dalton and Erik hopped back into their positions in the formation. "Two right," Maverick ordered just before two hit the next room. The team continued through the first floor of the hospital, clearing each room as they passed. The deeper they got into the hospital, the less ransacked the rooms seemed to be. Dalton's eyes lit up seeing the supplies in the rooms they were clearing. There were boxes of rubber gloves, gauze, and basic medical equipment just sitting in some of the rooms.

Maverick raised his hand once again, halting his team.

"Look at that," he muttered as he intensified the flashlight on his rifle.

Maverick was observant. He noticed the damage to that section of the hospital. The overhead lights were broken, deep scratch marks decorated the walls, and dry streaks of blood lined the floor.

"Keep your eyes open. We need to find that med room and get the hell out of here."

Maverick's flashlight shone down the dark hallway. Contemplating his next move, Maverick took a deep breath. He knew the risk of continuing down the hallway. All signs pointed to an encounter that he would rather avoid. It was the unknown. There could be one beast in the building, or it could have been a hundred. Although he was prepared to encounter other humans, he did not have the manpower to take on a pack of beasts if that situation presented itself.

"Let's move," Maverick ordered before advancing into the dark abyss. Only slivers of sunlight were able to reach this portion of the hospital, doing little to lighten the area. "Give me two right."

Dalton and Erik hit the next room, stumbling into the small area over an item that blocked the threshold.

"What the fuck was that?" Erik asked.

Dalton did not have to say a word because the stench of death in the room answered the question. Human remains blocked the doorway. Limbs were completely ripped off one of the bodies, and another appeared to be decapitated.

"Stay focused," Dalton uttered, noticing that Erik's focus was on the bodies rather than clearing the room with him. "Check this out."

A medicine cart sat in the corner of the room. Dalton darted toward the cart, ripping the doors open. "Bingo!" he yelled out, revealing the contents that filled the cart. Erik snapped out of his daze to see why his friend was making so much noise.

"What the hell?" Erik said after seeing the load that was left in the cart. "How is this stuff still here?"

Gunshots rang out in the hallway, followed by yelling. Dalton pushed the cart away and headed for the door. Just as he went to peek into the hallway, a large black blur flashed by the doorway. Seconds later, another blur passed.

Maverick let a flurry of shots fly out of his rifle as the black furry creatures rushed him. Jace followed up with a few of his own. A loud roar was let out as bullets ripped through one of the creatures. Dalton and Erik also popped out to join the fight. All four of the men let shots rip as the second beast made its way toward the entrance.

"Bravo team, you got contact coming your way."

The beast busted through the front door. The strength of the beast sent the doors flying off the hinges and into the street. The hideous creature began sniffing the air, picking up a sent. Blood and saliva dripped from its sharp teeth. A single shot from a sniper on the roof put the creature down easily as the bullet tore through its head. The beast immediately dropped.

"Nice shot," Darren said. "Alpha team, what's your status?"

"We're good," Maverick replied over the walkie-talkie. "Keep your eyes open, fellas. There could be more of them."

"Mav, that room we were in had a med cart that's fully stocked."

"Ok, we'll just have to hit grab that stuff and go."

"Just that? Let's keep going."

"No. It's not worth it."

A noise came from another room up ahead. Maverick immediately locked on it, and his team did too. They carefully moved forward, advancing on the room. Maverick hesitated, not knowing if more beasts were waiting on the other side of the door. "Give me two left."

Dalton and Erik stacked up on the door.

"Slow it down," Maverick ordered in a low voice. "Swing it open and cut the pie. Don't rush in."

Erik gripped the knob on the door and slowly turned it. The door began opening, and Erik swung it open. Dalton was perched up over his shoulder, ready to attack anything that came out of the room. A few seconds went by, and the doorway was still clear. Dalton looked back at Mav, who gave him a nod. Erik and Dalton entered the room.

"Contact!" Dalton yelled out.

"Don't fuckin' move!" Erik yelled. "I'll blow your fuckin' brains out."

Both men had their guns trained on two subjects who were tucked in the corner. One of them was sprawled out on the ground, and the other had his hands raised in the air. The young man with his hands raised was sure not to make a move. "Who are you?"

"My name is Levi."

"What the hell are you doing in here?"

"I was trying to get this guy some help," Levi replied. Kyle was still a bloody mess and appeared to be unresponsive. He had no idea what was taking place in the small room. His breathing was labored, and his body was numb.

"What's your status?" Maverick asked from the hallway.

"We got two subjects in here," Dalton replied.

"It sounds like we are about to have company, so let's get out of here."

CHAPTER

19

Lori was a few steps behind Jin as they headed to the medical ward. She noticed the fast pace in his steps. He was walking with determination. She could not help but think about the conversation she had with Abraham. This was a similar conversation she had with Lee before the first group left The Association. She did her best to convince them to stay, but her pleas fell on deaf ears. She was hoping history would not repeat itself. Although Lori knew that she could be useful to The Association, in the back of her mind, she knew that she was not a doctor. This meant that without Abraham, she was not really sure what her fate would be.

"Thank you for assisting me with this, Lori," Jin said as they reached the medical ward. A tiny grin spread across his face as he looked back at her.

"No problem, Doctor Jin." A tiny smile accompanied her response. The tiny smile dropped away when she spotted the door at the end of the room. *That's the room Abraham was talking about,* she thought. The closer they got to the door, the more anxious she became. Lori always stuck by Abraham's side, so like him, she had not had too many encounters with the beasts. She also was not privy to all information that was shared between the heads of the research team.

Jin opened a door to a small room. Inside was an empty classroom. There were only two desks and two chairs in the room. There were boxes of office supplies in the corner of the room. Printer paper, pens, staplers, scissors, and more filled the boxes. On one of the desks were three stacks of handwritten notes. These were the notes Jin had Abraham take about the last experiment and also some of his own. "I need these lab notes copied."

Lori glanced at the stacks of notes that Jin wanted her to copy. Each stack was about two feet tall, and she knew it would take her about two days to organize and rewrite everything he wanted. "I'll be down the hall if you need anything," Jin said before exiting the room.

"Doctor Jin."

"Yes, Lori. What is it?"

"I want to be more than an assistant."

"What do you mean?"

"I mean, I'm not stupid. Being an asset is valuable in this place. I need to be valuable if I want to survive in here."

Jin laughed. "You are starting to sound like our friend, Abraham. I'm guessing that is what your little quarrel was about when I stepped in the room."

"Yes. I want to be better. I want to be more valuable. I want to do more than just take blood pressures, give out medication, or copy notes. I want to be a doctor."

"Well, how do you propose we make that happen?"

"You can let me do more than take notes. I can help do small operations and surgeries. You can teach me and then let Micah know about my progress."

"Isn't that something Doctor Abraham should be doing?"

"Yes, it is, but he will never agree to it. That's why I'm asking you."

Jin took a deep breath, then stepped back into the room. "Lori, logging this data is a very important job. You wouldn't be here if I didn't think you were valuable."

"I hear what you're saying, Doctor Jin, but that's not good enough for me. I have to be able to do more than this."

"You will be able to do more than logging data, but right now, we are in very trying times. We are performing very serious experiments, and we need people we can trust by our side."

"I can be trusted, Doctor Jin. Please let me help you with more than just copying notes."

Dr. Jin was reluctant to take Lori up on her offer. Judging by the reaction he got from Abraham, he was not sure if she could stomach the experience. However, he needed assistance. He needed someone by his side to properly document each step that was being taken while creating the formula and the different stages of the mutation. The notes had to be precise so he could replicate the process if need be. "Are you sure that you're up for this?" he asked sternly. The change in Jin's tone was a bit concerning.

"Yes. I'm ready."

"Well, let's go."

Jin usually worked alone, but recently; things had become overwhelming. In the past, technology was his partner. He would record his experiments and research sessions and come back to them at a later date when documenting the steps. Times had changed, however, and there was not much technology in his reach. The Association had access to generators but powering up a computer or charging an iPad was not more important than keeping the lights on and necessary appliances running. He had to make do with what he had in front of him. And at the time, it was Lori.

She followed him into another room. The closer they got to the room; a muffled voice seemed to be coming from behind one of the doors. Lori couldn't tell which room the voice was coming from, but it was getting louder. When they first arrived at The Association, Lori had helped create the medical ward in the building. Alongside Abraham, their team helped turn the music wing of the school into a makeshift hospital. They created the medical ward for very sick individuals and those who were exposed to the chemical gas in some way. The rooms in the medical ward were equipped with restraints, so if a mutation did occur, the rest of the members of the group would not be in danger of an attack from a beast. But now, the medical ward had a very eerie feeling to it.

Jin entered the room, followed by Lori. "Gentleman, is our subject ready?"

"Yes, he is, sir," one of Jin's gunmen responded.

What subject? Lori thought as she closed the door behind her.

"TYLER!" Lori yelled out, spotting her daughter's friend strapped to a chair. "What in the hell is going on?" Lori asked, running over to the teenage boy and checking his vitals. "Why is he in here?"

"Lori, please get over here," Jin requested.

"Doctor Jin, what is this?"

The sound of a gun cocking grabbed Lori's attention. She slowly stood up as both gunmen approached her.

"Lori, do we have a problem?" Jin asked.

"Yes, we have a problem. Why is Tyler in here, Doctor Jin?" Lori's voice began to rise.

"Lori, I need you to calm down. I'll explain everything."

"Please do."

"Well, seeing as though you are a part of the medical team here, you know all about this young man's condition. You also know that we have run out of medication to give him in order to control his seizures. As long as he continues to have these seizures at random, he is a risk to us all. What you don't know is that recently I have had a breakthrough with the mutation formula that I was working on. We are on the brink of a cure, Lori. A cure for those dangerous mutations. A chance to get back to our old lives. A chance to restore humanity. The only problem is that my breakthrough formula needs to be tested in order to guarantee its results. We already had one successful trial, and this young man volunteered to be a part of the next trial."

"Volunteered? My daughter told me that Tyler was instructed to come here. That doesn't sound like he volunteered for anything."

"Lori, I'm giving him the opportunity of a lifetime. An opportunity to be free of that disease that currently controls his life."

"Then, why is he passed out? Why is he not awake for this trial?"

"He was sedated. It's for his own good."

"For his own good or for yours?"

"For all of us," Jin insisted, stepping forward to place his hand on Lori's.

Lori pulled her hand back in disgust. She kneeled next to Tyler and ran her fingers through his straight brown hair. "What's going to happen to him?"

"To be honest, the first trial involved exposing the subject to a chemical gas. Once inhaled, the gas caused a slight mutation in that subject. We believe this new formula that we just created will not have the same mutative effects and would be able to possibly reverse the effects on fully mutated subjects. For this young man, I would like to use an injectable form and track the release of it within the human body. That's why I need your assistance with the documentation."

"So, you're going to turn him into one of those monsters? You can't do this."

"Lori, I didn't say that. We are simply going to give him an injection and document what happens to his body. That's the only way we can find out if this new formula is the cure."

"There must be another way to do this."

"There is no other way—"

"There's always another way!" Lori barked. "So, you're just going to kidnap our own people and turn them into monsters?"

"Just the ones with a low survival rate."

"What the hell does that mean?"

"Epilepsy, cancer, AIDs, hepatitis. There are people among us that are going to suffer and die because there is nothing we can do about their illnesses. We're running out of medications, and we don't have the resources to properly treat those people. Rather than letting them suffer, I'm giving them the opportunity to sacrifice. Their sacrifice will guarantee our survival."

"You're God now, huh? You get to decide who lives and who dies, while the rest of us just wait until the decision is made that it's our turn to become one of your little Frankenstein projects. Is that it?"

"You have no room to talk!" Jin snapped. "You have it good here. You don't know what it means to be out there trying to survive. You sit in this fortress and eat well, while the rest of us have to bear the burden of saving the world. You haven't suffered, Lori. You haven't been on the brink of death only to beg for your life to be spared. I have. I understand what it takes to survive in this world, and that's what we're going to do here. You either get in line or get out of our way."

Jin gave a head nod, and one of his gunmen pounced on Lori, pinning her to the ground. Lori kicked and screamed, hoping someone would hear her. The gunman placed his hand over her mouth, muffling her screams. Jin walked over to a table and opened a box, revealing three large syringes that were filled with a thick, black fluid. Jin wrapped a belt around the sedated teen's left arm and pulled it tight. Veins began to bulge out of his arm, and Jin wasted no time stabbing one of the needles into one of the veins and injecting the liquid.

"Ahhh, shit!" the gunman yelled after Lori sunk her teeth into his hand. She pushed him off her, causing his gun to drop. Lori grabbed the gun and slammed on the trigger, barely missing the gunman who was crawling on the ground. She held the gun up to the other gunman.

"Drop your gun," she ordered. The man complied.

"What—what's going on?" Tyler muttered, coming out of the sedation.

"Unbelievable," Jin said. "Lori, look. He's waking up from the ketamine. That's impossible."

"Tyler, listen to me carefully. These men are trying to hurt you. They injected you with something that's going to mutate you."

The teen could not believe what he was hearing. He was going in and out of consciousness. "Ms. Lori, I don't feel too good."

"I know, Tyler. It's going to be okay."

"Help me, Ms. Lori."

Lori's heart sunk into her stomach. Hearing Tyler's innocent voice sent her over the edge. "Release him—NOW!" she shouted at the gunman. The man looked over at Jin, who shook his head not to follow the order.

BANG!

"The next one will be in you and not that wall," Lori said. She slowly walked over to the table and closed the box that now held two syringes. "Now, release him."

The man wasted no time scurrying over to Tyler and cutting the restraints. The woozy teen stood up and stumbled over to Lori. "Listen to me, Tyler. Take this box and go to Abraham. Tell him that he needs to leave."

"But Ms. Lori—"

"GO!"

Tyler staggered out of the room with the box containing Jin's needles. He was still confused and did not understand what was going on, but he followed Lori's orders.

Jin carefully watched the teen, amazed that he was even able to stand. Normally, someone in his condition would still be nodded out in the chair. "You're making a grave mistake, Lori."

"Shut up. Doctor Abraham was right about you. You're not going to get away with this."

"Lori, I was just trying to save us all. You just released that boy into our encampment, and there's a possibility that he is going to mutate in a matter of minutes. Once he does, he's going to murder everyone in here, including your daughter. We still have time to stop him."

"I'm not stopping anything except you and everything you're doing in here. You will no longer hurt innocent people. I'm going to tell Micah everything."

"Go ahead and tell him. Did you forget that he's the same guy that ordered me to test those troops that we brought in? Oh yeah, the one thing you didn't know is that he murdered twice as many soldiers during the attack on the convoy the same day he brought me into this place. He's not your savior. So, whatever you think he's going to do once you tell him what's going on, I promise you it won't help your little situation."

Jin inched closer to Lori. "Put the gun down so we can talk about this. A few minutes ago, you just asked me how you could be an asset to The Association and working alongside me will definitely make you an asset."

"You're lying," Lori responded, switching her aim from the gunmen to Jin.

"I'm not lying. I can ensure your safety and the safety of your daughter. Nothing will happen to you two. Lori, make the smart decision. Think about your future. Think about her future."

"I can't. I can't let you do this."

"So, what are you going to do? Shoot me?" Jin asked, walking up to Lori. He raised his hands and stepped forward until the barrel of the gun was pressed against his chest. "Do it. Pull the trigger."

The tension in the room could be cut with a knife. Before Lori could decide, Jin sidestepped and gripped the outside of her wrist. Lori slammed on the trigger. The shots hit the back wall of the room. She kept slapping the trigger until the gun locked back. Once it did, Jin tossed Lori to the ground. Maintaining his grip on her wrist, Jin put Lori in an arm lock. Her screams traveled through the halls as he snapped her arm, breaking it at the elbow.

"Throw her in the other room with that mutant and let's go find that kid."

CHAPTER

20

The smell of death lingered in the air. Kyle could barely open his eyes. His eyelids seemed as if they were being held shut. It felt like the weight of the world was spinning him down to the ground. Gunshots rang off in the distance, and suddenly, his eyes popped open. Orange smoke surrounded him. The smoke was the vessel for the toxic gas that caused the mutations. Kyle could not locate the source of the smoke. He coughed, trying his best not to inhale the smoke. His eyes began watering, making it difficult for him to see. Kyle pushed himself up, barely able to stand to his feet. He continued coughing. Kyle staggered as he tried to escape the smoke. Surprisingly, the wounds that left him crippled seemed to not affect him in the moment.

Kyle was able to get his legs under him and took off in a full sprint. In his mind, it was a full sprint, but in all actuality, it was a light jog. The gunshots rang off again. They seemed to be getting closer to him. His heart was racing out of his chest. Even though he was jogging, Kyle could not escape the toxic smoke. It was getting thicker and began filling his lungs. Kyle stopped in his tracks, coughing up a lung. His stomach turned, and he vomited. His body began to heat up. Kyle felt like his skin was on fire.

The world was closing in on him. Kyle dropped to his knees and vomited again. This time, blood came up, along with the contents from his stomach. Everything began to spin. Kyle fell face first into the pool of vomit. His body slammed against the hard concrete as he began violently seizing. The seizure lasted about two minutes.

After the seizure subsided, Kyle tried to get up off the ground. He placed his hands under his chest to push himself up. He watched as his fingernails began to slowly grow, ripping away from his cuticles. The hair on his arms thickened, completely covering his skin. The gas that once choked him up, was now having no effect on him. A sudden craving for meat came over Kyle. His mouth began to water. A mixture of saliva and blood dripped out of his mouth. A sharp pain shot through his mouth as his teeth began growing in his mouth. Kyle screamed.

"Hey, are you okay?" a soft voice asked.

Kyle popped up from an obvious nightmare. He tried to sit up in the bed, but his back was aching. His body still felt like it was on fire. Sweat poured down the side of this face. He was panicking. Kyle's head swiveled from left to right as he surveyed his environment. There was no sign of the thick smoke and no gunshots going off. He also looked down at his body, relieved to see that his hand was normal and no longer a furry claw. Kyle was grateful to be alive.

The dusty window curtain was blowing back and forth as a cool breeze crept through the cracked window. A woman placed her hand on Kyle's forehead. He was burning up. She placed a cool, wet rag on his forehead and walked over to open the window more. After making sure everything in the room was to her liking, she stepped out of the room. Kyle turned over on his left side to alleviate the sharp pain that was shooting through his back. With the window fully open, the breeze was alleviating.

"You need to rest," Maverick said.

Kyle never noticed that Maverick was standing at the head of the bed. "Where am I?" Kyle asked.

"You are in a safe place." Maverick walked over to the window and looked out.

Kyle stared at the man, who he was not familiar with. Kyle spotted the shredded, thin, blue-line, American flag tattoo that draped Maverick's arm. He knew if he ever met the man before, he would remember that tattoo. The tan man continued looking out of the window. A red Phillies baseball cap covered his head, and a thick, brown beard almost hid his lips. The flag tattoo represented the two things that Maverick dedicated his life to, which were his country and his career.

After the military, Maverick jumped right into the police academy. From the moment he sat in his first class at Valor Hall to the moment he received his first bravery accommodation, he shined like a star. Maverick was fearless and stood up to every challenge that came his way. He was born to be a leader, and it showed as he navigated through the new world. If it were not for him, the current safe haven that they were in would not exist.

"I wanted to be here when you got up, but you really need to get some rest. You are pretty banged up. It's going to be a while until you get back on your feet."

"I don't think I'll be able to rest for a while," Kyle responded. Between the back pain and the high-grade fever, he was very uncomfortable.

"Take this." Maverick walked over to Kyle and placed a prescription bottle in his hand. "The kid you were with in the hospital gave them to me. He said they were helping with the pain."

Kyle nodded. He struggled, trying to open the pill bottle, which was a task that Levi took over during their short stay in the hospital. Maverick was quick to pick up on Kyle's body language. He took the bottle out of Kyle's hand and cracked it open. He placed two of the painkillers in Kyle's mouth and followed up with a glass filled with cloudy water to wash them down.

"Thank you," Kyle muttered in agony.

"Listen, get some sleep, and when I return, I would like to ask you a few questions."

"Ask me them now!"

"Are you sure?"

Kyle nodded.

"I wanted to know if you could tell me more about the place you are from. I tried to ask the boy, but he said he didn't know much about you. Is that true?"

Kyle nodded again. "The place that I came from is called The Association. I don't know much about them. I was only there for a short time. Their group is up in the northeast."

"What else can you tell me about them?"

Kyle scooted himself up a bit. "The Association are monsters. They killed my family."

"And by the looks of it, they tried to kill you too. I'm assuming they are the ones that did this to you."

Kyle nodded his head once again, confirming Maverick's suspicions.

"The boy said there were some people looking for you back at the church. Was that The Association?"

"Honestly, I don't know. The last thing I remember is being in the truck and then seeing . . ." Kyle paused, thinking about Jacqui.

"Seeing what?"

"Nothing. I don't even remember."

"It's okay, my friend. Just tell me why The Association did this to you. What did you do to them?"

"I killed one of their leaders."

Maverick let out a deep sigh. It did not take a rocket scientist to figure out how much heat was now going to be on Kyle. This is exactly what the other members feared would happen. It was bad enough defending their territory against The Underlings and other small militia groups but being on the radar of another enemy is the last thing they wanted to do, especially when it was an outsider that was causing the tension.

"Why'd you kill their leader?" Maverick asked suspiciously.

"I did it because she is the one that had my family killed. You don't understand who these people are. They are terrorists."

"Kyle. I hear everything you are saying. But I just can't afford to take your word on this type of situation without some sort of explanation behind it. For you to kill a leader of any group, there must be a particular reason for it. It sounds like the death of your family was that reason, but how do I know that you aren't the terrorist in this situation? How do I know that I won't be the next leader that you try to kill?"

Kyle watched as Maverick pulled out a hunting knife and clenched it while resting his hand on his lap.

"You can put that away. I'm not your enemy. I can tell you all about their operation. You can make the determination yourself."

"Well, you better start talking."

"So, the day I met these monsters, I was home. They had a small group and were raiding our neighborhood. House by house, they would go in and take what they wanted, including innocent lives. I was in the house with my wife and daughter when they attacked our home. I tried to fight them off in a gun battle, but they had weaponized that chemical gas that caused the evacuations."

Maverick frowned. "What do you mean they weaponized it?"

"They had it filled in canisters. Tossing it in different houses, including mine. They pumped the gas into my home, and my daughter mutated." Kyle paused, and his head dropped. Taking a deep breath, he continued, "Once my daughter mutated, she killed my wife, and I was forced to kill her to protect myself. I ended up finding my way into their headquarters. At the time, I didn't know that it was the same group. Once inside, I saw everything. They have a doctor in there that is experimenting with the gas and mutating our troops. He had soldiers locked in cages, and they are killing them one by one. These people are sick. They are operating out of the old Northeast High School."

Maverick sat back in his chair. "Northeast?"

"Yup. The school and the blocks surrounding it. They have it blocked off pretty good too."

Maverick tucked his knife back in the holster and hurried out of the room. Kyle tried to turn his head to see what Maverick was doing, but the sound of the

148

door slamming let him know that his guest had left. Kyle returned to his most comfortable position as the painkillers began kicking in and doing their job.

Maverick busted back in the room moments later, and this time, he was accompanied by Dr. Lee. Maverick plopped back into his seat, but instead of having his knife, he held a map in his hand. He held the map up and showed it to Kyle.

"Are you telling me that the people you are talking about are stationed at this location?"

Kyle took a look at the map and saw The Association's territory marked off. He sat up despite the agony it put him through and grabbed the map from Maverick. "Give me a pen."

Maverick handed him a marker. Kyle tried to remove the cap from the marker but was unsuccessful. "Here, give it to me," Maverick said before taking it back. "Show me what you were about to mark."

"That's the entrance," Kyle said, pointing to Cottman Avenue on the map. Maverick marked it. "It's heavily guarded," Kyle said. "All of this right here is nothing. I think they burned the buildings down so they can be occupied."

"That's dumb. If they burned those buildings, that eliminates their chances of expanding their footprint. Why would they do that?"

"It's for visibility. They don't want to give their enemies the opportunity of getting that close to them. Plus, they aren't focused on expansion. They want to eliminate everyone else, including the innocent."

"If that's the case, then I can only assume that they have burned everything that surrounds them, not just in the front. Can you show me how far their reach goes on here?"

Kyle and Maverick spent the next thirty minutes going over the map. Kyle accurately pointed out The Association's borders and their interior workings, such as the location of the lab, vehicles, and everything else he remembered. Dr. Lee hovered over the two men in amazement. She was impressed by Kyle's recollection of the territory but also to the sophistication of The Association's operation.

"Oh, I'm sorry. Kyle, this is Dr. Lee. I asked her to join us because I wanted her to take a look at your injuries, but I also told to her that you mentioned that this organization had a doctor on scene."

"Yes, they did."

"What was the doctor's name?" Dr. Lee asked.

"I can't remember."

That wasn't the answer Dr. Lee was looking for. She needed to know if her suspicions were correct.

"Can you describe the doctor?" Maverick asked.

"Umm. He was a short, Asian man. He had like salt-and-pepper hair. He was annoying. I wanted to put a bullet in him once I found out about the troops."

"I think that's him. That's Jin," Dr. Lee said to Maverick.

"Wait, you know him?" Kyle asked.

"Something like that," Dr. Lee replied. "So, what exactly was he doing with the troops?"

"I think he was the one that weaponized the gas and was testing it on them. He had them all locked in cages like animals. By the time we saw them, they were all mutated. He was studying them, but I don't know what exactly he was doing. Like I said, he was annoying, and I wanted to kill his ass."

"I need that research," Dr. Lee whispered to Maverick. "If he is doing tests, I'm sure he's doing them both ways. He has to have the cure for the mutation. That's probably what his studies were focused on."

Maverick took a minute to process everything he was hearing. To the other two in the room, this information wasn't shocking, but Maverick was a bit in disbelief. "So, you mean to tell me that they can control the mutations?"

"No. I wouldn't say control the mutations. They just found a way to bottle up the gas that causes the mutations. They put them in the form of smoke grenades."

"Have you ever seen them cure anyone? Has anyone turned back human after being mutated?"

"Not that I know of. They didn't seem like the type of people that were concerned in that type of research anyway. But like I said, I wasn't there that long."

"We'll be right back," Maverick said, standing up and walking to the door with Dr. Lee.

"What do you think?" Maverick asked.

"I think we need a way into that place so we can get Jin's research. It could possibly speed up our process.

If we can do that, then that's one less problem we have to worry about. We wouldn't have to worry about the mutations at all. Imagine if one of our teams comes in contact with one of the mutated creatures, and they had a way to transform that creature back to a human being. That would be revolutionary."

"What if they don't have the cure? You heard what Kyle said. He never saw them reverse the mutation."

"He also said he wasn't there that long. They could have done it and just never made him aware of it."

"We don't even know if they have anything that would help us. We don't even have a way in to their compound. Kyle said that the leaders of that group don't want to expand, so showing up to their doorstep would be a death wish."

"You don't know that. They could welcome us if they knew our value. Together, we could change the world. I'm sure if I saw Jin, I could just talk to him, and we can work together to find a cure."

"We already tried this. We've sent people out there and never heard from them again."

"This time would be different."

"You may be willing to risk lives on a hunch, but I'm not. They won't care about our value. They are probably just going to try and take what we have."

"Well, what if we gave them something they wanted? Maybe then they would let us into their place to get the research."

"What makes you think we have something they would want? I'm sure they have everything we have.

Shit, they may even have more than us. If they are doing this type of research, that means they must have built a lab of some sort. There is probably nothing we have that they don't."

"They don't have him," Dr. Lee said, pointing to the room that Kyle was in.

Maverick was initially speechless. He walked over to the room and peeked in, making sure that Kyle hadn't miraculously gotten up from the bed and overheard their conversation. Seeing the battered man still in the bed cleared his conscious. "Absolutely not," Maverick muttered. "I'm not sending that man back to that place. They are going to kill him. I don't want that type of guilt on my heart."

"Why not, Mav? This is one man. One man that we don't know from a can of paint. He could be the key to us returning this world back to normal. We can go back to law and order and stop living like savages. Why pass up an opportunity like that?"

"Because that's not who we are. If that's the case, we might as well go in that room and kill him ourselves because that's exactly what they're going to do. We can't just send a man to his death and not think there won't be any repercussions."

"How many people have you killed, Mav?"

"Too many."

"Exactly. There is already blood on your hands. Blood that you will never be able to wash off. That's how death works. It stays with you forever. But in this case, you won't be doing the actual killing, and it would be a sacrifice to save humanity. That won't be guilt. There would be nothing to feel guilty about."

"That's easy for you to say. You are a doctor. You sit back here and do the easy work, while my team and I fight every day to protect this place. All you have to do is say you need something, and we are the ones that go out and get it for you. So, I don't want your lecture about sacrificing for humanity because some of us do it every day."

"So, you're saying that I don't do anything. No, I may not walk around toting guns like you, but I have had to make very tough decisions. How dare you try to downplay my contributions to this place!"

"I'm not downplaying anything. I appreciate your work. I appreciate everything that everyone does here. I just don't agree with you on this matter."

"Maybe this is something we take a vote on because this is bigger than me and you."

"Why are you assuming that those people are going to give us anything if we turn him over. His death won't guarantee us anything."

"I think you should at least entertain the idea. It won't hurt."

"I think our focus should be on updating everyone's maps and sending a scout team out to see what information we can gather. Once we do that, then we can focus on how to infiltrate their group."

Dr. Lee grabbed the map from Maverick and headed out.

CHAPTER

21

Jin stormed into Abraham's room. *I'm going to kill them both*, Jin thought as he scanned the room. There was no sign of Tyler or Abraham. Jin quickly searched the room, going through both Lori's and Abraham's personal belongings. One of the gunmen assisted Jin and helped tear the room apart. The other gunman ran to notify the other members of the security breach. They were about to lock down The Association.

He couldn't have gone far. The entire room was turned upside down, but there was no sign of the box that Lori gave Tyler. "I want every single room searched until we find them." Jin and the gunman went door to door, checking the other rooms. Some of the rooms were occupied, and the two still pushed their way in each of them, conducting searches. The occupants of those rooms were left wondering what precipitated the random shakedowns.

"Is everything okay, Doctor Jin?" Sierra asked when she spotted the doctor and gunman coming out of her room.

"I'm looking for Doctor Abraham."

"Oh, I just saw him."

Jin gripped the young woman. "Where is he?"

Sierra scowled as Jin's tight grip squeezed her arms. "I saw him down by the supply room."

"Was he with Tyler?"

"I don't think so. I only saw Doctor Abraham."

"Let's go," Jin ordered the gunman. He released Sierra and took off down the hallway. He could not let those syringes leave the encampment. With those samples out of his hands, Jin would have to go back through the entire process of redeveloping the formula and creating more samples. Jin was playing back the events that took place with Lori. He could not get his mind off Tyler's immediate reaction to the injection. Jin wanted to get the teen back in the lab to run tests because Tyler was not going to be the same with that serum in his body.

"Doctor Abraham, it burns. My body feels like it's on fire," Tyler muttered as he stopped to catch his breath. The teen was exhausted. His chest felt as if it was tightening up.

"What's wrong with him, Doctor Abraham?" Charlotte asked.

"I don't know, Charlotte, but we have to stay quiet. Emma should be pulling up with the car soon. Once we get out of here, we can figure out what's wrong with your friend."

Abraham crouched down behind the bench at the baseball field. The school that The Association deemed as their headquarters had three large sports fields located in the rear. Charlotte and Tyler ducked behind the bench with Abraham. Charlotte was still in shock. One minute, she was in her mother's room trying to get answers from Abraham, and the next minute, Tyler came busting in the room with blood dripping down his arm.

"Where is my mom?" she asked Abraham. He looked over at the concerned girl but did not have an answer for her. "I'm sure she's on her way," he lied. Lori and Abraham did not see eye the eye when it came to their future with The Association. Based on their last conversation, Abraham did not expect Lori to go along on this journey with them. He continued ducking behind the bench. The fields were not well lit, so it was easy for Abraham and the teens to go unnoticed. There was not much time before Jin and the other members of The Association flushed them out.

A charcoal gray Nissan Altima sped across the fields. It was hard to spot the vehicle because of its color, and the operator did not activate the headlights.

As the Nissan made its way to his location, Abraham popped up from behind the bench. He eyed up the driver, ensuring that he was able to get positive identification. "Right on time!" he yelled out.

Charlotte was next to pop up from behind the bench. She and Abraham assisted Tyler into the backseat of the Nissan. "We have to get out of here," Abraham said.

Emma peeled off, whipping the Nissan back across the field. She was one of the members of The Association who assisted a previous group when they decided to escape. She worked on a search team, so she easily had access to the vehicles and knew the blind spots of the guarded territory. She headed toward one of them now. With Micah pulling resources for the hunt, it was not hard to go unnoticed inside the walls. Even if a problem surfaced, Emma had a bodyguard with her. It was her boyfriend, Austin. Austin sat in the front passenger seat with a loaded rifle. He was ready for any type of confrontation that would present itself. Like his girlfriend, Austin played a specific role in The Association. He was assigned to one of the security teams and used his position to scope out the areas of weakness inside their walls.

"It looks like everything is still clear," Austin muttered with his head on a swivel. The young man guided Emma to a weak spot in the encampment border. This was caused by the rapid expansion of The Association's territory. When Micah ordered the walls to be put up, all of them were not properly secured, and they surely were not checked on a consistent basis. This was the case at one of Austin's security posts. He and his partner often explored the world beyond the walls of The Association when they were supposed to be working.

While the wall was being built, there was one particular spot that was not as secure as the rest of the wall. The lack of materials at the time contributed to this overlooked section. With the removal of a few posts, Austin and his partner were able to create an opening that was large enough to fit a sedan through. They often journeyed out, using the opening to come and go as they pleased.

Austin was depending on his partner to have this spot ready for him. When he and Emma assisted the first group out, no one ever discovered the method of their escape. This allowed the couple to prepare for this moment. Emma saw the sudden flash of headlights in the distance. She headed straight in the direction of the lights, still riding in complete darkness. Austin had a sawed-off shotgun resting on his lap. One thing about certain members of The Association was their ruthlessness. Austin knew when the time came, he needed to be ready to defend the mission. With the shotgun tightly tucked, he was more than ready to do so.

The headlights that were once in the distance flashed again, guiding Emma toward them. As she drove closer, she spotted a blue Toyota Corolla parked along the security wall. Inside was Nick, Austin's partner. Nick was securing the escape by ensuring that no one interfered with their plan. It was a straight shot for Emma.

Austin grinned as the Nissan passed through the narrow opening. Something was changing inside the walls of The Association, and it was not just the attack on Adina. Members were starting to feel like prisoners behind the wall. Being told when they could eat, what they could do, and when they could step foot outside of the walls was driving some people insane. This was not freedom, and it wasn't the future that Micah promised. Some enjoyed the safety and security that The Association offered, but others could no longer bear being under Micah's rule.

"Which way do I go, Austin?" Emma asked as she began putting miles between the Nissan and The Association.

"I think you bust a right when you get to Castor Ave. Let me check." Austin jammed the shotgun on the side of the seat and pulled open the glove compartment. Under the rations he had stuffed in the compartment was a small hand drawn map of the area. This map was created strictly off memory. Whenever Nick and Austin journeyed out, they documented the streets they took along the way. They included landmarks, such as drawing the burned down gas station that served as the point of no return. It was the end of the burn zone, which were the buildings around The Association that Micah had his people set fire to. This ensured that the buildings remained unoccupied. Micah's theory was that no one would be able to strategize an attack on The Association and use the surrounding buildings as cover and concealment. Entering the burned down buildings now was a risk in itself. One step could send them falling through a charred floor and to their death.

"Yeah, it's Castor," Austin confirmed, running his finger down the stained sheet of paper.

Emma followed the directions, whipping the Nissan down the street. Abandoned cars filled the roadway. She did her best to maneuver around them, all while maintaining her speed. Emma was not one to play it safe. The lack of manpower inside The Association meant that Micah and his search teams were still out. The last thing Emma wanted to do was run into them. It would be a fight for their lives if they did.

"Doctor Abraham, where's my mom?" Charlotte asked.

Abraham paused at the question. He was not sure of Lori's fate and was even more unsure of the perfect response to give Charlotte. "Your mom is going to meet us at our destination," he lied. Abraham could not bring himself to tell Charlotte the truth. Her mother was supposed to be in the car with them, but instead, she was in grave danger. Emma looked back and shot Abraham a look. She knew the truth and disapproved of Abraham not revealing this truth to

Charlotte. She continued down Castor Avenue. "Send the signal, Austin," she ordered.

Austin reached into the center console of the Nissan and pulled out a flare gun. He pointed it out of the window and fired it into the air. The group just alerted their friends of their location and now possibly their enemies too.

CHAPTER

22

The popping in the distant night sky caught Micah's attention. The blast of the flare in the sky was followed up by another, miles away. The calm of the night began to box him in. He was running out of time. Reality slowly began to set in. Kyle was slipping through his fingers. It was like they were hunting a ghost. A ghost that escaped death every chance he got, and Micah doubted his efforts to catch this ghost.

"Was that from the camp?" Londo asked, running up to the van that Micah was standing up against.

"I don't think so," Micah replied. "It seemed pretty close, though."

"That looked like a signal."

"I agree with you."

"Do you think it's him?"

"That would be impossible. There's no way he would have gotten that far in such a short period of time. Plus, who would he be signaling? He was a loner. It would be suicide for him to head back to anywhere that was close to The Association."

"A loner according to who?"

"According to the people he came with. They all keep saying that he was alone when they ran into him out in the streets."

"And what makes you believe them? Micah, don't be naïve—"

"And don't end up in a casket." Micah scowled, pressing a sharp blade against Londo's neck. "You need to mind your manners. The next time you speak out of line, I'm going to cut your fuckin' tongue out. Do you understand me?"

Londo nodded his head in agreement. Micah slid the blade down and pushed Londo.

"I didn't mean any disrespect, boss. I was just saying that maybe he has a team. Maybe he's a part of those rats that inhabit the underground. They could easily hide him down there."

"Do you think I'm stupid or something? You don't think that I considered that as one of the factors? Look around you. Why do you think I brought so many soldiers with us? We're going to tear this city apart."

Micah walked off, staring at the sky. Although he knew it could not have been Kyle that sent off the flares, that did not stop him from wondering who set them off. As composed and strategic he thought he was, Micah was not thinking right. He was focused on the hunt and not on the protection of The Association. He literally brought a small army with him for the second wave.

"It's funny seeing you cower in fear," Wolff said, approaching Londo.

"What?"

"Micah had you shaking in your boots, big boy. He said he was going to cut your tongue, right?" Wolff laughed.

"I'm not worried about that. It won't happen again. Trust me."

"Oh, I bet it won't. He's got you in check."

"Whatever." Londo walked off, going to check on the other members who just arrived.

"You know we're going to die out here," Wolff said calmly, stopping Londo in his tracks. Londo turned and shot the Irishman a deathly stare. "I know you see it. This is a suicide mission. We split up our numbers to chase one man when there are so many other groups out here. None of this makes sense. Why the fuck did we leave Adina back at the camp?"

"She's guarded."

"But not by the best. We are all here, chasing our tails."

"Well, if you don't like it, then do something about it. I've never been fond of a man who just ran his mouth and didn't back it up."

Wolff dug inside the pocket of his vest and pulled out a loose cigarette. He wedged it in his mouth and flicked a match to light it. Londo watched the cigarette smoke drift into the wind as Wolff took a few drags and looked up at the stars. "I'll never forget the first day I met Adina. She was so smart and powerful. The moment I heard her speak, I knew she was a leader. She was focused on the bigger picture. She understood what needed to be done to accomplish her goal. That's exactly why I followed her and obeyed her. And now look at me. On the hunt for the man that shot her when he shouldn't have even been with us. We never allowed people to infiltrate the camp, but you and your leader did."

Londo stepped forward. "Micah is your leader, not Adina. You need to understand that. I won't tolerate you disrespecting him."

"He's disrespecting us. By having us out on this wild goose chase."

"If you would have done your job, we wouldn't be out here. I suggest you take a look in the mirror before deciding who to blame for our current situation."

Wolff took another drag and blew the smoke in the air. To him, a cigarette was like gold. When others scavenged for food, he was more focused on looking for cigarettes and medication. Wolff always found a way to take the edge off. "I'm not here to argue with you. I'm just presenting an opportunity to you."

"An opportunity to do what?"

"To rule this city, just like Adina. We should head back to the camp and plan our next moves. No more of this bullshit."

"So, you don't want to find this Kyle guy?"

"I'm not saying I don't want to find him. I'm just saying that he shouldn't be our top priority right now. I'm fine with putting a search team together that will go find his ass, but what I'm not fine with is taking seventy percent of our people and artillery and bringing them out here. It just doesn't make sense."

Londo looked around. Wolff was right. When Micah sent for the second wave of members to join them, he ensured that they had the top dogs from their security team come out. All their eggs were in one basket, and they were beginning to crack. Micah had his people tearing blocks apart, looking for Kyle. The effort was impressive, but the results were a concern. In Londo's mind, there was no way that Kyle made it out of the radius they were checking. Even if he was dead, they would have found the body by now. Londo agreed that the smartest move would be to head back to the camp, but after the run in with Micah, he thought it best to keep his mouth shut about the situation.

"Listen, I know we don't get along, but you know this doesn't make sense. We can't let this incident crumble the foundation that was built. We can hold off and fortify for a while. Let's figure things out."

"You talk too much."

"Fuck is that supposed to mean?"

"It means you need to keep your mouth shut and learn how to follow orders. If you don't like the decisions that are being made for The Association, feel free to leave. If you stay with us, you are no longer allowed to speak your mind. No one cares what you think."

"And what will happen if I choose to leave?"

"Then, you'll die."

CHAPTER

23

"I just don't know why he's so stubborn," Dr. Lee said, placing a lighter under a tin can. The can was filled with rainwater that had been collected by the group. "He takes everything so personal."

"That's who Maverick is," Dalton replied. "He doesn't care what anyone else thinks. If it's not his idea, he doesn't want to go with it. You should have seen that hospital. There were so many meds and supplies in there we couldn't even carry it all back. And that was only in those two rooms. We didn't even get to the other portions of the hospital."

"That's unbelievable."

"I know. All we had to do was to clear the rest of the hospital to see if any of those mutants were still in there, and that place could have been ours for the taking."

Dr. Lee laughed. "I hate that you call them mutants. Every time you say it, I immediately think of Wolverine and Cyclops. It's like we are battling the X-Men."

Dalton chuckled. "Shit, I wish they were the X-Men. I'd be on their side. No offense, but this side is boring. It would be me and Magneto. And my headquarters would be that big ass hospital. I'd even give you a whole floor so you could do all of you doctor shit."

"Is that so?" she asked, turning her eyes from Dalton to the water in the tin can that had come to a boil. Dr. Lee took an oven mitt and grabbed the can, pouring the hot water into two mugs. Two mint leaves were in each mug.

"Hell, yeah. We need you doing that stuff. The work you do is essential."

Dr. Lee's heart skipped a beat. Hearing Dalton say those words was unexpected but reassuring. She needed to hear them. It was completely opposite from her trying to convince Maverick of her worth. "Well, I appreciate you saying that because sometimes I feel like the work that I do doesn't mean much around here."

"Are you kidding me, Doc? I don't want you to ever think that. You know what? I'm going to make sure you get that entire floor in the hospital."

Dr. Lee laughed. "That would never happen. Maverick already said that we wouldn't be expanding that far. It's okay, though. I'm perfectly happy with the setup I have now." Dr. Lee was pleased with the space that Maverick set up for her. She mainly operated out of an old dialysis facility, and she also had access to one of two urgent care buildings. Although they were not fully stocked hospitals, they did have medical equipment and supplies that allowed her to create two research labs.

Dalton lifted one of the mugs and blew on the mint tea before taking a sip. "Can I tell you a secret?"

Dr. Lee gave Dalton a suspicious look before answering, "Of course, you can."

Dalton looked around before leaning in and whispering in Dr. Lee's ear, "We're leaving this place."

Dr. Lee almost spit out her tea. Her eyes widened when she heard the words that Dalton muttered. "What do you mean you're leaving?" she whispered back.

He smiled. "A group of us are going back to the hospital. We're taking it over."

"Are you serious?" she asked. A part of her was concerned, but she was more so intrigued. Dr. Lee was in disbelief. As Maverick mentioned, she did not spend much time outside their safe zone, so she really did not understand how dangerous Dalton's mission was going to be. "I can't believe it. Does Maverick know about this?"

"Hell no, and I hope you don't go running to him."

"I won't, but don't you think it's important that you let him know that you are expanding? That way, he can plan the expansion properly. That's a lot of miles to cover between here and the hospital."

Dalton laughed. "Doc, you're funny. This isn't an expansion mission. I'm taking a group, and we're going to be doing our own thing. The hospital will belong to us, not The Saviors. But the good news is my offer still stands. If you want to join us, you'll get a whole floor to yourself. You'll have complete control over your work. You'll be able to do whatever you want."

Dr. Lee took a minute to process what she was hearing. The thought of operating in a hospital seemed like a dream. She imagined the technology and supplies they would have access to, assisting her with research, but also the level of medical care they could provide to people. She thought about the women who had to deliver babies who would have the opportunity to give birth in an actual maternity ward rather than a room in the urgent care facility. "How many of us would be going?"

"Right now, it's about twenty of us. Our plan is to take over the hospital, and then we'll come back to get others. We'll extend an invitation to anyone willing to join us. To live a freer life rather than being confined to the rules of The Saviors."

"The rules aren't bad here, though."

"Are you kidding? They tell us how much food we can eat, what we can drink, and what missions we can go on."

"That's true, but it's only to ensure that we have enough rations to last us," Dr. Lee replied. She hesitated to tell Dalton that the rules he was referring to were her recommendations for the group. She instructed Maverick to have the food rationed. The group was able to begin planting and growing foods and herbs, but Dr. Lee was a planner. She did not want to ever get to a point where they ran out of food, so even though they were maintaining, she planned for the worst-case scenario.

"I don't want to be told what to do. I'm not a child, and there's no way I'm going to sit here and let another man tell me how much food I can eat. I'll eat as much as my belly can hold if I want," he announced.

Dr. Lee smiled. "That's understandable. I think you should really wait to make the decision to leave here. If you want changes to be made, why don't you just tell Maverick? I'm sure he can accommodate any of your needs."

"I don't want to be accommodated. I also don't want to have to ask for anything. I shouldn't have to. When we get to the hospital, there will be no rules. You'll do what you want. This is still the land of the free, so we'll live like it."

Dr. Lee's smile masked her true thoughts. She wanted to tell Dalton the truth about the rules that The Saviors had in place, but she felt that she would look like a hypocrite. In one conversation with Maverick, Dr. Lee could get everyone's rations increased, but she knew that would not be enough to convince Dalton not to leave. However, it was still worth a try. She knew that Dalton could not be the only member of the group who felt this way. She was going to put some things in place to make life with The Saviors easier for everyone. "So, when's the big day?"

"Tomorrow."

"Tomorrow? That's not too soon?"

"Nope. The sooner, the better. I want to get to that hospital before someone else has the opportunity to take it over."

"But no one has taken it over in all this time. Isn't that weird?"

"Not to me. The way I see it, it's a bunch of scary motherfuckers like Maverick out here, so they probably didn't understand the value of being in that place. But that's fine because I see it. We'll be heading out around midnight. We can meet here if you plan to join us."

"Okay," Dr. Lee reluctantly replied.

"Trust me—you won't regret this."

CHAPTER

24

Lori stepped back, doing her best to stay still. She watched as a mutation crawled around the room. Lori's mouth dropped to the floor. The mutation was part of Jin's most recent batch of serums. Black blood dripped from the mouth of the mutated man. Lori had never seen a mutation like this. She was used to the creatures being large and furry with sharp claws and fangs.

The creature in the room with her had a completely opposite look. It was completely bald. Its skin appeared to be tight and calloused. The creature still had sharp claws and fangs. It varied from being on all fours to standing. Deep scratch marks covered the floor.

Lori felt like her heart was beating out of her chest. Fear covered her, and it seemed as if the creature could sense it. It began inching forward in Lori's direction. She crawled backward, trying to get out of the path of the beast. It stood on its back legs and let out a loud shriek. Lori covered her ears, but the shriek was causing a painful ring that traveled from her eardrums to her head. She could not help but scream in anguish.

The creature dropped on all fours and lunged toward Lori. She dove out of the way, causing the creature to crash into a metal shelf. It bounced right up and let out another shriek. The creature lunged at her again. Lori rolled out of the way. The creature crashed into the door. A metal piece of the shelf was under Lori's hand. She gripped the long metal piece and sized up the creature. "Back up!" she yelled.

The creature stood on its back legs again. Lori swung at the it, striking the creature in the side. The creature jumped up on the ceiling. "Stay back." The creature crawled around the ceiling, circling Lori like a vulture. Lori clenched the metal, ready to strike the creature again. Another loud shriek caused her to drop the metal and place her hands over her ears. The shriek traveled through the entire building.

"What was that?" Jin asked.

"I don't know," Brody replied, trying to figure out where the noise was coming from.

Jin looked around the field. "Brody, check the building! We'll keep checking out here. They couldn't have gotten far."

"Copy."

Brody headed back into the building. Another loud shriek echoed through the building. Brody sprinted through the building with his gun out. Members of The Association exited their rooms, also trying to determine the source of the shriek. Brody did not know where the shriek was coming from, but he was certain that it had to be coming from a mutation.

As Brody passed the rooms, he spotted members standing at the hall that led to Jin's experimental wing. "If you are looking for the noise, it came from down there," one of them said.

Brody advanced into the wing. He anticipated finding a large mutation at the end of the wing, but there was nothing. At the time, there was just silence. He put his ear up to each door as he worked his way down the hall. There was still nothing. Suddenly, a woman's scream grabbed his attention. Brody ran directly to the room it came from and kicked in the door.

Lori busted out the room and ran into Brody. She was stuck between two enemies. With no weapon in hand, she had no idea how she was going defend herself against The Association or the creature. Brody grabbed Lori and pushed her into one of the empty rooms he passed. Lori pushed and kicked Brody, hoping to get him off her. Brody was strong. Her strikes did not faze him. Brody pinned Lori to the ground. "Stop fighting me," he whispered.

Lori's eyes cut to the hallway and widened. The creature from the room was creeping in the hallway. Brody saw the expression on her face and slowly turned to see what had her spooked. He spotted the new mutation slowly crawling on the ceiling. Brody's heart began thumping. He took shallow breaths. The door to the room they were in was wide open, and there was nothing stopping the creature from seeing them. They did not want to make any noise that would give away their location.

The creature paused on the ceiling and began sniffing loudly, picking up a scent. *What the fuck is that*? Brody could not explain what he was looking at. The grey, calloused skin that covered the creature's body, black eyes, and sharp claws was enough to send a chill up anyone's spine. It was not so much the appearance of the creature that concerned Brody but the way it moved. In a way, it was stealthy, besides the loud sniffing and ear wrenching shrieks.

In the distance, screams were heard followed up by gunshots. One of the guards from The Association was coming to assist Brody when he spotted the creature in the hallway. He ripped off two more shots before the creature let out a loud shriek and began charging at him. The creature jumped down from the ceiling to the floor, then back up to the ceiling, making it difficult for the guard to get a steady shot. Another guard turned the corner and began sending shots toward the creature. The 9mm rounds struck the creature's calloused skin but did not slow down its stride. It dove toward the first guard, knocking him to the ground. Its claw sunk into his shoulders, puncturing his skin. It then swiped at the second guard, who was still firing on the creature, with no effect. The large claws ripped through the man's face and neck. He screamed in agony and backed up toward the wall. Blood poured down his face.

The creature focused back on its first attack. "Get the fuck off me!" the guard yelled in pain. The creature let out another shriek in the man's face. Black blood dripped from its mouth and into the guard's face. The creature then chomped at the man, devouring his face with bite after bite. Its sharp teeth and fangs ripped his face off, chunk by chunk. "What the fuck!" the other guard yelled as he took off. The creature wasted no time pursuing him.

Once again, it jumped from the ceiling to the wall during its pursuit. Although the members of The Association heard the screams coming from the guards, they also heard the shots. They assumed whatever was down the wing was taken care of by the guards. More guards popped up and began ordering members back in their rooms. Some followed the instructions, and others remained in the hallway, being curious.

"Run!" the injured guard yelled when he turned the corner. He was holding his face, but blood continued pouring out. It happened so fast, the creature bounced on his back and took a chunk out of the back of his head with one bite. Panic and fear spread through the building. The other guards began firing, but it was too late. The creature could not be stopped. It bounced around biting and clawing anyone who remained in the hallway. No matter where anybody was in The Association, the screams and gunshots reached their ears.

"What was that?" Brody asked.

"I should be asking you that question," Lori responded.

Brody climbed off Lori and allowed the woman to stand to her feet. Lori immediately took up a defensive position. She was ready to fight. Jin left her in that room for dead, and she was certain that Brody was sent to finish the job. "What are you doing? We gotta get out of here," Brody said.

"We?"

"Yes, we. We have to link up with Nick and the others."

Lori hesitated. "So, you're working with Abraham too?"

He laughed. "Of course, I am. Now, let's go, slugger."

Brody peeked out of the room. There was no sign of the creature or the other members of The Association. The two stepped into the hallway. In a such a short time, the creature had destroyed the wing. Claw marks were all over the ceiling and floor. Blood was splattered all over the walls. The body of the creature's first kill was centered in the hallway. Brody looked back at Lori. "We got no choice but to go this way."

Screams could still be heard coming from the residential side of the building. The two could not see the carnage, but the creature was mauling anyone it came in contact with. Bodies were dropping left and right. Rather than heading toward the carnage, Brody and Lori took the stairs. They got to the bottom floor and exited the building. Gunshots roared as soon as they walked out. The loud shriek sounded again. They both covered their ears, hoping to muffle the creature's torturous scream.

"Let's go," Brody said once he spotted the guards firing on the creature. This was the perfect distraction for their escape. The two took off toward Nick's post. Members of The Association were either actively combatting the creature or hunkered down, trying to avoid it. The wall that surrounded their territory was meant to keep mutations out, but now it was caging everyone in. With guards leaving to assist with the defense against the creature, all posts were unmanned, except Nick's post. He sat in the blue Toyota, waiting. He heard the commotion in the distance but did not concern himself with it. He did not know what the shrieks were, so he figured the gunshots were between Brody and other guards.

A knock at the passenger window startled him. "Hello, young man. Have you seen Dr. Abraham?" Jin asked.

Nick stepped out of the Toyota. "Dr. Jin, I don't think it's safe for you to be out here."

"Oh, don't worry about me, young man. I asked you a question. Have you seen Dr. Abraham?"

"Uh, no. No, I haven't. Is there a reason I would be seeing him?"

Jin looked up at the opening in the wall. "Yeah, I would say that there is a very good reason you would be seeing him."

Jin walked toward Nick and rolled his sleeves up. Nick backed up slowly. His hand rested on his sidepiece. The old 9mm Ruger® was more than enough to put Jin down. Jin continued advancing. "I'm going to ask you one more time: where is Dr. Abraham?"

"I don't know what you're talking—"

Nick's statement was cut short once he heard the cocking of the pistol that was shoved against the back of his head. The guard who was accompanying Jin had snuck up on Nick. The guard pushed Nick's hand away from his Ruger and removed the gun from the holster. "It looks like you just walked yourself into a sticky situation. Get on your knees."

"Why are you doing this? I told you I did not see where Dr. Abraham went." The guard pressed the gun harder against the back of his head. Nick dropped to one knee.

"You know what's funny? Almost every guard in this place left their post except for you. There's a mutation running around our camp, and you are over here, playing it safe. And out of all places, you're sitting at an opening in the wall. I find that very coincidental. And I don't believe in coincidences."

"I don't know what to tell you. I didn't know any of that was going on."

"I know what you can tell me. The truth."

"You can't handle the truth," a voice said from behind.

Jin turned around. "Lori. How the hell did you make it out of that room?"

"I don't think that matters."

"Well, I beg to differ. There is currently a mutation on the loose. At first, I thought it was our little friend that you helped escape but now that I see you, I think it's the creature that you were locked in the room with. If that's the case, I believe that matters a lot."

"Not really. Do yourself a favor and let Nick go so we can leave."

"Oh, so my suspicions were correct. He is a traitor, just like you."

"You're the only traitor here. Like I said, let him go."

"Or else what?"

"Or else I'll put a bullet in your head," Brody chimed in while popping out from behind a tree.

"Wow," Jin said when he laid eyes on his subordinate. "Today is just full of surprises, isn't it?"

"You can say that," Brody responded.

"That's good to know. Unfortunately, I'm going to have my comrade over here put a bullet in your friend's head. Afterwards, I'm going to make you two my next test subjects. I'm going to enjoy watching you suffocate from the gases that I'll force into your lungs. Your blood will boil in your veins as you scream to stop."

"That all sounds good, but I doubt that's going to happen," Brody said. "Your comrade is going with us."

Jin turned around to look at the guard. He was no longer pointing his gun at Nick but instead at Jin. "You can't be serious. How were they able to get to you?"

"I think the question is, how didn't you know? You pride yourself on being so smart, but somehow, your dumbass couldn't see what was happening right under your nose."

Jin remained silent. The gears were already turning in his head, and he already began plotting on how he was going get revenge on them all."

Nick stood up and walked over to the wall. He began slowly pushing it open. He walked by Jin, bumping him when he passed. The guard still had his gun aimed at Jin.

"We don't want to have to kill you, Doc. Take this opportunity to get out of here."

"You think I'm going to just walk away and let you escape? You took my serums, and I need them back. You're not leaving until I get—"

The loud thump from the guard's gun hitting Jin on the side of the head made everyone cringe. The doctor never saw it coming and was knocked out cold.

Gunshots were still going off, sounding like thunder in sky.

"Let's get out of here," Brody said. "Nick, you got the flare gun?"

"Yup."

"Good. Now, let's go find our friends."

CHAPTER

25

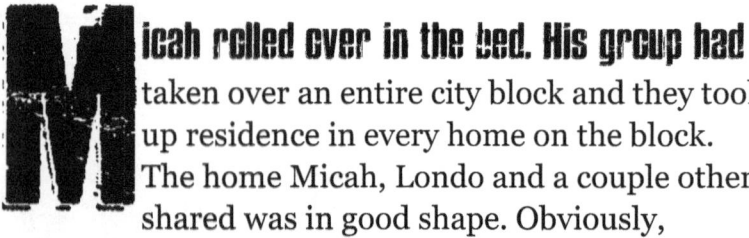icah rolled over in the bed. His group had taken over an entire city block and they took up residence in every home on the block. The home Micah, Londo and a couple others shared was in good shape. Obviously, someone had cleaned the place out, when it came to food and supplies but luckily, they did not destroy the older model townhome. The full-size bed was perfect for Micah to get a good night's rest; however, his mind was still on Kyle. No matter how comfortable the bed was, Micah could not sleep. He was quickly running out of options and had yet been successful in catching his prey. The last thing he wanted to do was show back up to The Association with avenging Adina.

Sunrays shot through window and beamed directly on the bed. Micah squinted his eyes and raised his hand in front of his face to block the sun. Loud chatter could be heard coming from the main level of the home. His head was pounding. It had been days since he had slept, and the fatigue was beginning to creep up on him.

KNOCK! KNOCK! KNOCK!

"Who is it?" Micah asked, as he slowly sat up in the bed.

"Londo," the voice behind the bedroom door responded.

"Come in."

Londo busted through the door. Sweat dripped down his face and he was panting like an old dog in the peak of summer. "They're gone, boss."

"Who's gone?"

"Our people. Half of them left."

Micah popped up, out of the bed. "What the hell you mean they left."

"Big Bill just came to me this morning after no one showed up to back him up on the morning security detail. That was Ricky's job to do, so I went looking for him. When I checked the spot that they were staying in, I noticed Ricky was gone. Him and everyone else that was in the home. Then I checked other spots and it was the same thing. Half of our people are gone."

"What the fuck," Micah yelled. The drywall crumbled as his fist blasted through the wall. He followed up with a few more punched into the wall, before turning back to Londo. "Where the fuck did they go?"

"I don't know but I think they went back home."

"And why the hell would they do that?"

"Wolff."

"Wolff? What about him?"

"I got into an argument with him last night and he said a few things that I didn't like. Going home was one of them. I'm guessing the others followed him."

"So, you knew they were all going to leave, and you didn't it was important to tell me?"

"I didn't think he was going to do it. He went on this rant about us chasing our tails and suggested I head back home with him. I told him that anyone who leaves will die. My message was clear."

"And obviously the message wasn't received." Micah pushed pass Londo and headed into the hallway. He checked the other bedrooms before making his way downstairs and out the front door. A part of him wished he were dreaming, but unfortunately it was a harsh reality.

Wolff was not the only one who felt that the mission they were currently on was pointless. He wasted no time gathering those that wanted to leave and heading back to The Association. Wolff wanted an update on Adina. He needed to know if his leader would survive, because he could not stand following orders from Micah. Even Dannie took the opportunity to sneak back to The Association by blending in with the others. He knew that he could not provide Micah with the information that he wanted, and it was only a matter of time before they left him for dead.

The black tactical boots slammed on the pavement, as Micah stormed down the street. The pounding of his head became more severe. He grimaced as he did his best to fight through the pain. He carefully checked each home, hoping that Londo's suspicions were not true. His search only revealed betrayal. His numbers had been cut in half and he did not know what else was in the mind of those that left. He could not understand what was more important than finding the man that shot Adina.

Micah slammed the front door of one of the homes, as he exited. Londo stood in the middle of the street and watched his leader. Micah looked at him with defeat in his eyes. He still did not understand the motive. Londo slowly approached.

"So, what's the plan?"

"The plan is not going to change. The mission stays the same. We are going to find that scavenger and skin him alive. We'll continue the search with the people that stayed with us. We're going to find this guy soon."

"What about the men and women that left?"

"When we're done, we'll skin them alive too."

CHAPTER

26

"I promise you all, this is going to be the best move you all ever made," Dalton announced.

The small group following him was eager to get to this "promise land" of endless supplies he could not stop bragging about. Although The Saviors provided a sense of security and protection for their territory, there was a small number of members who wanted them to be more aggressive and more dominant. Some thought The Saviors were playing things too safe. They believed The Saviors had the numbers to slowly take over the city, but Maverick wanted to be cautious about each move that was made. He was very thorough when deciding who was allowed to enter the group and ensure he got rid of people who broke the rules. Dalton was one of those people who wanted the group to be more dominant. It did not take him long to gather up more like-minded members and head back to the hospital. The thought of leaving all those supplies behind clawed at his mind since they completed that mission.

"It's just up here," he said.

Dalton was only able to snag a few guns away from the encampment, one of which he had aimed at the front door. The others were distributed to those in the group who felt comfortable using the weapons. The group definitely was not as skilled as the team that Maverick put together for the original supply mission. This did not matter to Dalton because he trusted his skills with a handgun and would not hesitate to take action. In the back of his mind, Dalton felt guilty that he was not completely honest with the group. He bragged about the supplies that were in the hospital and the potential they had to grow in the building, but he failed to mention the mutated beasts that the Alpha team encountered during their mission.

The group approached the hospital. Dalton spotted the front door with the broken window. He opened the door and shined the flashlight of his handgun down the hallway. He smirked when he saw nothing but emptiness. Dalton's description of the building did not match what the group was currently looking at. The hospital was eerie. Without the daylight, the hospital was pitch black. The moon sat behind the clouds, not assisting in illuminating the building.

The shattered glass cracked under their feet as they stepped inside the building. Some of the members were in possession of large candles, which they lit before stepping in. The flickering light of the candles bounced off the white walls in the hospital, allowing the group to see inside the building. Having some sort of illumination calmed the members. They were so used to the constant lighting that The Saviors arranged in the safe zone. There were people designated to make the candles and others who insured they were lit throughout the night and replaced them when they were about to go out.

Dalton led the group but not like Maverick. He had his gun up and was ready for a threat, but he was so ecstatic to be in the building that he was not focused. He peeked into the first room, which was the one that he and Erik cleared at the beginning of their mission. It looked exactly how they had left it. He then checked the second room.

"Welcome to your new home," Dalton announced when he re-entered the hallway.

The other members of the group looked around and began cheering. It was the start of a new beginning. Each member began running and claiming their rooms. Dalton was the last to take his room— intentionally. That was his way of showing the group what kind of leader he planned on being. He stepped into the hospital and threw his belongings in the corner of them. Ariel walked into Dalton's new room and handled him a candle. "Thank you."

"No, thank you. I am excited for our future."

"And the future will be bright. Our small group will grow into a large community. A community that will be prosperous."

"I can't wait to explore this place and see what we have. I bet the generators still work. We have to find a way to cut them on."

"I didn't even think about that. If we get the generators going, then we can light this place up." Dalton imagined the possibilities the group would have with power in the building. He knew it would not be hard to fill the building. "That'll be the first thing we do in the morning."

"Can't wait," she stated before stepping out.

Dalton sat on the hospital bed and kicked his boots off. He had to take it all in. Although this was what he planned to do, it was unreal to be in this moment. The pressure of being a leader was weighing on him, especially because he knew what lingered at the end of the hall. He thought about what excuse he would use once they rest of the group found out about the dead beasts. He did not want to cause any panic inside the building. *I'll just act like I didn't know they were there. Maybe I'll drag them into room so no one sees them.*

He grabbed the large remote that was connected to the bed and pressed the call button. He then reached over and rolled over the IV stand. Dalton was like kid, touching everything in the room. He filled the empty cabinets and drawers with items from his bag. Afterward, he walked into the bathroom. Surprisingly, it was clean. The first thing Dalton looked at was the toilet. Expecting it to be filled with urine and feces, he was surprised to see that the water was clear. The toilet had not been used, which was one of the perks of not getting one of the first rooms that were ransacked. He was certain that bathrooms in those rooms did not match his.

Dalton pulled back the shower curtain. He turned the faucet, hoping to see water drip from the shower head. *That would be too perfect*, he thought. The disappointment quickly went away when he spotted hospital soap, shampoo, and conditioner hanging in the shower. Dalton ripped open the soap, allowing the scent to escape the packaging and enter his nostrils. He then opened the mini bottle of shampoo. The fresh scent was intoxicating.

Dalton lifted his arm and smelled his pit, which was funky. It had been a while since he washed and even longer since he washed his clothes. Maverick wanted to preserve the rainwater that was collected for drinking, cooking, and cleaning wounds. He did not want to waste their water supply on bathing and washing clothes. Just in spite of The Savior's rules, Dalton took his clothes off. The stench of his body odor was overwhelming.

Dalton lifted the toilet seat and splashed water on his body. It was the most refreshing feeling he had felt in a long time. He dipped the soap into the toilet water and began rubbing the bar across his body. Dalton did not even bother washing himself up in the shower, but instead, he washed up right in front of the toilet. He splashed water on himself again, this time rinsing the brown suds off his dirty body. He ran the bar of soap around his body for a second time, ensuring he cleaned every area. On the second rinse, he was sure to splash water in his hair. Pouring shampoo on the top of his head, Dalton allowed the fresh smelling gel to run down until he dripped on his shoulders. He rubbed the shampoo through his dirty head and rinsed it out with toilet water.

Maverick can kiss my ass with his stupid rules. This is how we are supposed to live. Dalton raised his arm and smelled his armpit again. The sweet scent of the soap had masked the funk. His body odor was not completely gone, but a ten-minute bird bath was not going to do much against months of funk. *There's not even a towel in this room.* Dalton grabbed the sheet off the hospital bed and wrapped it around his body, using it to dry off. He was still in awe. His new life was off to a good start.

"DALTON!"

The loud scream of his name caught the new leader's attention. He threw on his pants quickly, grabbed his gun, and ran into the hallway. Water still dripped from his body and down his face. He was not sure who called his name. He looked down the hallway near the other member's rooms, but nothing stood out. Turning to the other end of the hallway, his eyes locked on a silhouette. Shadowy figures lingered around the end of the hallway toward the dark wing where the corpses of the beasts that the Alpha team killed were slowly rotting.

"Whoever you are, you have to leave. This is our building," Dalton ordered.

Three dark figures emerged from the shadows, one laughing at the order they had just received. Another had his mitts on one of the members of Dalton's group, Peter. The man was standing behind Peter, and his arm was wrapped around Peter's neck. Peter was a fifty-seven-year-old man who had retired from being a SEPTA mechanic. He spent his career repairing buses and trains, and now he was on a search to repair that damaged lighting in the building. His quest led him to cross paths with the three men. Peter was known as a tough and courageous man, so when Dalton heard Peter scream his name, Dalton knew something troubling had occurred.

"I'm serious. Let that man go and leave right now."

Other members of the group began exiting rooms to see what the commotion in the hallway was all about. This caught the trio's attention. Initially, they were not sure how many people Peter was with, but as they poured out of the rooms, the trio realized they were outnumbered.

"As you can see, this won't end well for you three. You have five seconds to leave here and never come back."

With a swift elbow to the midsection, Peter delivered a blow to the man that knocked him back on the floor. Peter took off running toward Dalton, only to stop in his tracks after a few steps. It happened so fast that no one saw when the knife was thrown, but everyone saw it sticking out of the back of Peter's head when he dropped to his knees and subsequently to the floor.

Dalton was filled with rage. He sent shot after shot at the three men. Four other members of the group came out firing their weapons also. The trio began retreating into the dark hallway. Bullets zipped past their heads, and some ripped into different parts of their body.

Dalton took off in a full sprint after the men and continued firing until the slide on the gun locked back. He hopped over Peter's body and disappeared into the darkness. Dalton activated the flashlight on the gun and scanned the area. *Where the hell did they go?* He immediately spotted the bodies of the beasts. There was blood all over this end of the hallway, making it difficult for him to differentiate the blood from the fresh wounds, which had dripped onto the blood covered floors. Dalton did not even know two of the men got struck when he was shooting. He took a minute to collect himself, realizing that he was alone in the dark hallway. The other members of his group never advanced into the darkness with him.

Dalton stepped lightly as he moved forward. He was cautious, checking each room as he carefully made his way up the hallway. He stepped past the two rooms that the Alpha team had raided during the supply run. That had been the farthest they went that day, so Dalton had no idea what was waiting for him past that point. He thought long and hard about whether to keep going or not, but fear got the best of him. "This is no time to be a hero," he mumbled as he turned around and headed back to his group.

CHAPTER

27

"How are you doing Dr. Lee?" one of the medical staff members said.

"I'm good. How are you?"

"I'm fine."

"How are our patients doing?"

"They are doing good. The one said he's still in a lot of pain, but all of his vitals check out. The boy seems fine. He'll probably be out of here in a couple days."

"That's good to hear. I'm going to go check on the boy."

Dr. Lee entered the medical ward. Although her main focus in the group was mutation research, she always stopped in on the medical ward to check on patients. The thought of having a whole floor to herself in the hospital was an unbelievable offer, but

Dr. Lee made the decision not to go with Dalton and his group. She understood most of the points that he made, but she did not agree with the "everyone can do what they want" mentality. There was no way she was going to start over with a group that was not going to be structured.

She showed up to the meet point at midnight, but she did not meet with Dalton. Instead, she watched from a distance to see who planned on leaving with Dalton. One by one, they showed. She was surprised to see the faces that were showing up, prepared to start a new life at the hospital. She was also surprised to see the number of members who were going to be in the group. It was less than twenty of them. There was no way that Dr. Lee was going to leave one of the safest locations in the city to go join a small group like this.

She entered the room that Levi was currently staying in. Levi watched as the door opened to his room, and in walked the forty-five-year-old Asian woman. Her dark hair was pulled back into a ponytail. A dingy lab coat was draped over her shoulders. She held a neat pile of clothes in her hand and placed them at the foot of the bed. "These are some clean clothes you can change in to. I also got you this," she said, tossing an apple to the teen.

"Thank you, ma'am." The teen wasted no time sinking his teeth into the juicy fruit.

"It's no problem at all. I'm Dr. Lee. What's your name?"

"Levi," he replied with a mouth full of apple.

"Oh, that's a nice name. Well, Levi, it looks like I have nothing but good news for you. Besides being a little dehydrated, it seems that you are a fairly healthy young man. Unfortunately, I can't say the same for your friend. What happened to him?"

"Honestly, ma'am, I don't know. I found him that way."

"What do you mean?"

"I belong to a church. I was in there with my friends, and I found him in the alleyway down the street from the church. Some guy was over the top of him, so I grabbed my bat and chased him away. The next day, a bunch of them came back to the church, and they ended up burning it down. That's how I ended up at the hospital with that guy. He was hurt so badly I didn't know where else to take him."

"What happened to your friends?"

"I don't know. One of them I told to run, and the others went missing right before the fire." With everything going on at the hospital, Levi never took the time to think about Sade, Cameron, and Jayven. He did not know what happened to them once the attack took place. There was a possibility that they made it out safe, but there was also the possibility that they did not make it out at all.

Dr. Lee saw how heavy the questions weighed on Levi. "But I guess once you got to the hospital, things got better. I heard there were a bunch of supplies in there, and it's abandoned, right?"

"Abandoned? Who told you that?"

"One of the members of the search team that rescued you told me that. He said the hospital was full of supplies, and it was still in pretty good shape."

"It is full of supplies, but it's definitely not abandoned."

"It's not?"

"Not at all. There are people in there and those monster things. We had to hide in a room the entire time so we wouldn't get caught. If it weren't the monsters creeping around outside the door, it was those guys. I heard them in there all the time, especially at night. Luckily, there were meds and supplies in the room we hid in. I went out once during the day to find food, and that's when I ran into those monsters. They were so scary. I barely made it back to room."

Dr. Lee was in shock. "A-Ar-Are you sure?" she asked, immediately worrying about Dalton and the other members who left with him.

"I'm positive. I heard everything while I was in there. There were nights when gunshots would wake me out of my sleep and other nights when I couldn't sleep because of the screams. There is nothing good in that hospital, ma'am."

Dr. Lee ran out of the room. Her heart felt like it was in her stomach. "Where is Maverick?" she yelled as she ran down the street. Tripping over the sidewalk didn't stop her from entering into a full sprint. The pointing of other members led her to one of The

Saviors training facilities. This specific facility was an old fitness gym. It was a no brainer to make it a training facility where members could exercise and train in hand-to-hand combat. "Where's Maverick?" she asked one of the guards who was standing outside of the training facility.

"What's going on?" Maverick asked, coming around the corner of the building. "Did something happen?"

"It's Dalton."

"What happened to Dalton?"

"He's in trouble."

"What are you talking about?"

"It's all my fault. I should have come to you earlier about this," Dr. Lee muttered. Tears began to fall from her eyes. She gripped Maverick's hand. "Please forgive me."

"You better start explaining why you need forgiveness. What happened?"

"Dalton left. He took some others, and they headed back to the hospital."

"What?" Maverick yelled. A vein popped up on the side of his head. "What do you mean he left?"

"He told me that he wasn't happy with the way things were being ran over here, so he packed up his things and headed to the hospital. I just got done talking to the boy that you rescued from the hospital, and he told me that it's not abandoned. He said there are people in there all the time."

"Why would he go back there? I already told him we weren't going to expand that far out."

"He wasn't expanding. He is planning on starting his own group."

"How do you know so much about Dalton's plan?" Maverick was not naïve. Dr. Lee was telling him too much about this situation. He was now skeptical of the woman who he recently had a disagreement with about Kyle's fate.

"I'll be completely honest with you. Dalton told me his plan and invited me to join him."

"So, why are you here?"

"I'm here because I believe in this place, Maverick. It's not perfect, but it is progress."

"That's not what I was referring to, Doctor. I want to know why you are in my face telling me about a group of people that voluntarily left to go do their own thing. Why would that be my concern right now?"

"They're still your friends, Mav—"

"Friends? Friends would have come to me and told me their plan. That wouldn't sneak off behind my back or keep secrets from me, then come running when they need to be bailed out."

The last comment stabbed Dr. Lee like a knife. "With all due respect, we don't have time to go back and forth right now. We need to go get Dalton and the others because they are walking into trouble, and they don't even know it.

CHAPTER

28

Dalton's eyes were bloodshot. He needed sleep. With the recent events, he could not risk letting his guard down. At face value, the three men entering the hospital seemed to be just a random encounter, but after the torturous conversation with Peter's killer, something did not sit right with Dalton or other members of the group.

"You told us this place was safe, Dalton. What the hell is going on?" Chuck asked.

Chuck did not bother glancing Dalton's way. He focused on scrubbing the blood from his hands. Chuck was a shoot first and ask questions later type of guy. He would not dare question Dalton's plan in public, but behind closed doors, he was curious.

"This place is safe. We just have to secure it," Dalton replied.

"Secure it?"

"Yeah. Once we secure this place, it will be fine."

"Those guys didn't come walking through the front door. They were already here. So, either you knew they were in here, or you lied to us all about this place being safe."

"I didn't lie. This place was safe. It is safe. We just have to secure it."

"There are only fourteen of us. Well, thirteen of us now that Peter is gone. There's no way we'll be able to secure a place this size. There are more entrances and exits than we have people."

"Well, you knew we were coming here. I told all of you this was a hospital. There's going to be a bunch of ways you can get in and out of this place. You're acting like I told you we were taking over a fuckin' food truck or something," Dalton barked.

Chuck threw down the bloody sponge. "Yeah, you told us we were going to take over a hospital, but you definitely didn't say it was going to only be fourteen of us making this trip. What the hell do you think we're going to accomplish with only fourteen people?"

"We'll recruit, my friend. Whether we have fourteen, thirteen, or twelve people, we will grow. All thirteen of us will do what needs to be done to survive, and soon, there will be 1,300 of us, then 13,000, and eventually thirteen million. We are the future."

Chuck laughed and picked the sponge back up. "You're starting to sound just like Maverick."

"Never. Maverick is soft. The Saviors are soft. I'm not him, and we aren't them. We are survivors, and this hospital gives us the best chance at survival."

"I hope so."

With a heavy heart, Dalton stood to his feet and walked out of the room. He was not too keen on the fact that Chuck compared him to Maverick. The last thing he wanted was to hear an "I told you so" from Maverick if his plan failed. He knew Maverick all too well. He knew that the leader of The Saviors would forgive them all and welcome them back with open arms. In Dalton's eyes, he had nothing to lose. If this plan did not work out, then they would head back to The Saviors and think of another one. He stared down the dark hallway, and the only thing that would playback in his mind was the first mission with Maverick and how Maverick took control of that situation and put those creatures down. It was nothing short of bravery at the highest level. Maverick sacrificed his own life to save everyone else, and that was what Dalton felt that he should have done for Peter. He felt like a coward for not going after the three men, when they had disappeared.

A part of Dalton wanted to turn back and lead the group back to their home, but he just could not leave all these supplies alone. His goal was to use the items as a form of currency. Even if it meant he had to barter with other groups, he wanted the power to do so. He formed two search teams composed of four members each to check the main floor of the hospital for more supplies. If they were going to head back to The Saviors, at least they would be stocked up when they did.

"Dalton," a female voice said lightly.

Dalton turned to see Maddie and her search team approaching him. Maddie was an ambitious young lady. She was a pharmacy technician in her past life, and she brought so much value to The Saviors by sharing her knowledge of medicine identification and distribution. Maddie was grateful when Maverick and his team defended her from an attack by savages who were breaking into the pharmacy she worked at. Because of Maverick, Maddie and her boss were saved, which allowed them to join The Saviors. Maddie's discrepancies with Maverick were more personal. With her knowledge, she felt that she should have been included in the prior mission to gather supplies, but Maverick thought it would be too dangerous for her to come with them. When Dalton returned and bragged about the endless amount of supplies that were left back at the hospital, Maddie took that opportunity to check out what medications were brought back from that mission. She was not impressed. She truly believed that her skills and knowledge would have allowed them to get more quality items. The lack of opportunity to be on missions was the driving force of Maddie's departure from The Saviors.

"What is it?" Dalton asked.

"You won't believe it. We found the cafeteria, and it's loaded."

"Are you serious?" Dalton's mouth dropped. She was right—he could not believe it. "What do you mean it's loaded?"

"There's still stuff on the shelves in the inventory room. A couple of the refrigerators have been emptied out, but one of them has stuff in it. The refrigerator has obviously been off for a while, but the stuff inside doesn't smell too bad. It's worth a shot."

"That's unbelievable."

Maddie tossed a small bottle of orange juice at Dalton. He caught the bottle and immediately examined it. The first thing he noticed was the expiration date, which was almost a year old. The second was the discoloration of the juice. It was a very dark orange that almost appeared brown. Dalton wasted no time cracking the juice open and gulping it down. It tasted just like it looked. Although tart, the old beverage was refreshing.

"Well, it's not too unbelievable. In the actual café, there are the remains of about thirty people. We can't tell how long they've been down there, but the bodies look old."

"It was probably those beasts that we ran into last time."

"Or maybe the gas got them all."

"Maybe. Well, anyway, take your team back down there and get the bodies piled up to the side. I'll gather everyone else up so we can have dinner."

"Are you sure that's a good idea? We could just grab a few items and eat in our rooms."

"No. We will eat as a unit, and we damn sure aren't going to be hiding in our rooms."

"Understood."

A part of Maddie was disappointed. She thought Dalton would be ready to tighten things up since they just lost one of their own, but the complete opposite was happening. Little did she know, he had a point to prove, and she was not going to stop him from proving it. Dalton went room to room, instructing people to head to the cafeteria. He even pulled the people who were standing guard at the entrances, replacing them with filing cabinets and heavy bookshelves that were used as barricades.

Despite discovering the medical supplies, Dalton felt the need to ensure his group that they made the right decision. He knew others wanted to return to The Saviors, and it was only a matter of time until they did. Watching them in the cafeteria was the feeling he was longing for. They were like kids in a candy store. The corpses in the corner of the room didn't even faze them.

"We should head back to the rooms," Maddie advised.

Dalton frowned and cracked open a small can of ginger ale. "No, we should eat and enjoy this moment," he countered. "I know you are upset about Peter. We all are. But this is what we came here for. To live, to survive, and to be free. Now, go join your friends and have a good time."

Maddie followed the advice of Dalton and headed over to the table with her friends. The group laughed and shared stories over their hot meals. One of the members was able to light a small fire on top of the stove, and another found a shelf full of baked beans. That was the meal of the day. The entire group continued enjoying themselves and their meal. The pile of human remains in the corner of the café didn't raise any questions. Society was to that point. Everyone in that room was used to seeing death.

Dalton enjoyed the view. He enjoyed watching the people who took the journey with him, seeing that the reward outweighed the risk. This was their new home.

BOOM!

The blast from the shotgun startled everyone in the cafeteria. Dalton and a few others dropped their food and drew their weapons.

"I'm looking for the one they call Dalton."

Everyone looked around at each other, wondering who just made the request and where he came from.

BOOM!

Another shotgun blast roared in the large cafeteria.

"Who is Dalton?" the man asked in a stern voice.

"Who wants to know?" Dalton asked, stepping forward.

"You can call me The Reaper."

Dalton chuckled. "I'd rather not call you anything. I'd rather you go back to whatever hole you just crawled out of."

"That won't be a problem. Just let me know where my men are, and I'll be on my way."

Dalton's eyebrows perked up. "Men? What men?"

The man's eyes locked on Dalton's face. "The men you shot at, Mr. Dalton. I had a few men in this hospital last night, and I was told that you and your militia shot at them. Luckily, one of them was able to escape with just a shoulder wound, but I want to see the other two."

"We didn't just shoot at those men for no reason. They killed one of my friends."

"Listen, Dalton, I'm not here for a debate. Just give me my men so I can leave."

"I can't do that."

"And why is that?"

"I don't know where your men are. They all got away."

Maddie and the others turned in response to Dalton's statement. They never noticed that the man immediately picked up on their body language.

"Is that true, Dalton?" the man asked as he exited the darkness and into the poorly lit cafeteria. He climbed on one of the tables, overlooking the entire group and the new food and supplies they had accumulated. "Listen up, everyone. Your leader has just lied to my face. I have no other choice but to assume that my men are dead. This means that someone has to answer for their deaths. I will give you all the opportunity to bring the people that killed my men to justice. This is the new world we live in. I call it accountability. You bring your people to justice, and I'll get out of your hair."

"What if we don't?" Maddie asked. "We didn't kill anyone, so what justice are you looking for?"

"My dear, you may have not killed anyone, but someone in here did. Your job is to bring that person or those people to me in the next ten minutes. If you don't deliver what I want, you all will end up the next batch of dead bodies to fill this room."

Chuck raised his pistol toward The Reaper. "What's stopping me from putting a bullet between your eyes and sending you to meet your fucking friends?" Chuck knew what was at stake. The last thing he was going to do was allow anyone to end up like Peter.

BANG!

The pistol fell from Chuck's hand. A .556 round traveled through his head, and his body quickly dropped. Screams filled the cafeteria as some of the members rushed to Chuck's side, and others armed themselves. Dalton looked up to where the shot came from, which was on the second-floor level directly above the cafeteria. Dozens of men and women flooded the second-floor area and the cafeteria.

"You all have eight minutes left to give me what I want."

Dalton did not hesitate to send shots up to the second-floor area. The Reaper let off a few shotgun rounds at the leader before dipping back into the dark corner of the room and disappearing. A fire fight erupted in the cafeteria. Members of Dalton's group exchanged shots with The Underlings. Bullets flew up to the second-floor landing, and bullets flew down to the main level. There were casualties on both sides. More screams were let out as bodies began to drop.

Dalton let off a few more rounds before his gun locked back. Unlike the night Peter got killed, Dalton was prepared to reload. He crawled under a table and reached into his pocket to grab the extra bullets that filled his pocket. He dropped the magazine out of the gun and began filling it. Pushing down on each round in order to slide the next in, Dalton was going to take it to the top. The last few rounds were a struggle to get into the magazine. A sharp pain shot up through Dalton's left side. His adrenaline was pumping, and he never noticed that he had been hit by one of The Reaper's shotgun blasts. The blast ripped off a chunk of his side, which was pouring out blood. Dalton dropped the three hollow-tip rounds. He mustered up the last of his energy to slam the magazine into the gun before cocking it and blindly sending shots up to the second floor.

A warm sensation hit Dalton's arm, forcing him to drop his gun. He screamed out in pain. It was not long before blood began pouring from the fresh gunshot wound. Although shots were raining down from above, this shot came from the main level. It was too late by the time Dalton's eyes trained on the men and women who had stepped out of the shadows. They fired more shots at Dalton and his group. Blood dripped down his lifeless body. That did not stop The Reaper from emerging from the darkness and putting another hole in Dalton. He then turned toward the other bodies and let off more blasts from his shotgun.

CHAPTER

29

At first light of day, five vehicles pulled up to the front entrance of the hospital. Two of the vehicles were full, but the others only had drivers. They were going to be the rides back for Dalton and the members who left with him. Maverick took a different approach during this mission because he knew what was at stake. If the information that Levi told Dr. Lee was correct, Dalton and his group were in trouble.

The team emptied out of the vehicles. There were thirteen of them total, and they were packing heat. Maverick was ready for war. "You three stay here with the vehicles and make sure no one comes in or out of this place. We'll go find Dalton and the others."

Maverick and his search team hit the ground running. They blasted through the doors with a purpose. The barricades that Dalton slid in front of the door were no match for the brute force that Maverick's team used to push their way in. Time was not on their side. Starting from the same location of their last mission, they knew the layout of that section of the hospital. They hit the rooms without hesitation and found exactly what they were looking for.

"NOOOOOO!" Erik yelled out after entering a room to clear it.

After hearing the scream, Maverick ran into the room. Peter's body was laid out across the floor. A sheet had covered his body, but his face was left exposed. Erik was on his knees. Peter was a good friend of his, and he had no idea that Peter left to be a part of Dalton's new group. Peter was a good soul and one of Erik's co-workers at SEPTA. He was always willing to lend a helping hand. He was pissed and wanted revenge. Maverick placed his hand on Erik's shoulder.

"We have to keep moving," Maverick muttered.

Erik picked up his rifle and headed back to the hallway. "It ain't looking good, everyone. We already found one body. We might be too late," Maverick stated. There was no response. Everyone's beady eyes just stared at their leader, hoping he was wrong. Erik just hung his head low. Maverick took up point and kept it moving. "Give me two left," he stated, allowing the members of his team to quickly clear the rooms.

"Give me two right." With a larger search team, it did not take Maverick long to work his way down the hallway.

Maverick let out a slow breath and cast his eyes over the familiar blood splatter that covered the walls. He also spotted the ricochet marks on the far wall from rounds he had sent flying at the mutated beasts. Maverick clenched the handle of his rifle as he shined the flashlight down the hallway. It was silent in the hospital. Goose bumps materialized on his skin. He had a bad feeling about being back in the hospital.

After facing the two creatures that popped up on the last mission, taking on a few more would not be all that difficult. The other members of the team grew impatient. They wanted to find the other members of Dalton's group before it was too late. The usual vocal members of the Alpha team were quiet. This had to be one of the hardest missions they ever embarked on. It was like reading a story and already knowing the ending.

The team was now in unfamiliar territory. Maverick scanned the hallway, and there were several doors that still need to be searched. Some of them were double doors, and the others were standard. Maverick's team went to work, clearing each one. They were focused. Even stumbling upon the medicine supply room did not get them off track. Their mission was to find Dalton and the rest of the group. There were two sets of doors left to hit on this floor, then they would have to start working their way up and down the six-story building.

"Give me two left."

The double doors flung open, and the room clearers froze in place when they spotted what was behind the door. "In here!" one of them yelled.

Maverick led his team through the doors and onto the second-floor balcony. He stopped in his tracks when he looked beneath him. Bodies were spread across the main level of the cafeteria in pools of blood underneath them.

"That's them!" someone yelled out.

For Maverick, it seemed like this moment moved in slow motion. The members of his team pushed past him to attempt to render aid to their fallen. They did not know how long the murdered group had been left rotting, but they were determined to provide some sort of life-saving efforts. The cafeteria looked like a war zone. A pile of rotting bodies was stacked in the corner, and the former members of The Saviors were all laid out, riddled with bullets. The cafeteria tables were completely destroyed, gunshots breaking them into pieces. The wooden tables did not do much as far as being used as cover. The bullets traveled right through them. The gruesome sight brought Maverick back to his time overseas in the warzones.

The members of Maverick's team were flipping tables over, clearing bodies from the debris, and checking pulses. They could do nothing but hope that there would be some sign of life left in the room.

Maverick watched as they went from person to person, knowing that meant that death had come to claim the souls of his people. Maverick stayed on point. He held his firearm up and was ready to fire as he inspected the room. He checked each crevice and each corner, hoping that Dalton and his crew were able to return the favor to their attackers. There was not even a drop of blood to be found from the attackers.

"Maverick, we got something."

Maverick quickly descended the stairs and ran over to his men, eager to see what they discovered. A slight groan caught his attention, followed up by another. He peeked over the men's shoulders and spotted a body that they had pulled from underneath one of the tables. "Maddie." The young woman was holding on to dear life. "Clear a space for her on one of these tables." Maverick's team responded promptly, clearing off one of the tables that had not been damaged and piecing together a first-aid kit from the supplies they had on them.

Erik and another member of the team lifted Maddie off the ground and placed her on the table. "Maddie, it's okay. I'm here," Maverick whispered.

Maddie groaned again. Her shirt and pants were soaked in blood. They did not know if it was from a wound or if she was covered in someone else's blood. He could tell that things were not looking hopeful. Maverick lifted Maddie's shirt, revealing three gunshot wounds to her torso. He slid his hand up her back. "There are no exit wounds. She needs surgery. We have to get her back to Dr. Lee." The others began scrambling to find a way to get Maddie to the vehicles.

The members of the team began dismantling the table. They planned on using the tabletop as a platform to carry Maddie to the vehicle. Maddie groaned and slowly opened her eyes. Her vision was blurry, and she struggled to regain consciousness. "Maverick," she muttered, recognizing his voice. The words barely came out of her mouth.

"Maddie, it's okay. We are here. We're going to get you help."

"It hurts." The words barely made it out of her mouth.

"Who did this?"

"The Re—The Reaper."

CHAPTER

30

Sade was heartbroken, and inside, she felt hollow. Although the injury to her arm was painful, the emptiness she currently had inside her hurt more. A part of her was grateful to had been snatched off the street because maybe this was the end. An end to the pain; an end to the misery; an end to the depression. The Underlings had finally got her and would end her misery. She would finally have the chance to reunite with her parents . . . in heaven.

Levi, I hope you got Jayven and Cameron to safety, she thought. Sade could not imagine what they were going through at the moment if they were all split up. She had no worries about Levi. She knew he could handle himself, but Jayven and Cameron needed the guidance. They would not be able to navigate this new world alone. *Maybe they got captured with me. Maybe they're here too.*

Despite the pain that Sade felt, she was also disappointed. Deep down she believed that a cure to the mutations was coming. She thought about the COVID-19 Coronavirus pandemic that crippled the world in 2020 and remembered that the United States Government had a vaccine completed and ready for distribution by the end of the year. She had the same hopes for this situation. Months had already passed, however, and there was not even a form of communication to know what was going on outside the city.

When she was brought to the encampment, Sade was taken to a townhouse that had been overseen by a woman named Latoya. Latoya used to be a teacher, and her husband was an electrician. This specific row of townhomes on the gird was dedicated to teenagers and overseen by adults with a background in education, social work, and other related areas. The leaders made sure that these homes, along with those that house the younger children and the elderly, were kept in the center of the encampment. This ensured the safety of the more vulnerable population. So, if there were an attack at the encampment, there were layers of security that the attackers had to go through before they could even reach these homes.

Latoya purposely gave Sade a spot in an upstairs bedroom that housed four other teenaged girls. The girls in this room were much more mature than others and were being groomed to take on other roles in the encampment once they turned eighteen. These roles included going on supply runs, checking inventory, caring for the elderly, assisting younger children with their education, construction, and culinary roles. Everyone had a role to play once they became an adult. There were also some teens who graduated to security details, but they were usually groomed by their parents for those specific roles.

Sade did nothing more than stare out the window. Although the other girls in the room were polite, Sade was not really in the mood to converse with them. They did their best to include her in conversations, but Sade did not participate in them. Her mind was only focused on how she was going to get away from this group and get back to the church. She needed to check on her friends to see if they were still alive.

"Sade, I brought you up some breakfast. You haven't eaten since you got here," Latoya said. She was holding a tray that held four stale crackers, a ketchup packet, and two tablespoon scoops of canned corn.

Sade did not even turn her head to acknowledge Latoya. She didn't know the woman, and they surely didn't know that Sade was a vegan. Sade just knew that tray was filled with some type of meat or dairy product. *If I have to die of starvation before these people murder me, then so be it.* Her focus was out the window, looking west toward the direction of the church. On the street, she could see people carrying out their daily duties. Children were out playing, people were walking around and talking to each other, and others were lugging around supplies. This sight was so foreign to Sade after being cooped up in the church for so long. This seemed to be the closest thing to what life used to be. It was unbelievable to her.

Latoya placed the tray on a table next to Sade. "Come on, girls. Let's head over to help Ashley with the toddlers. Sade, you can meet us out there if you want."

Sade's silence said more than her words could ever express. Latoya noticed this and wanted to give Sade her space. She took the other teens outside. Sade's eyes followed them as they hit the corner of the street and began mingling with the children who were outside playing.

She hopped up and grabbed the tray, devouring the crackers and corn in seconds. She ripped open the ketchup packets and poured the thick contents into her mouth.

"Slow down, champ," a soft voice said.

Sade turned and found one of the teenage girls standing in the doorway. The girl was Destiny. Destiny was not one of Sade's roommates. She roomed with the other girls who occupied the dining room of their townhome. Destiny always wore a gold chain around her neck with a cross pendant. She had been brought to the camp by her father, who was a firefighter. She planned on following in his footsteps one day, but he had other plans for her. He wanted his daughter to be in a safer environment during these times. Destiny was only seventeen years old, so he wanted to preserve as much of her teen years as he could. He did not want Destiny worrying about making adult decisions at that age.

Destiny's father pushed her to be a paramedic or nurse to keep her mind off wanting to be a firefighter. His hope was that she would see the reward in those career opportunities and stick with one of them. He had her shadowing other paramedics at the firehouse and going on runs when duty called. Destiny was always complimented on her quick learning abilities and professionalism. Those same skills were the reason she and her father were alive.

Destiny's father had a serious talk with Latoya and thoroughly explained his expectations for his daughter. Since the talk, Latoya sheltered Destiny and provided her with more nurturing tasks. Destiny did inventory work, assisted with cleaning duties, and she also led prayer groups for the young girls. Destiny more so preferred to be out in the field with the other medics, but her father denied the request.

"Sade is your name, right?" Destiny asked as she stepped into the room.

Sade did not respond. "It's okay. Just so you know, I'm a friend, not an enemy." There was genuineness on Destiny's face. Sade was confused as to why the teen was being so nice to her. What was the ultimate goal? She expected to have been tortured or killed by now, based on the rumors about The Underlings. They were known as a ruthless group, sometimes even performing public executions. So, Destiny's politeness was confusing and worrisome.

"Save the games. I know who you people are."

"You do? Well, I'm glad to hear that we have a bit of a reputation," Destiny said proudly.

Sade was disgusted. A part of her wanted to lunge across the room and take Destiny out. However, her injuries left her vulnerable and powerless. "What do you want?"

"I don't want anything. Why do you ask that?"

"Because everybody wants something."

"Not me."

Sade turned around and continued looking out the window. However, this time she was not looking at the activities that were taking place. She was staring at Destiny's reflection. Sade knew she would have to dig deep if Destiny made a move, so she was sure to keep an eye on her without being obvious.

"Who are you looking at out there?" Destiny asked, walking over to the window and looking out.

"Everybody."

"You're acting like you've never seen people before," Destiny said while laughing.

"I haven't seen people acting so normal since this whole thing has happened. It's weird."

"It's not weird. Sitting in a window and staring at people is weird." Destiny chuckled. "Come on. Let's go outside. I'll show you around."

Sade initially hesitated. Although Destiny seemed nice, Sade did not know her or trust her. "Where are we going?" she asked.

"Somewhere special where you can get some more food because I saw how you devoured your breakfast," Destiny replied while laughing.

Sade could not help but laugh too. Deep down inside, she knew Destiny was right. She was still hungry, and the items on that tray were not enough to satisfy her appetite. Destiny just made her an offer that she could not refuse. Being in the window was not the same as stepping foot outside. Sade was so used to only going outside for a reason. This was the first time in a while she went outside just because she wanted to. It also felt good to hold a conversation in a normal tone, rather than whispering to her friends inside the church.

She took time to just breathe and allow her skin to soak up the sun rays. The sound of cheerful laughter and casual conversations filled her ears. Sade smiled. She was at peace. She had envisioned The Underlings territory to be less pleasant. This scene seemed to be something out of a fairytale. It was joyful.

"Come on. I'll take you to one of the inventory locations."

"Why do you seem so excited to go to this place?" Sade asked after noticing how giggly and cheerful Destiny became.

Destiny stopped at the front door and turned to Sade. "You promise you won't tell anyone?"

"Tell anyone what?"

"There's a guy in here, and I like him. He just got here too. He's so mysterious and dreamy."

Sade laughed. She couldn't believe what she had heard.

"You can't tell anyone," Destiny pleaded. "I don't want this getting back to my dad. If he knew, he wouldn't allow me to come back here."

"Your secret is safe with me. So, tell me about your little boyfriend."

"Glad you asked. He's so perfect. His name is—"

"LEVI!" Sade yelled out.

Levi was shocked to hear the familiar voice when he opened the front door of the inventory facility. He was stuck, like he saw a ghost. Sade jumped into his arms and held him tight. Levi still could not move. Although Sade was in his arms, it did not seem like a reality. He never thought he would see Sade again. Being trapped in the church on the day The Underlings showed up was a scary experience for him. The henchmen spent very little time raiding the church, which made Levi worried about Sade because she was all alone out there with those men.

Destiny cleared her throat. Sade's arms were still wrapped around Levi. Destiny cleared her throat again, louder this time. "Oh, sorry. Let me introduce you two. Levi, this is . . ." Sade paused, realizing that she didn't know the girl's name.

"Destiny. I'm Destiny. Very nice to meet you."

"Well, hey, Destiny. I'm Levi."

"Oh, I know who you are," Destiny purred.

"You know what? I think I've seen you around."

"Yes. Yes, you have. I worked the inventory room a few times while you were also in here."

"Cool," Levi replied.

Sade wasted no time butting into the conversation. "So, where are they at?" she asked, looking behind Levi. "Where are Jay and Cam?"

"I was about to ask you the same thing."

"What?" Sade pulled Levi to the side. "They aren't here?"

"I haven't seen them."

"What happened in the church?"

"The Underlings came in. When I went in, I could not find Jay and Cam. Those men came in so fast there was not much I could do. I got my bat and went straight into the basement. They were searching everything, and then all I know is that I heard the beasts. Those men must have opened the wrong door and let them out. Then, there were gunshots and screams. I stayed in the basement until everything got quiet. I went back up to look for Jay and Cam, but there was no sign of them."

"Well, then, that means they have to be here because they must have taken them like they took me."

"What are you talking 'bout?"

"Isn't this The Underlings' camp?"

"Wait, you think we had some connection with those creeps?" Destiny asked, butting into their conversation.

"Umm, yes. That's exactly who I thought you were. All I know is that they pulled up to where we were at, and the next thing I know, I'm getting snatched up, and I end up here. What was I supposed to think?"

"Destiny, can I get a minute with my friend?" Levi asked.

"You can get anything you want," Destiny replied before lunging forward to give Levi a hug. Despite him not embracing the hug back because he was not expecting it, she enjoyed it.

Sade and Levi both laughed as Destiny entered the inventory room. "What the heck is up with that chick?" Levi asked.

"She likes you. Isn't it obvious?"

"She doesn't even know me."

"Well, apparently she knows enough to know that she likes you."

They both laughed and began taking a walk. It only took Destiny seconds to pop back out of the building and keep her eyes on the prize. Levi and Sade worked their way around the neighborhood.

"Where are we?" Sade asked.

"These people call themselves The Saviors. I think they're the good guys. They saved me, and obviously, they saved you. I've been around here a little bit, and they seem to be cops and troops. Think we're in good hands."

"Where the hell were they at this whole time?" Sade barked, stopping in her tracks. "There were cops out here, and they're just standing around while innocent people are getting murdered?"

Sade's elevated voice caught people's attention. "Calm down," Levi said. "It's more complicated than that. They said all these people were battling The Underlings every day. They are doing the best that they can. They have a plan."

"Well, whatever they are doing isn't good enough. We sat in that church for months while they picked and chose who they felt was worthy of been saved. Come on, Levi. Open your eyes. We went out every day, hoping someone would be out there that could help us. Where were they at?"

Levi did not have an answer for Sade. She had a point. He remembered how desperate they were in that church. At one point, they did not think anyone else survived but The Underlings. Every week, they spotted that group raiding stores and homes, leaving them damaged. Not once did they run into anyone who was looking to help.

"We have to go back," Sade said.

"Go back where?"

"To the church. We have to see if Jay and Cam are still alive."

"I told you I looked for them, Sade."

"You just told me a lot of things, but somehow, you're here, and they aren't."

"What's that supposed to mean?"

"Exactly what it sounds like."

CHAPTER

31

A massacre took place at The Association, and Micah's words were stuck in Wolff's head. He was not happy with the decisions that were made by his leader, and they ultimately caused dozens of members their lives. Bodies were everywhere, and Micah was nowhere to be found. Things had to change. Wolff took it as a sign of disrespect that Micah felt the need to empty out half of the manpower in The Association just to look for Kyle. If it was not for that poor choice, the guards would have possibly been able to stand up to the mutation.

"He's too fuckin' soft. Listen up, boys. This is what happens when you let your emotions get the best of you," Wolff announced. "Why the hell are we being punished? This is his fault. We were stuck here with

no defense, and they let one of the monsters slip in."
The tattooed fists of the Irishman pounded on the
table as several men looked on. "First, he let that
coward in our home. He invited those motherfuckers
into our castle and has the nerve to blame us for the
shit that went down. Then, we get placed here, and all
of a sudden, a monster pops up in here and slaughters
our people."

His pale skin turned red. Veins bulged out of his
neck, and his hands began shaking. Wolff had
erupted.

"So, what do you think we should do?" Bogdan
asked. Bogdan was a slim, Polish fella with a temper
just as bad as Wolff's. During the incident with Kyle
and Adina, Bogdan was back at The Association. Kyle
had taken his spot on the team for that particular run.
It was not often that Bogdan was not right by Wolff's
side. Alone, each of them was dangerous, but together,
they were like a ticking time bomb.

"First thing we need to do is get rid of these fuckin'
visitors. Then, we'll go look for that fuckin' monster
and make sure it doesn't come back in here."

"But Micah said they can stay."

"I don't care what Micah said. Matter of fact, I don't
even see him around. That means I'm in charge right
now. I'm Adina's second in command, and I say those
people need to go." Wolff removed the magazine from
the assault rifle that was slung around his neck and
checked it. The magazine was half-filled, which must

have been acceptable because he slammed it back into the weapon.

Bogdan stepped up, grinning from ear to ear. "Where the fuck are they at?"

"Follow me."

Wolff and Bogdan took the stairs down and exited the building. Just walking down the street annoyed Wolff. It was desolate. If it was up to him, the streets would still be filled with their men, and they wouldn't be wasting any time on the search for Kyle.

Bogdan kicked the door in on the one-bedroom apartment that was assigned to Marcus and Candice. "What the hell is going on?" Marcus asked, jumping up from the dusty folding chair that he was sitting on. He was confused as to why the door was just kicked in. "What are y'all doing in here?"

"It's time for you to go, big boy," Wolff ordered, pointing the assault rifle at the nervous man.

"What do you mean it's time for me to go? You were in the room when Micah said we could stay. We already told y'all that we didn't have anything to do with Kyle and whatever he did out there. I don't even know him like that. We aren't friends, we aren't family, and we have no type of allegiance with him."

"For some reason, I don't believe you. I think you know more than you're telling us, and I think Micah made the wrong decision by letting you stay. I'm here to make the right decision."

"You can't do this."

BANG!

The .223 round escaped the barrel of the rifle and struck Marcus in the leg. He screamed in pain. Candice ran out from the bathroom after hearing the shot. The running water she had on in the bathroom drowned out the other noise in the room, so she had no idea that they were being violently evicted from the apartment. She had decided to wash up quickly after their encounter with Micah and his goons.

Bogdan's eyes locked on the blonde-haired woman who was barely dressed. She had put her t-shirt back on, but her jeans were still in the bathroom. "Oh yeah, what do we have here?" Bogdan asked excitedly.

Candice was stuck. She saw the two men and their weapons, and she also saw Marcus on the ground holding his leg. It was as if she tried to speak, but the words never came out. She slowly back-pedaled to the bathroom. She didn't want to leave Marcus in the apartment alone with the men, but she also didn't think she served much of a purpose standing there partially clothed.

Bogdan toted a silver revolver that he pointed at Candice while slowly advancing toward her. "Slow down, sweetheart. The party just started, and I think you should stay and have some fun."

"Leave my wife alone, you piece of shit," Marcus muttered through the pain. Still holding his leg, he tried to stand up.

Wolff was quick to move, striking Marcus in the head with the rifle. The strike left the big man seeing double. "Stop!" Candice yelled.

"You really want us to stop?" Bogdan asked.

"Yes. We haven't done anything to deserve this."

"Well, give me a reason to stop. I think if you have something that could convince me to leave." Bogdan licked his lips and kept advancing on Candice with his eyes scanning her body. "Come here and let me get a taste."

"No. Leave her alone," Marcus mumbled, barely being able to get the words out.

Candice ran into the bathroom and Bogdan was quickly on her tracks. She slammed the bathroom door, but he dove into it shoulder first, blasting it open. Candice screamed and grabbed an old plunger that was resting next to the toilet. "Please don't hurt me," she begged.

"Listen, honey, I'm not trying to hurt you. I just want a taste, and I'll leave. I promise."

"Please don't do this. Just leave."

"I can't do that."

Candice had her run-ins with some evil men, but the evil she spotted in Bogdan's eyes was different. The tight bathroom didn't leave much room to maneuver. She backed up until she felt the wall behind her. Candice swung the plunger at Bogdan out of desperation. Bogdan ducked the swings and rushed Candice, pinning her to the back wall. Candice yelled for Marcus to help her. Little did she know, Marcus had a rifle pointed in his face.

Wolff laughed. He was enjoying the moment. "What do you think my buddy and your old lady are in their doing right now?"

Marcus didn't respond. His mind was racing. He had to make a move. Candice needed him. Her screams echoed out of the bathroom. Marcus could hear the struggle. He reached up and grabbed Wolff's rifle, almost pulling the man to the ground. Wolff held onto the rifle tight, refusing to let it out of his hands. He delivered two swift punches to the side of Marcus's head. Marcus countered with a body shot that rocked Wolff.

Marcus didn't let up. He delivered another body shot in the form of a right hook, then a left uppercut to Wolff's chin. Wolff stumbled back. The screams in the bathroom continued. Marcus charged Wolff, knocking him over the chair and onto the ground. As soon as Wolff hit the ground, Marcus limped his way to the bathroom.

As soon as he entered the bathroom, he saw Bogdan on top of Candice. She was struggling to get him off. Tears were in her eyes, and a fresh bruise was on her face. She continued fighting Bogdan. Marcus used his last bit of energy to pounce on Bogdan's back, knocking him off Candice.

He delivered two power punches, breaking Bogdan's nose instantly. Blood began pouring from his nose. With his pistol in hand, Bogdan pulled the trigger, trying to put Marcus down. The shot missed Marcus, and he delivered another blow to Bogdan.

Another shot went off. Marcus cocked back to deliver another blow to Bogdan's face but fell straight forward. A powerful strike on the back of the head by Wolff had knocked him out.

CHAPTER

32

This had been the first time The Saviors had called a meeting of the masses. Maverick stood on the roof of the urgent care facility with a bullhorn. He looked down at the hundreds of people who were staring up at him. Only a few people knew why the meeting was being called. Everyone else braced themselves for bad news. If the heads of their group were coming together, it could not have been for a good reason. It felt like a lump was sitting in Maverick's throat as he swallowed and held the bullhorn up to his mouth.

"Thank you all for coming out tonight. I have called you all here to relay some sad and disturbing news. It is with a heavy heart that I regret to inform you that thirteen members of The Saviors have been killed."

Chatter began traveling through the crowd. Heads were turning, as if people wanted to see if anyone they knew were among the deceased.

"Last night, those thirteen members decided that they no longer wanted to be a part of the family we have built. Those members were led by Dalton. I considered Dalton to be a good friend of mine, and I don't understand why he wouldn't come to me before making such a terrible decision. The group ventured off and attempted to take over the hospital. Unfortunately, it seems that another group had access to the hospital and may have ambushed our people. Although I am saddened by the events that took place, I am also angry. I am angry because I believe that some of you knew their plan to leave and didn't notify us."

Throughout the entire crowd, Maverick was able to spot Dr. Lee. His eyes locked on hers. Her heart dropped because she knew he was speaking directly to her. He was calling her out.

"I also believe that some of you had planned to join them." Maverick took a deep breath. "Their blood is on your hands!" he yelled. More chatter came from the crowd. "If you would have notified us, we could have sent reinforcements with them. We could have ensured their transition to the hospital was completed safely. But instead, they were all gunned down because you all chose not to say anything. So now, I am giving you a way out. If you do not want to be a part of what we're building here, you can leave. There will be no hard feelings. We cannot afford to have people in our group that are going to make dumb decisions and cause the death of ours. It doesn't make sense. So, if you decide to stay, you need to be in it for the long run. No more jumping sides or running off to do your own thing. Just leave now because we need to move forward. If you have any information on people who were supposed to be a part of Dalton's new movement, please come to one of us. We need to identify these people if they will not come forward on their own. If you have any questions, please contact the head of your respected department, and they will happily answer those questions for you."

Maverick stepped down off the ledge of the roof and headed back into the building. Maverick hoped the message got across. He made arrangements to have people in place to safely escort anyone who wanted to leave out of their territory. What he did not know was that Dalton recruited more than sixty people to join him. Most of them agreed with his ideology, but they were too scared to leave the comfort of The Saviors. Maverick hoped that he would be able to identify those people and confront them about their decision to stay or not.

"Why did it seem like you were talking directly to me?" Dr. Lee asked, entering the urgent care building.

"Because I was. You and anyone else that knew what Dalton had planned."

"How many times do I have to apologize? I didn't know this was going to happen."

"How did you not know? What world are you living in? People are getting slaughtered out here. That's why we took over this territory. We had to do something to keep people safe. You knew that when you joined us. And you joined us because you knew exactly what was out there."

"Dalton said it was safe."

"Well, Dalton lied to you. And you listened to him rather than coming me."

"I can't come to you. No one can."

"What the hell is that supposed to mean?"

"It means that you are a big reason why all of those people wanted to leave. You don't listen to anyone. No one can make a suggestion without it being an issue with you."

"Are you talking about the suggestion you made? To turn a man over to his death? Are you serious right now?"

"It was just a suggestion."

"Yeah, a bad one. Just like Dalton's suggestion," Maverick barked. "When we left that hospital, I told him exactly why we couldn't take it over, and then he goes back on his own to do it. You should have seen the bodies. It was a mess."

Dr. Lee shook her head. "I don't even want to think about it."

"Well, you need to think about it because you could have prevented it from happening."

"I could say the same to you."

"I'm not going to sit here and keep doing this. If you don't see how this all could have can been avoided, then I will talk to the other heads, and we will need to reconsider your position within this organization."

"You can't do that." Dr. Lee was furious. Although she knew about Dalton's plan, she did not feel that she was in any way responsible for what happened to them. Maybe it was her arrogance, but she did not want to be blamed for the massacre at the hospital.

"I need to go check on Maddie."

"Me too."

Both of them headed down the hall to check on the wounded woman. Maddie had undergone an operation to remove the bullets from her body. In a normal world, the procedure would have been an easy one, but doing it in the urgent care facility was a struggle. One of Dr. Lee's comrades was able to show her worth to the group by performing the operation. She successfully removed the bullets.

"How is she doing?" Maverick asked.

"The same. She's still out of it. We're still monitoring her vitals."

Maverick placed his hand on Maddie's shoulder. *She's a fighter*, he thought. He had faith that she would wake up. He needed her to because he wanted answers. He needed to know exactly what happened in the hospital and the identity of The Reaper.

"Keep me posted on her condition."

CHAPTER

33

"I think that's their car up there," Nick said as he pulled up to a Sunoco gas station. The Nissan Altima was running in the parking lot, sitting among a bunch of abandoned vehicles. All the windows to the gas station were shattered. The actual gas pumps were knocked over. A commercial truck was positioned on top of the damaged pumps. The scene was unreal. Nick pulled up next to the Nissan.

"Well, it's about damned time. I ran out of flares and didn't know how I was going to signal y'all," Austin said.

The occupants of the Toyota exited and greeted him.

"Where's Charlotte?" Lori asked. She was not concerned about anything else except her daughter.

"She's inside with Dr. Abraham and the others."

"Lori ran into the gas station."

"Mom!" Charlotte yelled out, dropping everything she was doing to embrace her mom. The two hugged so tight they would have to be pried apart to separate.

"I was so worried about you, Mom."

"I was worried about you too, baby."

Lori continued embracing her daughter. She happened to look up and see Abraham and Emma standing at the counter, looking at something. They had not even turned around to greet her. Charlotte's arms were still wrapped tightly around her mother. Then, Lori saw the legs. The legs were stretched out across the counter. "What's going on?"

Charlotte released her grip and stepped back. "It's not good, Mom."

"Is that Tyler?" she asked, walking toward the counter.

Abraham looked back and nodded. He and Emma stepped back, clearing a path for Lori. Her mouth dropped to the floor when she approached him. Tyler was almost unrecognizable. His hair had fallen out, and his skin seemed tight. Lori placed her hand on top of Tyler's hand. It was almost as hard as a rock and felt like it was on fire.

"Why is he so hot?"

"We don't know," Abraham replied. We did our best to try to cool him down, but the fever progressed through all of our efforts. We don't know what else to do for him."

"We have to do something."

"We don't even know what Jin put in his body. Without the time to analyze the notes and test the remaining serum that is in those syringes, there is literally nothing we can do."

"I can't believe this. Tyler, it's going to be okay. We are going to try and get you some help." Tyler slowly turned his head and looked at Lori. He used almost all his energy to crack a smile for her. Blood dripped from his mouth, and Lori back-pedaled. An image flashed in her head.

She had not put two and two together when she first looked at Tyler, but the dripping blood was the missing clue. The blood was black. Images of the creature that attacked her in the room flashed in her head. "We have to get out of here."

"Mom. Are you serious? We're not leaving until Tyler gets better."

"Honey, you don't understand. Tyler is not going to get better; he's going to get worse."

"You care to explain, Lori?" Abraham asked.

"Jin. Jin's serum. It causes a different type of mutation. Jin locked me in a room with one of them, and I saw it with my own two eyes. Tyler is turning into one of them. We can't be here when he does."

"Mom, we can't leave him."

"Charlotte, this is not up for debate. Tyler is mutating. When the mutation is complete, he is going to be unstoppable. It's nothing like the other ones. We just saw one of them up close and personal. Go ask Brody."

"So, you're telling me that there are more of these things running around?" Abraham asked.

"I don't know. We only saw that one. But knowing Jin, there could be more."

Abraham was concerned. Lori was right. Jin was not the type to only conduct one test. He limited the access to certain experiments for others on the research team. When Micah had them searching for a cure, Jin had all hands on deck. But there were times when he did research alone. He started that experimental wing without Micah's permission. The testing he did with the new serum was not approved because Micah was on the hunt. Jin took full advantage of both his leaders being missing in action.

Charlotte stormed out of the gas station in tears. Emma chased after her. Lori knew the news was going to hit her hard, but it was not an easy decision to make. It broke her heart to see Tyler this way. But she was terrified of what he was going to become. Lori knew time was not on their side. If Tyler was mutating in such a short period, it was only a matter of time until the monster came out of him.

Lori did not have much fight left in her. She remembered being back in the small room with the metal pipe. The same fear that overcame her in the room was coming over her now. She barely made it out of that situation alive, and she did not know if she could do it again.

"We received a flare signal back. Do you think it's worth trying to get Tyler over to their medical personnel? Maybe they can do something for him."

In her head, Lori could still hear the sound of the screams that echoed down the hallway. There was pain and agony in each of them. "No. We can't risk it. I refuse to have anyone's blood on my hands. If we take Tyler there and they can't help him, he is going to slaughter them all."

"You don't know that."

"I do know that. I can still hear them. I can still hear their screams, Abraham." Lori was shaking.

Abraham pulled her in. He could still feel her jittery movements even while she was in his arms. "Everything is going to be okay. I trust you. Whatever you decide, we'll do it."

"What about Charlotte? She'll never forgive me."

"In due time, she will."

So, it was decided. The group left Tyler in the gas station. The young man laid across the counter. The Nissan and the Toyota peeled off. The group was on their way. They had a ton of miles to cover until they hit their destination.

CHAPTER

34

Levi had reservations about Sade's decision. This was the first time in a while that he felt safe and did not have to constantly look over his shoulder. With permission from Maverick, he packed a bag filled with items from the inventory room. He knew he could not convince Sade to not make this trip, so he did not even try. Plus, a part of him felt guilty that he left Jayven and Cameron behind. Levi knew he had no other choice but to leave the church and take Kyle to the hospital, but Sade would be furious if she knew that was the reason that Levi did not take the extra time looking for his friends.

Levi got up to answer the knock at the door. "Are you ready?" Sade asked when the door opened.

"Yup. Let me just grab my stuff."

Sade stepped into Levi's rowhome. "You stay here all by yourself?"

"Naw. It was a bunch of guys in here with me, but I heard they left this place."

"Left? To go where?"

"I don't know. I think they were going back to the hospital. People are saying they probably got killed."

"Why did they want to leave this place?"

"I don't know. The short time I've been here, those dudes seemed to be running things for the teens. I don't know why they would leave."

Sade rolled her eyes. Levi knew that look all too well. Sade's resistance had just begun. "I see you still got that bat," she said.

"Yup. Hopefully, I won't have to use it."

The two stepped out of the home and started walking toward the camp border. Levi had already arranged for the trip that was approved by Maverick. After Dalton's situation, Maverick loosened up on the rules. Dalton leading that group to their deaths was a crippling hit for The Saviors. There were families who wanted answers, and other groups of people who wanted to feel less like prisoners to the camp. Maverick knew every move and decision he made was for the safety of the entire group, but he was not expecting the immediate resistance. So now, he allowed people to come and go freely as long as they told them where they were going and what they were going to do.

Sade knew she should not have been out, but her stubbornness got the best of her. She only had the use of one arm. The injured one was bandaged up and placed in a sling. Her determination to find Jayven and Cameron fired her up and made her ignore the pain. Levi had an eerie feeling leaving The Saviors camp and heading back to the church. There were so many questions he wanted to ask Sade but knew he would not like the answers, so he did not bother. He used his nailed bat as a walking stick as they headed down the block.

The walk to the church was not a short one. It would take the teens at least an hour to make it there on foot, and that would be if they were not all banged up. At the rate they were going, they would make it there in about two-and-a-half hours. A glance over at Sade revealed the determination. She did not complain one time about the walk. Matter of fact, she did not say much at all during the walk. The two teens remained observant during the walk. It was not the safest decision they had made, but there was no other way for them to get to the church.

After about twenty minutes into their walk, the sound of a running engine got Levi's attention.

"Someone's coming, he said, pulling Sade into an alleyway.

The two tucked tightly into the alley as a green Honda minivan drove by. The van was filthy, and they could not see inside, but they knew there was only one crew who was known to drive around the city during these times. The last thing Levi wanted was another run-in with The Underlings. The first two encounters, he got lucky, but there was no guarantee that a third encounter would grant him the same luck.

"Could you see who it was?" Sade asked.

"No. It was a minivan, but they drove by too fast for me to see the driver."

"Let's go," Sade said before exiting the alleyway.

Levi grabbed her arm and pulled her back. "Slow down. I know you want to find Jay and Cam, but we can't be reckless. Give it a minute to make sure no one else is around."

"Don't lecture me, Levi. I'm not the one who left our friends to die." Sade pulled away from Levi and exited the alleyway. Just as she did, the minivan reversed to their location. Sade attempted to run forward as the van reversed.

"Yo!" the male driver yelled out, rolling down the window.

Her heart was pounding out of her chest, and it felt as if she was about to lose her breath. Nevertheless, Sade continued sprinting up the block. The driver of the van slammed the gear shift into drive and followed her. Levi spotted this from the alley and chased after the van once it took off. Her sneakers slammed on the pavement as her stride shortened. Sade was gassed. She spotted another alley and slipped right into it. This time, she did not pop back out as quickly as she had done minutes ago.

Unfortunately, with the slight limp in her run, she did not gain any distance at all on the van. It was right behind her the entire time. The driver pulled up to the alleyway, and the driver got out in a hurry. "What are you running for?"

Sade pulled out a blade with her good hand. "Come any closer, and I'll cut you," she threatened.

"Hey, get away from her!" Levi yelled as he ran up with his bat positioned for a swing.

"Levi!" Destiny yelled as she exited from the passenger seat of the minivan.

Levi stopped as the teen ran toward him and jumped into his arms. "What are y'all doing?" Levi asked, pushing Destiny away from him. "Why the hell would you pull up on us like that?"

"We were looking for you two. Ms. Latoya saw you leave this morning, so I figured we would come be your backup."

"But why would you pull up on us like that?" Sade asked angrily. "Someone could have gotten hurt. What if I had a gun instead of this knife? I would have shot your friend right here."

"This isn't a game. I know y'all have been couped up in that little safe environment with The Saviors, but out here, it's life or death!" Levi shouted. "You can't just pull up on us like that. You can't pull up anyone like that."

"Sorry," Destiny muttered. "We were just trying to come along to help you."

"We didn't ask for help, and we don't need any help!" Sade hollered. "Go back home."

Destiny was nearly in tears. She and the driver headed back to the minivan.

"Hold on," Levi said. "We could use some help."

"We don't need it," Sade replied.

"Yes, we do. We still have a long way to go, and it would be quicker getting there in the minivan. Plus, you ain't even thinking logically. So, I could use the extra eyes and ears with me."

"You're not in charge of me, Levi."

"I didn't say I was. But it seems that you are out trying to get yourself killed. I'm not letting you drag me into a dumb situation. Look at you. You weren't going to do anything with that knife. Now, I'm getting in this minivan, and I'm going to the church to find Jay and Cam. You can come along if you want."

Levi walked over to the van and opened the side door. There were two other teens in the back of the minivan. They scooted over to make room. Levi waited for Sade to make her decision.

CHAPTER

35

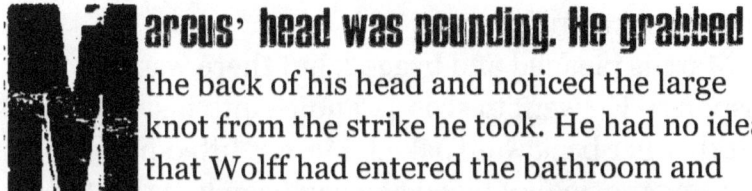arcus' head was pounding. He grabbed
the back of his head and noticed the large
knot from the strike he took. He had no idea
that Wolff had entered the bathroom and
knocked him upside the head with a rifle.
One minute he was going toe to toe with Bogdan, and
the next he was face down on the floor. Marcus
grabbed the toilet and pulled himself up. The gunshot
wound to his leg he bled so much that his jeans were
drenched. However, it appeared that it was only a
flesh wound. Marcus used the wall to support him as
he sat up and gathered himself.

"Candice, get up," he said, noticing that she was
still on the bathroom floor. It was time for them to
leave. Going back and forth with some of the top men

in The Association was not on his list of things to do. Marcus needed a plan to get himself and Candice out of the reach of The Association.

He removed his shirt, balled it up, and pressed it against his leg wound.

"Candice, get up, baby."

"Candice."

"Babe, get up."

Marcus pulled himself forward and flopped on the ground by Candice's side. He nudged her, but she did not respond. "Candice, wake up," he said, shaking her by the shoulders.

Candice's body was limp. Marcus shook her again, hoping she would wake up. He scooted closer to her and put his ear on her chest.

"No, no, no. Candice, get up. Don't do this to me. Please, wake up."

Marcus pleaded and begged, but there was no response. He went to scoop Candice into his arms and felt that her back was soaked. Marcus lifted her up and saw the pool of blood she had been lying in. He let out a loud scream as he held her in his arms. His heart skipped a beat, and tears began to flow from his eyes. They were uncontrollable. Seeing his wife filled with holes made him feel guilty. She was struck by the bullets that were fired during the initial altercation.

Marcus squeezed Candice's body and held it tight. He was in disbelief. "I'm sorry, baby," he whispered.

"Yeah, you are sorry," Bogdan said.

"Leave. I don't have time for this," Marcus muttered. He did not even bother looking up. He was a broken man.

"You don't get to decide what you have time for," Bogdan said, firing a shot at the wounded man. Marcus yelled out as the bullet ripped through his other leg.

"I need to know where your friend, Kyle, is hiding at."

"I already told you," Marcus groaned. "I don't know him."

Bogdan ripped off another round, this time sending the bullet into Marcus's good leg. Marcus screamed. "Stop. Leave me alone."

Wolff let out a devilish laugh. "Damn. You got him begging."

Bogdan approached Marcus, who was flopping on the floor like a fish. "This is the last time I'm going to ask. Where is Kyle?"

"I don't know."

Just as Marcus spoke his last word, Bogdan fired another round at Marcus. This time, the bullet struck him in the head, blowing his brain out of the back of his head. Marcus's body slumped over Candice.

"Was that necessary?" Wolff asked jokingly.

"Everything we do is necessary." They were the current leaders of the organization and needed to step it up a notch. There was no more of Micah's open-door policy. It was time to lock down whatever was left of The Association.

CHAPTER

36

"You're going to turn left up here at the corner," Levi said.

"So, what's the deal with this church? Why are we going there?" Neil asked. Neil was the driver and Destiny's cousin. The eighteen-year-old was also a part of The Savior's security squad. Although he was very timid during the encounter with Sade, Neil was well-trained with the .40 caliber Glock 19 that was strapped to his hip. His friends, Jameel and Terrence, were the ones in the back of the minivan.

"That church is our home," Sade responded. "I think our friends are trapped inside of there, and I want to get them out."

"Say no more," Neil said.

"So, what's the plan once we get there?" Destiny asked.

"The plan is you stay in the van, and we'll go inside and get their friends."

"No, Neil. You're not going to treat me like a kid," Destiny stated.

"It's not up for debate. Uncle P would kill me if something happened to you. So, like I said, you're staying in the van."

Jameel was right. Destiny's father, Patrick, didn't even know they left the camp. At that very moment, he probably thought she was running her shift in the inventory room. Destiny knew exactly what would happen if her father knew she was out on a rescue mission, let alone with a bunch of other teenagers.

"He's right, Destiny, it's best that you stay out of that place. It's dangerous, and we still don't know who or what is inside." Levi added.

Sade looked over at him. A grimaced look covered her face.

"What's that supposed to mean?" Jameel asked. "You said you don't know who or what is inside. What do you mean by that?"

Just as the young man asked that question, Neil pulled up to the church. The front doors of the church were wide open. Sade and Levi looked at each other, and both of their mouths hit the floor. The last time they had left the building, it was secured from the inside. The only way to enter the church would to have been by force. Neil slammed on the brakes once he saw the bodies that covered the street and entrance to the church.

"I guess this is what they meant," Terrence mumbled, seeing the street filled with the corpses of humans and mutated creatures. The other teens in the group had heard about the mutations, but none of them had seen them up close before.

"Make sure you guys are locked and loaded," Neil ordered.

"I thought y'all said this was your home," Destiny said.

"It is," Sade replied.

"Y'all lived here with all those things around you?"

"Those things are our friends and family," Sade retorted. "And they weren't around us—they were living inside the church with us. Someone let them out."

Destiny turned around in her seat. "What do you mean you were living with those things?"

"Exactly what I said. We lived there with them."

"Please tell me those aren't your friends out here on the ground too," Neil said.

"I hope not." Sade's mind was racing. She did the best she could to eye up the human bodies that were scattered around the church and in the street. She could tell by the statures of the bodies that most of them were adult males. *The Underlings*, she thought. She continued scanning the scene.

Levi was particularly quiet. The day of the attack on the church was playing back in his head. He could hear the doors slamming, gunshots, and screams. He could actually hear it all like it was happening right now. He was not sure what would be left of the church after The Underlings got to it. He still could not wrap his head around the disappearance of his friends. He knew Sade wasn't satisfied with his version of the events that took place that day, but he certainly remembered checking as many rooms as he could and his friends not being in any of those rooms.

The side door slid open. The teens exited the minivan and headed straight to the church. Destiny stayed put, and Neil left Terrence with her. Terrence was squirming in the backseat. His sweaty hands shook as he did his best to grip the small pistol. The Ruger .380 almost slipped out of the hands of the nervous teen several times. His head was on a swivel, but it was more so out of fear than anything else.

Terrence couldn't sit still. He hopped out of the minivan and posted outside of the vehicle with his gun up.

"What's wrong with you?" Destiny asked, opening the door.

"Get back inside the van. It's not safe out here," Terrence said. His voice cracked as he spoke.

"T, get back in here. You don't have to be out there."

"No. I'm not going to be a sitting duck for these demons. I heard Mr. Dalton talking about them one time. He said they can crush a car just by jumping on top of it. I'm not going to be sitting in there so one of those things can crush me like a bug."

"So, why are you leaving me in here to be crushed?"

"Because I'm going to protect you. This jawn right here may be small, but it packs a punch when I shoot it. If one of those things comes near me, I'll empty the clip on it. It won't even get close to the van."

The words sounded brave, but Terrence's body language told another tale. He also had a bit of a history when it came to having courage. Destiny remembered an incident in which a squirrel got into the inventory room, and Terrence fired five shots at it, missing all five shots. The leadership of the group were ready to strip Terrence of his weapon and security detail, but Destiny took the blame for the incident. She knew her father would pull strings with Maverick, and that was exactly what had happened. Terrence was able to keep his duties, and Destiny got a stern warning, but no other punishment was issued.

"Terrence, get back inside here right now! You aren't going to do anything with that little gun. Look how big those things are."

"Yes, I am. I'm going to kill one of those things."

"Thou shall not kill, Terrence. You know that's what the Bible says."

"I think the Bible was referring to humans, not these monsters."

"They are humans. Well, they were humans at one point."

"Shut up, Destiny. Do you want to live, or do you want to die?"

"I want to live, but I also want to go to heaven. Think about what you're saying and what you're planning to do. There's no coming back from that. You'll have to live with that forever, and at some point, you'll have to answer for those sins."

"I'll gladly answer for my sins. But I'll do it when I grow to be an old man. I'm not going to sit here and listen to you preach peace at a time when people are struggling to survive. And since you want to talk about your Bible so much, ask God to protect you because I'm going inside with the rest of them."

"Wait, don't leave me out here by myself," Destiny pleaded, watching Terrence run over to the church.

CHAPTER

37

"This is sick," Neil said as the group stepped into the church. He was so distracted by the pungent odor in the air and the gruesome scene that he did not have his weapon raised.

Usually, the young man was on point, but this was the first time he had seen anything this horrendous. The main level of the church was filled with the corpses of the mutated creatures. The teens were literally walking on blood and spent shell casings. It was a warzone. Human body parts were also scattered around the floor. The scene was the result of heinous attacks by the creatures.

"How do we know these things are dead?" Jameel asked.

"We know, because if they weren't, we'd be dead right now," Levi replied.

Levi poked the corpses as he passed to confirm what he had just told Jameel. This was the first time he had been in this portion of the church since the night everyone mutated. So many memories came back to him just standing in the aisle. He missed his parents and his old life more than ever. Seeing the church in this condition was a disgrace to him. He was ashamed.

"Check this out," Sade announced. She was standing next to one of the spray-painted ambulances that The Underlings arrived in. There was heavy damage to the front of the ambulance. It was used to drive through the front doors of the church during the raid. The scratches all over the vehicle showed that the creatures attempted to claw their way inside of the vehicle.

Levi ran over to the ambulance. "This is one of the vehicles that those men came in."

"Let's clear it," Neil said.

"We only have two guns. How are we going to cover it?" Jameel asked.

"You have three guns," Terrence added, stepping into the church.

"What the hell are you doing in here?" Neil shouted. "You're supposed to be protecting my cousin. Where is she?"

"I'm right here," Destiny said, walking into the church. The smell of rotting corpses immediately turned her stomach, causing her to vomit.

"This is why I told you to stay in the car. We don't have time for this. Come on, let's clear this vehicle."

The three, armed young men took up a tactical position and approached the ambulance. Sade moved out of their way, and Levi trailed them with his Louisville Slugger®. The ambulance had been driven directly down the main aisle of the church, which left them in an area of approach from their current position. With their guns pointed at the rear of the vehicle, they made their way up to the rear doors.

Jameel grabbed one of the door handles and flung the door open. The back of the ambulance appeared trashed. Neil climbed inside the back to double-check the vehicle. He discovered a few weapons and restraints that were left behind. "Yo, fellas. We are taking these with us," Neil said, throwing the found items out of the vehicle.

After clearing the ambulance, the teens continued through the church. Sade noticed all the damage throughout the church. The church had been riddled with bullets. The window to the production room was filled with holes. Initially, she was mad at Levi for what had happened, but walking through the church made her realize what he was truly up against during the raid. It was a miracle that he made it out of that place alive. Realizing this also made her worry more about Jayven and Cameron.

The blocked access to the rear of the church had been opened up too. Levi's anxiety was going haywire while he searched the back rooms. He did them in the same order as the day of the raid. Each room had been ransacked. There was no sign of his friends.

"Levi!" Sade yelled out from the basement. Levi sprinted to see what Sade wanted. Once he reached the basement, he saw her kneeling down over some boxes. "You believe they didn't even take my jerky?" Sade said to him, laughing.

Levi laughed too. "I guess those dudes would rather starve than be vegans."

The other teens laughed at the comment. "Can we please take this stuff back with us?" Sade asked Neil.

"Yeah, we can do that." Neil, Terrence, and Jameel began picking up the boxes of spilled goods and taking them out to the minivan.

"There's no sign of either of them," Levi told Sade.

"What does this mean? Did they get out like us, or were they taken? For all we know, they could have even been eaten by the beasts."

"Don't say stuff like that."

"Why not? It's the truth. Jay and Cam have nowhere to go, and they can't survive out here on their own. It's been more than a week since all of this happened. You know damned well that they couldn't survive out here for a day, let alone a week."

"Stop swearing in the Lord's house, Sade. You know I hate when you do that."

"The Lord's house? It looks more like the devil's playground to me. Take a look around, Levi. This place is a mess."

"Don't you think I know that? It's okay, though, because once things go back to normal, we are going to fix this place up and get it back to a place of worship."

Sade patted Levi on the shoulder and nodded before hitting the stairs. She appreciated his optimism, but she didn't have the energy to entertain it at the moment. She knew that she would never live a normal life ever again. The closest thing to it was The Saviors camp, and who knew how long that would last?

Sade struggled to climb up to her favorite place in the whole building. Getting up there with one arm was not easy, but she was able to do it. She was back on top of the world. She watched as the other teens carried her boxes out to the car. She ripped open a package of jerky and bit into the tough snack. Sade longed to taste the snack once more, and she got that wish granted. She lay down on the beam and looked up into the sky. Everything was changing so fast.

Below her used to be a pit of monsters, and now it was just a burial site. *Jay and Cam, I won't stop until I find you.* She took another bite. Levi looked and saw her good arm dangling from the post. He knew she would not be leaving without visiting her favorite spot. He, on the other hand, wanted to get out of the church sooner than later. Looking around at all the corpses, he couldn't even tell which ones belonged to his parents. The number of corpses he was looking at was significantly lower than the number of beasts that was originally packed in the building. Levi was not sure what happened to the rest of the beasts, but he had an inkling that there was a possibility of them returning. If that was the case, it was time to head back to The Saviors.

CHAPTER

38

"**You are crazy, you know that?**"

"Yeah, I know. I can't help it sometimes," Bogdan replied.

"You didn't have to kill that chick. You could have let her, and her pathetic man just leave."

"Me? You are the one that knocked out the big black dude. It didn't look like he was breathing. So, don't sit here and try to lecture me."

Wolff laughed. "If I didn't knock him out, he would have knocked you upside your head."

Bogdan held a cloth up to his bloody nose. Wolff placed his hand over Bogdan's nose and quickly snapped it back in place. Bogdan grimaced.

"Keep that rag on that crooked snout. I popped it back in place, but it's still going to leak for a while."

Wolff dropped a box of bullets on Bogdan's lap. Bogdan opened the cylinder on the revolver and dropped out all the empty casings. He placed the gun between his legs while he reloaded with his free hand.

"Hurry up so we can go get that pansy next."

"How the hell are we going to get him? He's in Adina's room."

"We'll just find a way to get his ass out of the room. When we do, we are going to put him down."

"And how exactly are you going to explain that to her?"

"I don't think it will be much to explain. Adina has a choice. The Association or the fucking pansy. If she chooses him over us, then she'll have a big problem on her hands."

Dannie watched as Star trotted around the room. Adina was still recovering, and as Dannie promised, he wasn't going to leave her side. The only time he stepped out the room was if he could not find someone to take Star outside for a walk, which was not really an issue. The anxious dog barked and clawed at the door.

"Get back over here. There ain't nothin' out there for you, girl," Dannie said.

Star continued to claw at the door. Suddenly, the door slowly crept open. Star took off out the door. "Hey, get back here," Dannie yelled, as he hopped up and began chasing after her. The last thing he wanted was Star getting out of the building. Dannie jetted down the hallway and made a sharp left turn around the corner. Just as Dannie hit the corner, he spotted Star. She was wrapped in Bogdon's arms. "I apologize for my dog. She got out as soon as I turned my head."

"Oh, no worries," Bogdon muttered as he rubbed his hand across the top of the dog's head.

A knot formed in Dannie's stomach. He noticed that Bogdon still had not released Star. He just continued rubbing her head. He slowly inched forward, hoping that the man would get the hint and release his dog. However, Bogdon stood his ground and continued giving Dannie a sinister look. Dannie continued toward Bogdon when suddenly a sharp pain shot through the left side of his face. He stumbled onto the ground. Wolff emerged from an open door, delivering another punch to the side of Dannie's face.

"Where is he?" Wolff asked.

"Where is who?" Dannie asked after spitting out a glob of blood.

"Your friend. The one that shot Adina. I want to know where he is."

"He's not my friend."

Wolff delivered a swift kick to Dannie's midsection. "Where is he? Wolff yelled.

"I don't know."

The pain Dannie felt was excruciating, especially after Wolff kicked him again. "I'll give one more opportunity to tell me the truth," Wolff declared, as he slowly pulled out his blade. Dannie knew no matter what he said, this would be the end. He pushed himself with his left hand and then rolled over.

BANG! BANG! BANG!

The shots from the .380 pistol were aimed at Wolff. After the first kick, Dannie had pulled the small pistol out of his pocket. The second kick almost caused him to drop it, but he held on tight; knowing it was his form of defense against Wolff. Star barked and came running down the hallway. Both Wolff and Bogdon took cover after the shots when off. Bogdon dropped Star and ducked behind a pillar. He pulled a gun from his waistband and gripped it tight. He took a deep breath and popped out from behind the pillar. With his finger slapping on the trigger, Bogdon sent several rounds down the hallway.

Wolff popped out from the room with a rifle in hand. He was ready to put holes through Dannie like a slice of Swiss cheese. When entered the hallway, he noticed it was empty. "Where is he?" Wolff barked.

"I didn't see where went. I tried to light his ass up."

"Go find him. I'll check these rooms."

Bogdon sprinted down the hallway and took off around the corner. Wolff eyed up another open door that led to a room right across from the one he took cover in. He held his rifle up, ready to attack as he stepped in the room. "Come one out, if you're in here. The more I gotta keep hunting you down, the worst it's gon' be for you."

Wolff kicked over a desk that was pushed against the wall, but there was no sign of Dannie. The old classroom was still filled with the small student desks and a bookshelf that sat in the back corner of the room. Everything was clear except the bookshelf. Wolff crept up to the shelf, as he listened intently. He waited for the sound of the slightest movement, ready to strike. There rustling coming from behind the shelf. He walked lightly, trying his best not to give away his location.

Once Wolff got up to the bookshelf, he carefully placed his left hand against it. His right hand continued to tightly grip the rifle. He was licking his chops, ready to slice Dannie up. The rustling continued. Wolff pushed the bookcase over, hoping to trap his prey. Instead, a stray cat ran from behind the crashing bookshelf. Wolff checked under the shelf and there was no sign of Dannie.

A large explosion from outside rocked the building, shattering the windows in the room. Wolff dropped to the ground as the glass spread across the floor and onto his back. His ears were ringing. He popped up and looked outside, only to see members of The Association scrambling around outside. Wolff quickly exited the room and ran out of the building to find the source of the explosion. Smoke and flames surfaced from the front gate. Other members of The Association ran toward the front gate.

"What the fuck going on?" Wolff yelled, running toward the gate.

"Someone drove a car into the front border, and it blew up," one of the men replied.

The car was an older model Ford Crown Victoria that had be driven directly at the entrance to The Association. Wolff immediately thought it was Dannie trying to make an escape. The vehicle was still on fire and smoking, as he reached the front gate. He noticed the vehicle was on the outside of the gate trying to get inside the camp. "Find me the person who did this."

Wolff had his suspicions on who would perform such an act. His first thought was Dannie, but his next was Micah. They left their leader in the streets, and this could be his way of sending a message to those who chose to return home. Wolff wasted no time investigating the damaged Ford. There would surely be some type of evidence inside that could help him figure out who drove it into the gate. The flames were still shooting out, making it difficult for him to approach the vehicle but he circled it from a distance. There was no sign of a body inside the vehicle.

"Wolff, over here!" someone shouted. Wolff looked down the street and saw a man approaching with his hands up. Dressed in all black, the man kept his hands raised in the air as he approached. Wolff's rifle was pointed directly at the male, but he didn't pull the trigger.

"Stop right there," Wolff ordered. He looked over and flagged a team with him.

Wolff took his time advancing toward the male, making sure to scan the area. He had to make sure this was not some sort of ambush. If anyone popped out with any surprises, Wolff was ready to put them down. The small team that joined Wolff also had their guns trained on the mysterious man. This caused a smile to spread across the man's face. He was happy to receive the warm welcome from The Association.

"Get the fuck out of here," Wolff barked. He could not believe what he was seeing. Better yet, he could not believe who he was seeing. "Dale?"

"Surprise, motherfucker!"

"What, you rose from the dead, you crazy son of a bitch?"

Wolff let his rifle hang and extended his hand. Both men shook hands and embraced each other.

"They told us you died."

"Who told you that?"

"Rob and Benny. They said you got attacked by some of those fuckin' beasts, and you didn't make it out."

"Is that right? That's what they said, huh?"

Wolff scrunched up his face. "What? Is it not true?"

"Well, let's just say I did die, but now I'm back."

Wolff looked back to his men. "Do y'all see this? He's back from the dead. The return of the infamous Dale."

"The Reaper."

"What?"

"The Reaper. Dale is dead. This is the return of The Reaper."

"Interesting. The Reaper. I like it. So, what brings you back, old friend?"

"I need to speak with Micah. I have a proposition for him."

"Micah isn't here right now."

"Where is he?"

"He's out on a scavenger hunt. He took a bunch of our people with him. If you need something, you can go through me because I'm in charge."

"You're in charge? Where's Adina?"

"She's inside."

"So, why are you in charge if she's in there?"

"It's a long story. Let's just say that she isn't currently fit for her duties."

"So, where exactly did Micah go?"

"He went on a run really quick."

"A run? Since when did Micah start going on runs?"

"This one is a very important one, and he doesn't want to risk any mistakes being made. Somebody attacked Adina and Micah's out looking for the guy."

"So why the hell are you here and not out there looking with him?"

"Because he is small minded, and I'm focused on the bigger picture. Micah has gone crazy. He tried taking all of our resources for his lil' bullshit hunt, but we weren't doing shit but wasting time. That dude is long gone and for all we know, he's probably dead. I lit him up when he was trying to get away."

"I'm actually surprised to hear this," The Reaper replied as he rubbed his chin. "Micah has always known there was a split in loyalty when it came to The

Association. Why in the world would a king ever leave his castle unattended."

"Because he should have never had the throne. It's mine now and we're going to do things a lot different around here. The way Adina always wanted it."

"Well, if that's the case, I come bearing a gift."

"Another gift, besides that burning car you smashed into the front gate?" Both men laughed.

"Yes. Seeing as though you have found yourself with new responsibilities, I am here to provide you with an army."

"An army?"

"Yes. Hundreds of men and women that are willing and ready to follow orders."

"Where did you find these people?"

"Below the surface, with the rats. They've been down there for a long time, and they are more than deserving of a new home. I want this to be their home but if it's too much for you to handle, then we'll find somewhere else to call home."

"Not at all, friend. Your people are more than welcome to join us. But they are your people, and you should be the one to lead them. I want you to be by my side. Let's get rid of this stupid hierarchy that this place had before and let's rule these people together."

"That sounds like a plan. What about Micah?"

"Well I'm sure the next time I see him, he'll be trying to kill me for leaving him, so I guess I have to be the one to strike first. When they come back, we'll take them all out."

CHAPTER

39

The minivan pulled up to the borderline of The Saviors territory. Armed security slowly approached, identifying the occupants. It had been a few hours since the teens had left for their rescue mission. "Where the hell did y'all go?" a loud, boisterous voice yelled.

Destiny sank into her seat once she heard her father's voice.

"Uncle P, I can explain everything," Neil said, hopping out of the minivan.

"There's nothing to explain. Why was my daughter outside of the camp?"

"We just took a quick ride, Uncle P. It was nothing serious."

Patrick grabbed Neil, almost lifting him off the ground. "Listen here, boy, my sister has been very lenient with you and let you run free and do whatever you want. But when it comes to my daughter, you better believe that you don't get to take her anywhere without my permission."

"Daddy, get off of him!" Destiny yelled. The young teen was scared of facing the consequences of leaving without permission, but she wasn't going to watch her cousin get in trouble for her decisions. "Daddy, it's not his fault."

"Where did you go, Destiny?"

"I was going to take a walk with my new friend, and Neil offered us a ride so we would have protection. He also brought a few of his friends."

Patrick eyed up the minivan and saw the other three teen boys and snapped. The last thing a father wanted to see was his daughter going missing, and when she came back, it was with a group of boys. "I'm only going to ask you one time: what the hell were y'all doing?"

Neil was scared to answer the question honestly, but he had no other choice. "Uncle P, Destiny's friends went up to this church off of Rising Sun Avenue to look for some other kids that they thought might be dead. We went up there, and those kids weren't there, but we were able to snag some food and weapons out of that spot. That's it. That's all we did."

"Food and weapons out of a church?" Patrick asked skeptically.

"Yes, sir. You can take a look in the back of the van. All of the stuff is back there."

The large man pushed his nephew back on the ground and stomped over to the minivan. The other teens all ran out of the way. They did not want to face the wrath of Destiny's father. He opened the back and spotted the supplies that his nephew mentioned. He examined the weapons first, impressed with the load that was brought back. Then, he looked through the boxes of Sade's snacks.

Patrick ripped open a pack of the jerky and wolfed down the dry snack before frowning in disgust. "You could have left this crap back where you found it. It tastes like cardboard."

The teens all laughed at the comment, including Sade. "It's vegan. It's good for you," she said.

"Well, it tastes bad for me," he replied. He turned to Destiny, who was trying her best to avoid eye contact with him. "You're grounded, young lady!" he yelled. "Now, come on. Let's go. You, too, Neil."

Destiny marched away with her father. Other members of the camp had gathered around to see the parenting show. It was all smiles and smirks in the audience.

"How do you get grounded during an apocalypse?" Terrence joked.

The other teens laughed.

"Is he always like that with her?" Levi asked.

"Yup. Mr. P does not play about his daughter. Destiny is usually up in her room when the rest of us hang out. He has her paranoid. He also has Ms. Latoya check on Destiny constantly to make sure that she's following his rules."

"That's insane. I feel sorry for her," Sade added.

"Well, that's enough of this spectacle. Where do you want us to take this stuff?" Jameel asked.

"Am I allowed to take it to my room?"

"Not really," Levi said. Fill your bag up to the max, and I'll put the rest up in the inventory room." Sade cocked her back, trying to process what Levi had just suggested. "Come on, Sade. You can't just hoard things in this place. We have to share with everybody the same way they share with us. Nobody is going to touch this nasty stuff anyway. You're probably the last vegan on earth."

"Whatever. I don't know how much longer you meat-eaters think you're going to last in this world. You better start eating those creatures," she said while chuckling. "I'm sure mutated meat tastes like chicken."

Sade began stuffing her backpack with snacks. Levi reached into the back of the minivan and grabbed two pistols, tucking one into Sade's bag. "Keep this with you at all times," he whispered. She nodded in agreement. The other one, he placed in his bag. Levi figured it was time to upgrade from the bat. Although he never fired a gun before, he realized that he would not get far with just his bat.

The Saviors camp was very structured. Maverick only wanted certain people carrying weapons.

Everyone could not be trusted. Although no one had betrayed the group in a formal sense, Dalton was not the only person to have their own personal opinion about how the group should be running and what they should be doing. Some people were welcomed back with open arms after leaving, but there were others who never made it back at all. Levi was taking a risk by arming himself, but that was a risk that he was willing to take.

The teens drove the minivan over to one of the inventory rooms and began unloading. Sade stepped into the room, amazed by the products that were on the shelves. "You mean to tell me they got all this food stocked in here, and that lady only gave me crackers and ketchup?"

"We have to eat in portions. That's the only way we can guarantee that the food will last," Terrence said. "Maverick said if everyone just ate what they want, we'll be out of food in a matter of months."

"Who is Maverick?"

"He is one of the leaders of this place. I think he used to be a cop or something like that. It's a few dudes at the top, and they make all the rules. Maverick is just the one that puts everything together."

Sade was impressed. She was starting to see what Levi saw. It was so much different than the life they lived in the church. Going back to the church gave her closure, but the disappearance of Jayven and Cameron still needed to be solved. She still wanted to find her friends, but she just did not know where to look.

"Why do you look like you're up to something?" Levi asked.

"We need to go back."

"Go back where? The church? We just searched that entire building, Sade. There was no sign of them in there."

"So, where could they be? They have to be in one of those buildings. You know they wouldn't have gone far. I'm sure if we keep looking, we'll fi—"

"We did look!" he barked. "And we found nothing. I'm sure if we go back there and look some more, we still won't find anything."

"So, you just want to give up?"

"No. I'm not giving up."

"Let me ask you a question. Did you even try to look for me?"

"That's not fair to ask. You know that I tried looking for you."

"So, why is it so easy for you to give up on them? They're not just our friends, Levi. They are the only family we have left."

"Don't you think I know that? I was the one that was there, Sade. Not you. I was the one getting shot at and left in that church to die, not you. So, stop with the lectures."

A hard smack knocked saliva out of Levi's mouth. "How dare you say that to me?"

Levi held his face and watched as Sade stormed off.

C.L. LOWRY

CHAPTER

40

Sade sat in her room in tears. The other girls had not come back from performing their duties yet, so she had the room to herself. Levi's words cut like a knife. *So, that's how he really feels about me*, she thought. *He feels that I left him*. Although she had ran off to her room, she was parked right at the window with her eyes on her friend. He was still unloading the minivan with the others.

Sade held her injured arm. The incident from that day was now playing back in her head. She did not remember much after falling through the awning, but she did remember the gunshots. She did remember how scared she felt and how Levi's words made all that fear go away when he told her to jump the roof.

"You must be grounded, too, huh?" Destiny asked, walking into the bedroom.

Sade quickly wiped the tears that were running down her face, but the pools were still in her eyes, and her nose had turned red.

"What's wrong?" Destiny asked, running over to Sade and embracing her.

The tears just began flowing down Sade's eyes. She was pouring her heart out on Destiny's shoulder. The tears were contagious because they started falling from Destiny's eyes too. The two teens were letting it all out. They spoke no words; it was just tears.

Hours had passed, and Latoya returned to the home with the other girls. Patrick had tracked her down and gave her an earful after chastising the kids upon their return. Latoya understood Patrick's parental instincts, but she also knew Destiny's potential. She did not even realize everything that the teens witnessed today. What the adults thought was just an adolescent rendezvous was actually a life-changing experience. None of the teens would ever be the same.

Latoya entered the home, looking for Destiny. She wanted to have a chat with the teen following the conversation she had with her father. Destiny wasn't in her assigned area. *I know this girl didn't sneak out of this house when she knows her dad just grounded her.* Latoya looked all over the first floor, but there was no sign of Destiny. She even asked some of the other girls, but they hadn't seen her.

Latoya walked upstairs and peeked into the room Sade was assigned to. She saw the two girls laid out on the floor, sleeping like babies. Latoya smiled. After that initial encounter with Sade, she was happy to see her making friends.

Latoya decided to clean up the girls' belongings so that the other teens wouldn't bother them. She picked up Sade's bag, and most of the contents fell out, including the snacks and the handgun that Levi tucked inside. Latoya was disturbed by the discovery. She ran out and headed to Maverick.

"We have a problem," Latoya said, standing in front of Maverick, Seth, Helena, and Noah.

Most people in the camp had interactions with Maverick, but not many people interacted with Seth, Howard, and Noah. The four individuals were structured like the different branches of the United States Military, and they oversaw all the operations within their respected branch.

With his law enforcement background, Maverick was in charge of the day-to-day operations outside the camp. This included putting together search teams and rescue teams and strategizing offensive tactics. Seth had a military background and was in charge of the camps defenses. He put together teams who protected their territory but also worked on defensive strategies and the expansion of the group and their territory. Helena was a medical expert. She worked closely with the doctors and nurses in the group to keep members healthy but to also get other members trained too. Noah controlled everything else, including the inventory, housing, and other elements that were specifically geared around the lifestyle of each member of the group. None of them worked exclusively by themselves because an action in one area seemed to have an effect on the other three areas, so it was important that they had effective communication and transparency. Most people saw Maverick as the leader of The Saviors because he was the most vocal out of the bunch, but in reality, The Saviors had solid leadership.

"What is it? What's the emergency?" Noah asked.

The four heads of The Saviors sat at a round table in an old event hall that they had transformed into their headquarters. Latoya threw Sade's bag on the table.

"What is this?"

"Open it up. I found it in the new girl's room. I think she stole these items out of the inventory, and I have no idea where she got that gun from. I saw her talking to that new boy that works in inventory as well. This isn't good."

"What are you saying, Latoya?"

"I'm saying that there may be an issue here. I talked to Patrick earlier. He's one of the firefighters. He told me that his daughter was out with those kids and that they took her to some church. They didn't ask anyone for permission to leave the camp, and who knows what they were doing or trying to do out there at that church?"

"As you know, Latoya, since the Dalton incident, people are allowed to leave the camp at their own free will. Those kids leaving doesn't mean that they necessarily did something wrong," Maverick said.

"But I was told that Dalton and the people that murdered him were all slaughtered. What are we going to do about that?"

"Who told you that?" Maverick asked, slamming his hands on the table and standing up.

Latoya flinched at the action. She didn't mean to blurt out that information because she wasn't privileged to know the details of that mission. Maverick was fuming because someone on his team was leaking information to Latoya.

"Maverick, have a seat. You can work out that issue later," Helena said. "I would like to have a discussion with these kids and figure out if these allegations are true."

"And what if they are?" Latoya asked. "What are we going to do about it? We can't just let them stay here. They are dangerous."

"Oh, come on. This is ridiculous. They are just kids. We haven't even heard their side of the story yet. Maybe there's a perfectly good explanation for this bag," Maverick said.

"Is this girl on one of your search teams, Mav?" Seth asked.

"No, she's not."

"And she's not a member of any of my security teams, so tell me how she got her hands on a gun."

Maverick took a deep breath. Seth did not hold back with the sarcasm, and Maverick was not in the mood for it. Ever since the Dalton incident, Maverick felt that his leadership was always in question. He was sick of taking the blame for individual actions. "I don't know how she got that gun."

"That is precisely why we need to bring her in and question her about it."

"I just want to go on record to say I don't agree with that."

"Why not?" Latoya asked.

"Look at Dalton and the people that followed him. It is no secret that people are starting to feel like prisoners in here. So, now you want to start having a formal court system and accusing people of crimes that don't exist? We don't need that type of division right now."

"There are rules in here that need to be followed," Seth countered. "Without rules, there will be chaos. If we start having chaos in here, then we are no different than those savages out there."

"And if we treat our people like prisoners, they will continue to leave, and there will be no one left."

"You have to do something. The rules state that members must be trained and given permission to carry weapons. Are you suggesting that we allow this girl to break the rules?"

"No, I'm not," Maverick pleaded. "Just give me the chance to talk to her. I'll find out where she got this stuff from."

"Even if she says that the gun fell out of the sky, she knows that there are rules to follow in this place."

"Well, that may not be true," Latoya added. "She was a bit standoff-ish, so I haven't gone over the rules with her yet."

"Exactly. So, how can she break the rules if she doesn't even know them?"

Seth was irritated. He wanted a zero-tolerance policy in the camp. Any chance he got, he proposed that the camp be run with a military structure, but he was always outvoted by the other leadership. He knew times were changing. The more mistakes that occurred, the sooner the others would start seeing things from his perspective. Seth did not want the members of the group to have as much freedom as they were given. He believed that the camp was vulnerable, and it was only a matter of time before someone slipped and caused a lot of damage.

Maverick and Seth were always clashing. Maverick was more strategic, and Seth craved power in the worst way. They both wanted the same goal, which was getting the world back to normal and re-establishing the government, but they had two different opinions on how to reach that goal. The current structure that was set up for The Saviors was the only thing they kept the camp from dividing into two groups.

"Latoya, do me a favor and go get the girl," Seth ordered. "I'll send one of my men to go get the boy. We're not going to play politics. The safety of the entire group is at stake right now, and we need to know what's going on with these two."

CHAPTER

41

Levi and Sade sat across the table from the leaders of The Saviors. The teens were nervous. They did not know who three of the leaders were. Levi recognized Maverick, but Sade had never met him. Sade's bag was emptied out on the table. Levi's eyes were locked on the gun that he gave Sade. Sade's mind was racing trying to figure out how her items got in the room. Levi's heart was beating out of his chest. Although he was nervous, it was not just about the gun on the table. He also had one hidden in his room.

"Do you know why we brought you two here?" Seth asked.

Sade and Levi both looked at each other, but neither responded to the intimidating man's question.

"We need to know where you got all of these items from."

Sade and Levi both stayed silent. Levi looked at Maverick, who had his head down. The other leaders had their poker faces on. Levi could not read the room. He was not sure where the conversation was going. The teens were smack dab in the middle of an interrogation and did not know why.

"You two are new here, and we know you couldn't have gotten these items on your own. We want to know who helped you steal this food from our inventory."

"Steal?" Sade hollered. "We didn't steal anything. This is my stuff."

"Your stuff?" Seth scoffed. "You don't have any stuff in here. We took you in, and we have rules."

"I don't care about your rules. I didn't ask to be here."

"Young lady, you need to calm down and show some respect," Helena advised.

"He just accused me of stealing. Where is my respect?"

"You are a child. I don't owe you any respect!" Seth yelled.

"Everybody, calm down," Maverick said. "We don't want another Dalton situation on our hands," he muttered to the other two. "Let's hear them out. Where did these items come from?" he asked in a soft voice.

"The church," Levi answered.

"Your family's church?" Maverick asked.

"Yes, we snuck out and went over there to look for our friends. Someone had set a fire to the church, and there were a bunch of bodies inside. We took what we could carry from inside and brought it back. There were weapons and food, so we grabbed some stuff for ourselves and took the rest to the inventory room."

Maverick looked over at the other leaders.

"How do we even know that any of this is true?" Helena asked.

"You can ask Destiny's dad. He caught us when we came back. He opened the van and saw everything. He even ate some of my vegan jerky," Sade replied. Both Levi and Sade smirked, remembering the reaction on Patrick's face when he ate the jerky.

"Vegan jerky?" Helena asked.

"Yup. I'm vegan, so it's hard for me to eat in this place. Luckily, I found my jerky at the church. It's right there on the table."

Helena looked at the items on the table. Maverick walked over and picked up one of the items. It was the vegan jerky. He grinned and tossed it in front of the other leaders. "You two can head back to your rooms. We'll talk later."

Levi and Sade did not want to risk Maverick changing his mind, so they exited quickly. She did not even bother asking to get her belongings back. "What are we doing?" Maverick asked the others. "We're just going to sit here and accuse these kids of something they didn't do?"

"How were we supposed to know that they snuck out?" Helena asked.

"You could have just asked them."

"They are kids."

"So what? This isn't the nineties. These kids aren't just sitting around watching cartoons. They are different now. They have seen and gone through so much. Probably more than you."

"Excuse me?"

"Have you even tried to have a conversation with some of these kids in here? They are mature and eager to help out. Maybe you could recruit some of them to assist you in medical."

"We don't need kids. We people with experience. Kids don't have experience."

"But you can train them."

"I don't have time for that. I'll leave that up to you three," Helena responded. A nasty scowl spread across her face. "So, let me guess. They don't have to follow the rules? They can just have weapons around other kids?"

"They have to know the rules in order to follow them. I'll tell you what. They can be with me. I'll train them."

"You're going to train these kids to be on one of your search teams?"

"That's exactly what I'm going to do."

"Well, good luck, Maverick. And just remember if something goes wrong, it's on you and not us."

Maverick did not bother to respond. He put all the items back in Sade's backpack. He returned everything except for the gun, which he tucked in his waistband. He opened the door and felt a thump behind it. He pulled the door back, revealing Levi and Sade. "What are you two doing?" he asked.

Both teens stood up straight, and Levi pushed the door to close it. "So, you're going to train us, huh?"

"Oh, so that's what you two were doing. You were eavesdropping on my conversation." Maverick smiled.

"We just wanted to know what you were going to say to them."

"Especially that mean lady," Sade added. "I don't know what her problem is."

"Her problem is that you two are hardheaded. She doesn't want to be bothered with a couple of kids that don't want to follow the rules."

"A wise man once said that you have to know the rules in order to break them," Levi responded.

"Oh, really? And who is this wise man that you are quoting?"

"Nobody really. Just an old fart that has three bossy friends." All three laugh.

"Well, this old fart just got your friend her stuff back." Maverick tossed Sade her backpack. "Make sure you two go get some rest. We start training early in the morning."

CHAPTER

42

It was the morning, and a stray cat was walking across the stone wall. The white and orange cat was so dirty it looked gray. The cat was thin, a result of weeks of not eating. Just like every other creature, the cat was on the search for food. Hopping from stoop to stoop, the cat was on the prowl. A small mouse or a bag of trash would have been more than enough to satisfy the feline's appetite.

The cat continued wandering down the street, sniffing the street, hoping to pick up a good scent. The filthy feline hopped over a fence and into a junky backyard. An arrow was fired and tore through the side of the cat. It let out a painful scream and flopped around. The more the cat flopped, the deeper the arrow became inserted through its body.

Suddenly, the cat stopped flopping and just lay on its side. The cat panted for a while before becoming lifeless. Maverick walked over to the scrawny cat and lifted it by the arrow. "See now, this is why we train," he said. "You don't eat if you don't train. In our case, we all don't eat if we don't have people who train."

Levi was impressed. He picked up the bow that Maverick fired the arrow from. It was worn down but obviously still functional. The device fascinated him. He pulled the string back and let it go, pretending as if he was shooting a target.

"You know that cat had as much right to live as we do," Sade said to Maverick.

"That is true, young lady, but I also know that we won't live unless we eat."

"But you let us bring rations from the inventory room in our packs. We can just eat that stuff. You didn't have to kill that cat."

"If I allowed you to just eat the rations, you will always depend on them to survive. What we are doing out here is training. Training you for the present but also the future."

"Can you teach me how to fire this thing?" Levi asked.

Maverick tossed the cat at Levi's feet. "Sure, but before we get into that, I want to see you skin this cat."

"I can't believe this. I'm out," Sade said, walking back into the building. Maverick's crew had cleared out a retail store which was now being used as one of their training facilities. The 1,500-square-foot building had been cleaned out. The main training that was conducted in that building was room clearing tactics, close quarter combat, and weapons training. Sade walked inside the building. She did not feel the need to watch the cat get slaughtered. Seeing it get shot with the arrow really irritated her.

Maverick handed Levi a knife. Although he did not care to cut the cat open, the young man was excited to have the training. No one noticed, but Levi was growing into his own. Between the encounter with The Underlings to the situation at the hospital, he had been exposed to a lot in a little bit of time. He experienced what it meant to be a leader, and he did not feel like he lived up to the role. Levi looked up to Maverick and respected how Maverick stood up for him and Sade. If it were not for Maverick offering to train the two teens, The Savior's leadership would have voted to have the kids banned from the camp.

Levi did not forget how Sade acted when they first left for the church. He came to the realization that he had to upgrade from the bat, which was why he hid the gun in his room and put one in Sade's bag. Levi was preparing himself for whatever sticky situations he might encounter.

His hand shook as he held the knife to the neck of the deceased feline. "Keep your hand steady and give me one slice straight down the center," Maverick ordered. "Don't cut too deep. Just enough to get under the fur."

Levi stuck the blade of the knife into the neck of the cat and sliced it straight down. Maverick reached in and began peeling the fur-covered skin back, exposing the meat of the animal. Levi carefully watched each step, then peeled the other side. Levi was grinning from ear to ear. He was proud of his accomplishment and so was Maverick. However, Sade was not of fan of the lesson. She reluctantly watched her friend and his new teacher from a window, but she could not see much. Levi's back was to her, so he could not see her, and she could not see him skin the cat.

"Good job. Now, all you have to do is cut off the head, and we'll be done with this lesson."

"Is there a certain way I do that?"

Maverick chuckled. "There aren't too many ways you can cut a head off. My only advice would be to use a bigger knife, but unfortunately, we only have that little pocketknife, so make it work."

Levi did not need to hear another word. He took the knife and began hacking the cat's head off. Hack after hack, he slowly caused the head to separate from the body. The skinned fur was attached to the head like a cape. "That was easier than I thought."

"No one said it was going to be hard. All you have to do is pay attention, and you can learn any skill in the world."

"So now, what do I do with this head and fur?"

"Do whatever you want to with it. That's yours."

Levi was proud of his accomplishment, but he was also mindful of his friend's feelings. Sade loved animals. She was a lot more forgiving now than she was prior to the world changing. Although she did not agree with all the means of survival, she still understood having to survive. Nonetheless, Levi wanted to be somewhat respectful, and he walked around the corner to dispose of the cat remains.

"Now that you got it skinned, I'm going to show you how to make a fire so you can cook your meal."

Levi followed Maverick as he gathered some branches and stones. Levi made a mental note of the sizes and types of items that were picked up. Sade was standing outside when they returned with their material. She watched intently as Maverick carefully set up the items and prepared to make the fire.

He meticulously placed down stones to make a barrier and then dropped twigs, bark and dry leaves in the center of the stones. He was impressed by his tender nest. Using a small knife, Maverick cut a notch into a piece of fireboard. He slid a large branch into the notch and began to roll the shaft in his hands rapidly. Embers began to form on the fireboard. With the branch between his hands, he continued rolling it back and forth. Maverick softly blew on the embers and placed the fireboard in the nest. He continued blowing until the embers lit the twigs and dry leaves.

Sade and Levi carefully looked on, watching exactly what Maverick was doing. He was exposing them to an entirely different style of living. Neither of them had even seen a fire started like this in person. It was always in a movie or on television.

Smoke began to appear from the pile, and soon after, there was a small fire. Maverick gently blew air onto the small flame, causing it to spread around the rubbish and grow.

"Sade, do you have any questions?" Maverick asked.

"I have plenty, but none about the fire," she replied.

"I'm sure you do." He laughed. "We are about to cook, so maybe it would be best if you waited back inside."

Sade walked back inside the building. Maverick pulled out three branches and began setting them up. Two of the branches were shoved into the ground around the flame. Each of those branches had other branches coming from the top of them. The third branch was slid through the body of the cat.

Maverick placed the third branch between the other two and over the flame. "The key to a good meal is constant rotation," Maverick said. "At this distance from the flame, this meat is going to cook slowly. Every three minutes I want you to rotate it."

"Yes, sir. When will I know when it's done?"

"We'll keep checking it and make sure the meat has cooked through."

Sade looked around the building. She walked over the creaky floor wondering what the building was used for. For some reason, she liked it. It reminded her of when her father bought their new apartment. She loved the space she had before the furniture was put in. She would be running around with her friends all the time. For some reason, the empty building gave her a warm feeling inside.

She also thought about the fire that Maverick just made. She wanted to mimic the training she just received, so she retained all of the information he gave them. She grabbed the nap sack that Maverick told them to pack. She reached in and grabbed a pack of her jerky. It was lunch time for her.

Levi rotated the cat over the flame. His mouth began to water thinking about sinking his teeth into the warm meat. Maverick just watched the young man. He was quite impressed with the teen's willingness to learn and to adapt to the training environment. Although this was just the beginning of the training, it was a good start.

CHAPTER

43

Levi pulled the string back on the bow, then released, letting the arrow fly through the air. The arrow stuck into a wooden fence. An old paperback book that sat on top of the fence was the target, but Levi was happy with the result of his shot. It was his first time using the weapon, which was why hitting the book was not that big of a deal for him.

He loaded the bow again, pulling the string back and letting it fly. The second arrow struck the fence just slightly to the left of the first arrow. Sade laughed. "What's so funny? You can't do any better than that."

"It's only one way to find out," Maverick said. "Let's see if Sade was paying attention."

Sade stepped next to Levi. Due to the injury to her arm, Maverick preloaded the crossbow he let her train with.

Sade carefully aimed the crossbow and pulled the trigger. The arrow struck the book, knocking it off the fence. "Oh, snap!" Maverick yelled. "She's a natural."

Sade gave Levi a goofy look.

"That's not fair. I have this old bow, and she gets to use that fancy one. If I had that one, I would hit the book too."

"Put your money where your mouth is," Sade said.

"What are we talking?" Levi asked.

"Your pack snacks. If you miss, you'll give me your snacks. If you hit the book, then you get my snacks."

Levi thought intensely about the offer that was put on the table. "How about we up the ante a little? If I miss, I will give you, my snacks. If make it, you have to eat the next meat we catch."

"Deal."

"Whoa! Are you sure about this, Sade?" Maverick asked, knowing Sade was a vegan.

"I'm 100% sure. He's not going to hit it."

"We'll see," Levi muttered.

Levi grabbed the crossbow from Sade. Maverick picked up the book and removed the arrow from it. He handed the arrow to Levi, wondering if the young man was paying attention when they were given the loading instructions. Levi loaded the crossbow. The book sat at the top of the fence, and the teen took up aim on the target.

Levi pulled the trigger on the crossbow. The arrow struck the fence just under the book. Sade burst out laughing. Maverick followed.

"I'll be taking these," Sade said, picking up Levi's pack.

"You got any more excuses you want to use?" Maverick asked.

Levi ignored the question and walked up to the fence. He removed the arrow and reloaded it into the crossbow. He walked back to Maverick and took up aim on the book. This time, he took a deep breath before pulling the trigger.

Both Sade and Maverick were watching closely. Levi pulled the trigger again, and this time, the book fell off the fence. The arrow had grazed the book, knocking it over. Levi took a quick walk to pick up the arrow and the book. Sade and Maverick looked at each other, confusion on their faces.

"You know you already lost the bet, right?" Sade asked him.

Levi did not respond. He put the book back on top of the fence and took up his position. He reloaded the crossbow and aimed at the book. Levi was determined to hit his target. Not because he lost the bet to Sade but because he was on a mission to become better in every way possible.

Levi fired the crossbow for the third time, this time striking the book and knocking it off the fence.

"It seems that the third time is a charm," Maverick said.

"Yeah, I guess so. Let's just hope I get three tries when one of those giant fur balls is in front of me. "

"Don't worry. When that time comes, you'll be just fine. They are a much bigger target than that book." Maverick took the crossbow from Levi and handed it back to Sade. "Let's get some reps in so this starts becoming second nature for you two. Levi, you have to learn how to work the standard bow."

"Now, this isn't a competition. We have to always work together so that when one of us falls short, the other is there to get the lethal shot. Two shooters are always better than one. So now, you both will aim at the book, and you both will take your shot when I say threat. If it is done correctly, you won't even know which shot was yours. The key is to have them both as close as possible. No shooter is perfect, but you don't have to be a perfect shooter to kill something or someone."

Maverick walked behind the two teens and yelled out, "On the line!"

Levi and Sade lined up next to each other.

"Shooters ready."

Both teens aimed at the book.

"Threat."

Both arrows struck the book. The teens cheered. They began jumping for joy, celebrating their hit.

"Reset," Maverick ordered. "Back on the line."

The training continued until both teens put up more than 100 shots with the bows. There was something about the survival instincts that both teens had that made them different from any other teen Maverick or his peers had trained. Neil was very structured when it came to training, but Levi and Sade had natural skill. Their decision-making seemed to reflect a bit of wisdom as well.

"So, when do we get to go on our first mission?" Sade asked before biting into her vegan jerky.

"Well, you won't be going on any missions until we fix that little arm of yours," Maverick responded. "It would be too much of a risk that I'm not willing to take."

"That's not fair," she responded.

"Life is not fair. You are healing. You have to get your body back to a 100% before you can go out on a mission."

"But she went with us to the church," Levi added. "That was like a mission."

"That wasn't like a mission. If one of those mutations attacked you, you would probably be dead. They are strong, fast, and relentless."

"So am I," Sade muttered.

Maverick saw the look in Sade's eyes. She was going to go on this mission one way or another. "We have a big mission coming up. More than likely, we'll need all hands on deck. Before then, we'll do a few supply runs back to the hospital to get your feet wet. Let's see how you two do on the runs, and if I like what I see, I'll let you tag along for the mission."

CHAPTER

44

The Nissan and Toyota slowed down as they made their way down Frankford Avenue. As one of the main roads in the northeast section of Philadelphia, the group figured this had to be the flare location. Their only instructions were to follow the direction the flare came from, which would lead them to a safe position.

"This can't be the location," Emma said as she looked around the area. It was an abandoned neighborhood. The sedan bounced as they drove over the debris-covered roadway. The evening breeze carried a slight scent of rain. Gray clouds began forming in the sky.

"Well, it looks like a storm is brewing," Brody muttered as he pulled up next to the Nissan. "We're going to have to clear out one of these buildings, so we have somewhere to stay."

Emma and Abraham nodded their heads in agreement. "Brody, you're with me. Let's clear out this laundromat. I doubt anyone would come searching in here, so we should be safe," Emma said.

"How long do you think we'll have to stay here?" Brody asked. "We only have enough food and supplies to last us a week."

"Well, I'm hoping we won't have to be here that long."

The two checked their firearms, ensuring they were loaded, and headed to the laundromat. As with other properties in the area, the front glass windows of the laundromat had been shattered. Most of the washing machines and dryers had been ripped down and taken apart. It was common for people to destroy machines in hopes of getting certain parts from them. In a world that has been destroyed, cash is nothing more than pieces of paper. Food, weapons, and supplies were the new currency. This new form of currency also included parts. There were always groups that tried to regain a sense of normalcy, even if that meant having the capability to wash their clothes. Those were the little things that made significant differences in people's minds. However, others wanted the parts for different reasons.

"Who in their right mind would trash a laundromat out of all places?" Brody asked as he stepped over damaged mechanical parts to enter the building. "I understand raiding the grocery stores and gun stores, but what would you possibly need out of here?"

"The same people that stocked up on toilet paper during the COVID-19 pandemic. You remember how crazy everything was that year. They have now evolved from toilet paper to detergent and fabric softener."

The two laughed. They scanned the building, which was barely in a livable condition. Besides most of the machines being knocked over and dismantled, a part of the ceiling had caved in, and there was heavy water damage to the floors. The group would have to do some heavy lifting to make the building safe for their visit.

The soft, rotted floor sunk in under each of Brody's steps. If it were not for Emma, he would have backed out of the laundromat and found another property to inhabit. He imagined scavenging through some of the homes on the block and finding food and supplies. His mind drifted at the thought of plopping down on a soft bed and falling into a deep sleep. Unfortunately, those thoughts would have to remain just that, as his reality included molded walls and a sketchy ceiling.

"This place is clear. It looks like this is our new home for now," Emma said.

"Oh, great. I think I'll let yall have this place, and I'll just sleep in the car."

"What's wrong? Big, bad Brody doesn't want to be a team player?"

"Nope. I'm going to sit this one out. The seat cushions in the car are much softer than the floor. I don't feel like waking up tomorrow with a jacked-up neck."

"It seems like The Association had you spoiled," Emma replied sarcastically. "You're acting like those little sleeping bags they gave us were king-size mattresses or something."

"They were better than this nasty floor. I would kill to get my sleeping bag back. However, since that isn't happening, I'll be in the car. If you need me for any reason, just let me know."

Brody walked outside and gave the others the signal to come in. They wasted very little time grabbing items out of the car. Aside from the two sleeping bags that managed to get packed in the Toyota trunk before the escape, there was not much to bring out. Most people in the group left home without knowing the plan already been put in place. They did not have time to pack their belongings before hopping into the getaway cars.

"Wow, this place has seen better days," Abraham muttered.

"I could say the same thing about us," Lori responded. "Never in a million years would I have expected to be fighting for my life against monsters and humans." She had not been the same since the last attack. Nevertheless, she still replayed those events back in her mind. The rancid odor entering her nostrils as she stood face to face with the test suspects. Her heart pounding out of her chest, not knowing if she would ever escape the room Jin locked her in. Not knowing if she would ever see her daughter again. The thoughts brought tears to her eyes.

"What's wrong, mom? Why are you crying?"

"No reason, honey," she lied as she wiped tried the wipe the tears away.

"It's Tyler, isn't it. You miss him too?" Charlotte asked. She wrapped her arms around Lori, holding her tight. Large bags had formed under Charlotte's eyes from the ride over. The moment the group left the gas station, she bawled her eyes out the entire ride. She missed Tyler so much and felt guilty for leaving him.

Lori felt the same guilt but just magnified. Tyler begged for her help when Jin had him restrained to the chair, and Lori felt like she let him down. Despite assisting him in escaping from The Association, Lori failed at her promise to fix whatever Jin injected into Tyler's body. More tears poured from her eyes as she thought about what the mutation would do to the young man. Leaving Tyler was not an easy decision for anyone in the group to make. He was special to them.

Lori and Charlotte followed Abraham into the laundromat. They were a bit surprised in the selection of the building, once they spotted the ceiling and floors, but no one made an argument. They were more concerned about their safety than anything else. The bags from their vehicles were placed in the back of the laundromat. Emma had already designated the aisles of the laundromat as the sleeping areas. Their only task now was to clean the aisles up from the parts and debris left behind.

Just as the group was getting themselves settled inside the laundromat, a tan minivan came screeching to a halt just outside of their location. Emma and Brody had dropped the supplies they were bringing inside and drew their weapons on the vehicle. The odor from the burning rubber began filling the air. The driver's side front window rolled down, and the driver stuck a flare gun out of the window. Brody and Emma slowly lowered their weapons. "We've been waiting for you," the driver said as he placed the gun on the front passenger seat.

"Well, we are glad to see you," Brody responded.

The driver honked his horn three times and stepped out of the minivan. The group was surprised to see it was just a teenager. He immediately locked eyes with Charlotte. "Is everything okay?"

Charlotte wiped her eyes and nodded her head. "Yes, everything is fine. Unfortunately, she just lost a good friend," Abraham stated as he stepped forward to greet the teen. "Hi. I'm Abraham. I'm a doctor," he said, reaching out his hand for a shake.

"Nice to meet you, Abraham. I'm Neil." The teen stuck his hand out and completed the shake.

Abraham took a step back as he watched three more vehicles pulled up behind the minivan. Nick stepped forward with Emma and Brody. All three of them were armed but chose not to remove their weapons. The vehicles were packed. To their surprise, armed lookouts began exiting some of the neighboring properties. The group thought they were alone when they were being monitored the entire time. "What is all of this?" Abraham asked.

"This is our welcoming party," Neil asked. "We're going to take you back to our camp, and we can't risk being outnumbered if someone attacks us.

Abraham gave the teen a nod. In the back of his mind, he could not help but wonder if he had left The Association for a similar version of the same environment. He glanced back at Lori with a concerned look on his face. It was as if she could read his mind because she felt the same way. The group appeared to be heavily armed and had vehicles and a way to fuel the vehicles.

"Abraham!"

He turned at the sound of the woman's voice that called his name. It seemed like all his concerns went out of the window in that split second. "Lee?" he asked as he began running toward the woman that was exiting an off-white GMC Envoy. "I can't believe this."

Abraham wrapped his arms around Lee as the two gave each other tight hugs. Abraham and Lee worked together at The Association, and she was a part of the first group that ever escaped from the territory. During her time with the organization, she saw through the false narratives that the organization's leaders tried to paint. On several occasions, she overheard conversations between Micah and some of the members of the research team. She remembered being threatened by him to try and find a cure for the mutations. At that point, she teamed up with a few others and planned their escape. Before she escaped, she warned the other doctors and medical staff about what was truly happening inside the territory. She did her best to inform trustworthy people of her plan to escape, but most of them were fooled by the leaders of The Association. They were led to believe that they were now living in a sanctuary, and outside of the walls was nothing but chaos.

Lee did not let those narratives deter her and her group from exploring the world outside of The Association. After discovering the Saviors, she vowed to go back to The Association and get others, so the Saviors implemented the location marking with the flares. With this system in place, people did not have to wander the streets and hope to be alive at the end of the day. Instead, people would come to locations and be met by The Saviors before being taken back to the camp.

"How have you been, my friend?" she asked.

"I have been well, up until this point," Abraham replied. "Things have gotten a lot worse since you left."

"How so?"

"Jin. He's out of control."

Lee was not too surprised to hear that name. During her time at The Association, she was under one of Jin's research teams. He was one of the reasons she wanted to leave. "What has he been up to? Was he able to find a cure for the mutations?"

"No, he wasn't. To be honest, I don't even think he was looking for a cure."

"What do you mean? That's all that Micah wanted. Every day he barked at us to find a cure."

"Exactly, but something happened to Adina, and Micah left."

"He left?"

"Yes, and he took all the guards. Everything was so secretive, so we didn't have any details. So, with Micah gone, Jin took the opportunity to use one of the medical wings as his personal lab. He altered the chemical gas over there and performed experiments on some of the members."

"What do you mean he altered it?"

"He created another gas and a serum from a creature's blood. Apparently, he was able to create a different type of mutation."

"Are you fuckin' serious? Why would he do that?"

"I don't know. He's insane. He even tried to kill her," Abraham said as he shot a look over to Lori.

Lee looked at Abraham's entire group. They were drained. Lori was still clutching onto Charlotte, Brody, Nick, and Emma were on edge, and Abraham seemed petrified. "We have to stop him."

"I agree. How good is this place you'll be taking us to?"

"They're not perfect, but they are good people."

"Do you have people that could help us perform tests?"

"Yes, I do. What tests do you need?"

"We were able to get some of Jin's serum. We need to test it ASAP and find a way to reverse its effects on people. We also need to talk about a boy that we left at the gas station a few miles back."

"Don't worry. I'll take you to Maverick and the others. Then, we will get your group a meal and figure out a plan to stop Jin."

CHAPTER
45

Look at that," Micah said as he turned the corner with the remaining members of his search team. They were all packed into four vehicles. Wolff was sure to take the majority of the vehicles back to The Association, when they left.

Londo was riding shotgun and could not believe his eyes. Although he stayed with Micah for the entire search, deep down he was skeptical on whether they would actually find Kyle. "That's the truck," he blurted out, spotting the wrecked Chevy Silverado.

The four vehicles pulled up to the Chevy, which was flipped on its side. The search team poured out of the vehicles and into the streets. Micah had a team of fifteen men and women with him, and they all converged on the truck. "I want him alive," Micah announced as he approached with his team.

Everyone was armed and they were ready to start firing, especially Londo. Just because Micah wanted Kyle alive, that did not mean that he wanted him unharmed. Londo was ready to do damage and avenge Adina.

"Slow it down," Micah ordered. He spotted the trail of blood the was coming from the vehicle. He also noticed the spent shell casings the covered the street. Everything in the neighborhood reflected chaos. "Clear the truck and make sure you cover each other."

Micah's team surrounded the truck. A team of four cleared the vehicle while the others watched their surroundings. With all the destruction around them there was no telling if a threat was going to pop out. "It's empty boss," Londo yelled out. "There's a lot of blood in here though."

Micah kneeled and looked into the truck. *There is no way he survived after losing this much blood*, he thought. When he looked past the Chevy, he spotted bodies that were sprawled out in the street. The bodies were all in front of a church which had extensive fire damage. The body of one of the mutated creatures was also on the bloody pavement. "Hey, let's move on this church," Micah ordered. He and his team advanced on the damaged church, being cautious at the front doors. The last thing Micah wanted to do was leave any stone unturned. Finding the truck that Kyle was driving was a small victory for him, but he needed to get his hands on Kyle.

The church was dark. Micah's team lined like a firing squad in front of the broken front doors. The sun dipped behind some large clouds, which made it difficult to see inside of the wreckage. It appeared that during the fire, the top levels had caved in on the main levels. Micha and his team had no idea how many bodies were crushed under the wreckage. The only thing that peaked through the rubble was the black ambulance.

"What do you think happened here?" Londo asked.

"I can't tell."

"Do you think he was involved."

"More than likely. But did you see how much blood is in the truck?"

"Yeah, I saw it. You think he's alive?"

"I doubt it. Nobody is surviving from losing that much blood. At some point, I need to stay realistic when it comes to this hunt. I've already lost my people and I think we should head back and see how things are going. What about the ones that left?" We'll figure out what to do with them once we get back."

"And what about Wolff. I think he is the one that led them all back.?"

"We'll kill him in front of the others to send a message. Treason will always be punishable by death. He got a pass for allowing this bastard to get to Adina, but he won't get a pass for this. I want his head on my mantel and his body fed to his followers."

Londo gathered the team and they loaded back up in the vehicles. This time Londo drove and Micah rod shotgun. He could get his mind off the Chevy. He had gotten so close to capturing Kyle, but he was a little too late. From the looks of it, somebody else may have gotten to him first.

The ride back to The Association was rough. Micah felt like a failure and now he had to punish one of his own people. He was not looking forward to his encounter with Wolff, but he knew it was time to set the tone. If he let Wolff get away with this act, there is no telling what the disobedient man would do next.

Dark clouds filled the sky, and the sun began to set. Micah and his team were on the strip back to The Association. As they pulled up, they noticed a large number of vehicles pulled up outside the gate. "What the hell is all of this?" Micah asked.

"It looks like we have company. I've never seen these vehicles before," Londo responded.

"I've seen that one before," Micah said, pointing to the black ambulance. "It was one just like it inside that burnt church. Stop here and let's make sure everyone is on point. We don't know what the hell we are walking into."

Londo slowed the vehicle down. They stopped about 200 feet away from the front gate. The burnt car was still crashed into the gate. As Micah and his team approached, people began flooding from inside the walls and also from the vehicles. "Who the hell are these people?" Micah asked as he watched the Underlings crowd around the front entrance.

"We're about to find out," Londo muttered as he gripped tightly on the shotgun he was armed with.

The Underlings just stared at the team as they approached. Micah and Londo were a few steps ahead of the rest and halted when they spotted a familiar face. "Welcome back," Wolff said.

"What is all of this?" Micah asked.

"This is The Association. Well, it's currently under new management."

"Who are all of these people?"

"These are our new friends. They came to join us, on our mission to take over the world. Unlike you, some people actually enjoy being here. It's a good thing we came back too because somehow one of those mutations got loose inside the buildings and there is nothing but bodies in here."

"Well, get to your post and let's make sure none of them return. We have to fortify this gate too."

Wolff laughed hysterically. He looked over to the others who also began laughing. Micah and his team were confused. There were hundreds of strangers around them, and they all began laughing.

"What's so fuckin' funny?" Micah asked.

"The fact that you think you're still in charge. You don't get to go out on your little excursion and then come back, barking orders. We don't answer to you anymore Micah. There's a new sheriff in town."

Micah's eyes locked onto a subject that stepped up, from behind Wolff. The large hood on the black trench coat was pulled over his face. A rifle was slung across his chest and skull gas mask was draped across his shoulder. The Reaper slowly removed his hood, shocking Micah and his team.

"Dale?"

"Back from the dead," The Reaper said.

"What is going on?"

"I'll make this quick. Me and Wolff here are the new leaders of The Association. My friends here go by the name of The Underlings and will be joining this movement." Loud cheers erupted from The Underlings.

"Where is Adina?"

"Adina is exactly where you left her? Is she even alive or are you just in denial and holding on to her body?"

"The doctors that were caring for her, I want to speak to them."

"Well, your lead doctor ain't caring for shit but himself. Word on the street is that he has been creating more of these smoke grenades. I need them all."

Micah was confused but tried his best to remain composed. He was not sure what The Reaper was referring to, but he planned on finding out sooner than later. He looked in the distance and saw Jin making a getaway towards one of the rear buildings.

"Well, if you let me in, I will get them all for you," Micah asked as he took a step forward.

The Reaper raised his rifle and sticking it in Micah's face. A chill went up his spine as he slowly began backing up. "You ain't coming in here," The Reaper muttered. "You are no longer welcome on our territory. Out of respect for Adina I'm going to let you live but the next time I see you, I won't be as generous."

Micah scowled at The Reaper. He could not believe the words that just came out of his mouth. Micah was never a big fan of The Reaper back when he was Dale, the head of Adina's search teams. The two men always butted heads because Micah believed that The Reaper was reckless. Little did he know, The Reaper was only acting under the orders of Adina. Micah felt the urge to draw his pistol and put The Reaper down, but they were extremely outnumbered. Londo was also craving for some action. He could not take his eyes off Wolff and vice versa. The two men despised each other and Londo was willing to risk his own life to take out Wolff.

Several small explosions went off inside behind the front gate, grabbing everyone's attention. A few members of The Association and The Underlings were injured because of the explosions, but the more serious concern was the red smoke that began seeping out from the grenade canisters. Micah quickly released the canisters that were hanging from his belt, releasing a thick, orange cloud of smoke in the air. All the members of The Association began covering their mouths, knowing the result of inhaling the toxic gas that was releasing with the smoke. The Underlings were not too familiar with the bioweapons that The Association created. They began dropping like flies.

The shotgun roared as Londo took a shot at Wolff before, dipping back into the orange smoke. The other members of Micah's team began firing at the Underlings too. The Underlings blindly shot back, but most were still dropping as the gas continued spreading. The Reaper donned his mask and let his rifle rip into the orange smoke. The scene was chaotic. Bodies were dropping left and right. He ran into the orange smoke, hoping to go toe to toe with Micah. This was a battle that he dreamed about.

More shotgun blasts went off, followed up by more explosions. Both the red and the orange smoke became thicker. Members of Micah's team had also released their canisters and donned their masks. The Reaper fell forwarded after being struck in the back of the head with a shotgun. Londo jumped on top of him delivering several more blows. The Reaper grabbed Londo by the neck and Londo reached down and began tugging at The Reaper's mask. The Reaper continued to try to choke Londo but was quickly overpowered. He grabbed the handle of his rifle and pulled the trigger. Unfortunately, none of his rounds struck Londo. He tried bringing the rifle up higher, but Londo pushed down on his arm.

The Reaper quickly grabbed the back of Londo's mask and pulled it off. Londo panicked and began throwing punches at The Reaper. Two of his strikes landed and broke The Reaper's mask. The two men tried their best to hold their breath as the thick smoke surrounded them. Londo delivered another blow to The Reaper but missed and struck the ground. A sharp pain shot through his knuckles and wrist. That was just enough of a distraction for The Reaper to Londo off him. The two men stood and Londo gripped his shotgun, aiming it center mass on his target. His finger slid onto the trigger and then a second later slid off. Londo dropped the shotgun and held his hands up to his neck. Blood poured from the fresh wound to his neck. Wolff used all his strength to pull the hunting knife from Londo's neck and stab it into his back. Londo was too busy tussling with The Reaper, he never noticed that Wolff crept up behind him.

Both men fell to the ground. Londo hit the ground hard, as his severed carotid artery sent blood squirting out of his neck wound. Wolff was also down. The entire right side of his body was covered in blood. His right arm was also ripped off from Londo's initial shot from the shotgun. Wolff did not let the severe injury stop him from getting to Londo.

CHAPTER

46

The blasts of gunfire and agonizing screams
continued to fill the air. The chemical gas that
disseminated through the red smoke resulted in
the countless casualties on both sides. It was
still unknown what damage the chemical gas in
the orange smoke had caused. The orange smoke
contained the same gas that caused mutations in some
and death in others. Bodies were covering the floor
and it was only a matter of time until the mutations
would occur.

Jin knew that he was a wanted man. The Reaper
sought after Jin's knowledge of the chemical gases and
Jin knew after that knowledge was obtained, there
would be no further use for him. The Underlings were
already taking anything they wanted. They were

raiding the living quarters of The Association members and pilfering through the supply rooms. It was sickening. Jin immediately headed to his lab, to save his hard work and test results. He knew the smoke canisters that he let off would soon go empty and once the smoke cleared, the war would continue.

The doors to the laboratory were standing open. "What the hell are you doing?" Jin asked angrily. There were members of The Underlings rummaging through the makeshift lab that Micah and Adina had assigned for the mutation research. One of the men was stuffing a bag with the canisters that Jin and his team created.

"Who the fuck are you?" the man asked.

"I'm the doctor that runs this lab, now give me my canisters," Jin said as he ran over and grabbed the bag.

The man swung a punch at Jin, which was countered. He threw another, which Jin ducked and followed with a gut punch. The man dropped the bag and charged at Jin and attempted to tackle him to the ground. Jin wrapped his arm around the man's neck as he was being tackled. Jin squeezed on the man's neck, holding him in the chokehold. The thin man's face turned red as he slowly began to lose air. Jin loosened his grip after being kicked in the face by one of the other Underlings. They did not even let him get back to his feet before they began attacking him. A few of their members jumped Jin and began stomping on him while he was down.

Jin did his best to cover up while in the fetal position. His adrenaline was high, so he could barely feel the kicks and the punches that were being delivered to his body. The beating continued for about a minute before the men ran out with the bag of smoke canisters and files that were on the table. Jin stood to his feet, after realizing that the assault was over. He scanned that lab, which had been ruined. He stumbled toward the wall and opened the door that led to the testing section of the lab. It was clear that The Underlings had not yet reached this portion of the lab because there were extra canisters on one of the tables that were untouched.

Loud roars echoed in the room. The mutated beasts that were caged wanted a piece of Jin. His test subjects banged against their cages and scratched at the thick metal bars. Jin ignored the beasts and headed to the center of the lab. His focus was gathering supplies and securing the remaining samples. He wanted to get rid of the lab and he no longer needed the beasts that he had caged. The last thing he wanted was The Underlings to piggyback off his hard work and claim his weapons as their own. Jin grabbed a set of bolt cutters and got to work before The Underlings returned.

"What do we have?" The Reaper asked as he waited by the vehicles that Micah and his team arrived in. With his mask broken, he made a quick exit to get out of the smoke. He enjoyed watching Londo meet his fate and was grateful that Wolff saved his life despite being disfigured.

"We have a bunch of casualties. Our people didn't have any sort of protection from the gas," one of The Underlings said.

"What about our prisoners? Was your team able to capture them?"

"Yes, sir."

"Ok, perfect. Let's go get – "

Before The Reaper could finish his statement, a large explosion occurred in the lab. The entire building had blown up and rocked the other buildings that were on the property. The lab was fully engulfed. A substantial amount of orange smoke filled the air as it exited the gaping hole that was created when the roof collapsed. The Reaper did not know what to expect. There were so many wounded and dead. There was also no sign of Micah. The last thing he wanted to do was surrender the territory he just obtained, but he also needed a new mask because the orange smoke from the explosion was quickly spreading like a sandstorm.

Loud roars could be heard coming from the burning lab as eight beasts emerged from the smoke. Their claws dug into the ground as they ran towards the first humans they saw. Smoke particles stuck to their thick fur. The beats began causing havoc on the surviving members of both groups. Gunshots began ripping off at the beasts as both sides focused their attacks on the mutations. A couple of the shots hit their targets and put two of the beasts down, but as the smoke spread, it became more difficult to see them. It as if the beasts were using the smoke to their advantage to strike the humans. They clawed through skin with powerful swipes, punctured arteries with deep bites and tore limbs from bodies with eases. It was a blood bath but both sides stood their ground and put up a fight.

The ground began rattling as everyone continued their assault on the beasts. The orange smoke continued bellowing out the building, as roars and howls came from a distance. Those who were on the outside of the gate heard the roars, that seemed to be getting closer by the second. A few beasts were spotted running into the territory as the orange smoke attracted them. They too joined in on the battle with the humans. The Reaper had witnessed this scene before. He knew that there would be more beasts coming towards the smoke. He reluctantly entered the black ambulance that was parked out front. Multiple vehicles took off just in time, as a stampede beasts headed to The Association. The sight was unbelievable. Hundreds of the mutations were making their way to the bellowing smoke. Both The Association and The Underlings were not prepared for what was coming their way.

...TO BE
CONTINUED

CONTINUE THE STORY BY CHECKING OUT THE FINAL BOOK IN THIS SERIES

SCAVENGERS

C.L. LOWRY

COMING NEXT YEAR

BONUS

CHAPTER

The stench of death was in the air. Dannie's head was pounding. He did not know where he was at. The last thing he remembered was being out with the group, and now he was in a dark place. He attempted to sit up but quickly realized that he was tied down. Sharp pains shot through his wrists and ankles. He yelled out in pain. He looked over to find the source of the pain and spotted the barbwire that was wrapped around his wrists. His first attempt to sit up caused the blades on the wire to slice his skin. Blood was trickling down his wrists and ankles from being sliced.

"Help me!" Dannie screamed out.

"Is that how my girlfriend begged for her life?" The Reaper asked, stepping into the room.

Dannie's eyes widened when he saw the man enter. A large hood was pulled up over the man's head that partially covered his face. "Help me. Please get this shit off my wrists."

"Don't beg. It's not a good look on you. You can't imagine my surprise when I saw you at The Association. I was in disbelief at first, but there you were running for your life after the explosions. Through all the chaos, I was given a gift from the gods of war and all I had to do was be patient and snatch you up when the time was right. Now, here you are." The Reaper pulled up a crate and sat on it. He was at the foot of the bed with his eyes locked on Dannie's face. "Do you know how beautiful fear looks on your face? I love it."

"Who the hell are you, and what do you want?"

The Reaper laughed. "I'm getting exactly what I want. Karma."

Dannie yelled out in pain again. He continued screaming for someone to help him. The Reaper continued watching him. He was admiring his work.

"You never answered my question. Did you make my girlfriend beg for her life?"

"Who the fuck are you?" Dannie asked.

"I'm your worst nightmare times ten."

"What the fuck do you want, you fuckin' creep?"

"I want you to answer my question," The Reaper said as he stood up. He grabbed the crate from the ground and struck Dannie's left ankle. The blades on the barbwire sunk into his skin, cutting deeper.

The scream that Dannie let out could be heard from blocks away.

"Now, can you answer my question?"

"I don't know you, dawg. Let me go."

The next scream that Dannie let out topped the first one as the crate was used to strike his right ankle. The barbwire was now embedded into both of his ankles. Blood poured from the new wounds. Dannie's body went into shock and the injured man lost consciousness.

The Reaper stood up and walked out of the room. The thrill behind the event had left the building. Dannie being passed out was way too easy in The Reaper's opinion. He wanted Dannie to be up during this encounter. He did not want one second going by that Dannie did not feel the pain that the Reaper was inflicting on his body.

As The Reaper exited the room, someone else entered. It was a woman. She walked to the foot of the bed and examined Dannie's wounds. The barbwire cuts were deep, and the blades were still embedded. She had a pair of wire cutters in her hand. She carefully clipped the barbwire around the razor edges that were embedded in Dannie's ankles.

Once the wire was cut, she carefully unraveled it from his ankles. Blood had soaked the wire. After the wire was removed, the woman took out a wide butcher knife. With a torch lighter, she heated up the knife. The hot blade of the knife was held to the side and pressed against the embedded razor edges, pushing them deeper into Dannie's ankle while the actual wound was being soldered. The smell of burnt flesh filled her nostrils as she continued working diligently to stop the bleeding. By the time she was done with each wound, Dannie was regaining consciousness.

Dannie grimaced, immediately feeling the throbbing pain of the second-degree burns on his ankles and the blades that were still embedded in his skin. The first instinct was to grab his legs and to somehow get to his feet, but the pain was too excruciating to move. He felt like he had woken up from a terrible nightmare, but it was his current reality. He did his best not to squirm. Although his legs were free from the barbwire, his wrists were still locked in.

"Hey, can you help me?" Dannie asked the mysterious woman at the foot of the bed.

The woman didn't say a word.

"Listen to me! I know the leader of The Association, and I can get you whatever you want. Food, vehicles, weapons. Whatever you need, I can get for you. Please let me go." Tears poured from his eyes, as he begged the woman to help him.

The woman bent over and carefully moved the clipped barbwire to the side. Dannie noticed the knife that was in her hand. He glanced down at his ankles, and his heart dropped into his stomach. The pain was agonizing. He could barely move his feet. There was no telling what type of damage the embedded blades were causing.

The woman smiled at Dannie before exiting the room, with the wire.

Seconds later, The Reaper re-entered the room. Dannie's eyes were trained on him. "Hey, you proved your point. Please, let me go. I was just telling your lady friend that I can get you whatever you want. Just let me go."

"And I told you already that I got exactly what I want. You know how long it took me to get to you?"

"What do you mean how long it took you? What is your beef with me?"

"This is so pathetic. I need you to guess what my beef is with you."

"Man, I don't have time for this. Let me go."

"It looks like you got time to me. It doesn't seem like you'll be going anywhere." The Reaper laughed and pulled his crate up to the side of the bed.

Dannie's heart still felt like it was in his stomach. Having The Reaper that close to him was extremely uncomfortable. The Reaper eyed Dannie's wrists, then his face.

"Why are you doing this, man?"

"I'm doing to you, what you have done to someone that I loved. You are going to pay the ultimate price for what you did to her, but first, you're going to suffer."

The Reaper pulled out a cellphone and powered on the device. He was able to give it a little juice, after having it plugged into an old generator. He held the phone up in Dannie's face, forcing him to look at the cracked screen. As soon as the video began playing, Dannie turned his head to look away.

"Do you remember now?" The Reaper asked after showing Dannie the video of him killing Dana. It was at that moment that all the memories came rushing back. It was the same room. They were back in the same room where Dannie had killed Jane Doe. More tears fell from Dannie's eyes.

Dannie could not believe he was back in that house, let alone the exact room that he took a life in. He knew there was no talking his way out of this situation. His demons had finally caught up to him. He needed to find a way to escape, and he needed to find it soon. He tried moving his legs, but the pain was unbearable. His wrists still had barbwire wrapped around them, and he did not want to take the risk of cutting his wrists deeper.

"Is there anything you would like to say?"

"What can I say? Obviously, you watched the video. I've been sitting here begging you to spare my life, but I know you're not going to do that."

"Tell me why I should spare your life."

"You're not going to sit here and treat me like a bitch. I'm not going to let you do that to me. If you're going to kill me, be a man and just do it already."

The Reaper took out the torch lighter and put it up against Dannie's left bicep. Dannie could not even get his next words out before the torch was burning the flesh on his arm. Dannie's screams pierced The Reaper's ears. A slight grin spread on his face as he continued to burn Dannie's left arm.

Dannie's body began convulsing. The barbwire around his wrists sliced into him as his body seized. This did not stop The Reaper from burning the flesh until he reached the bone. The Reaper stood to his feet and watched his victim continue to seize. Dannie's mouth foamed up. The odor in the room was stomach-turning and somehow it did not bother The Reaper at all.

"You're not going to get away that easy," he whispered into Dannie's ear.

A large icepick was swiftly taken out of The Reapers pocket. He used the item and began viciously stabbing Dannie in the torso. He then climbed on top of Dannie and with two hands on the weapon, he drove it downward into the body of his victim. Blood splattered on his face with each strike. This killing as so much different than any other. It was almost orgasmic for The Reaper as he continued stabbing. His eyes were trained on Dannie's face, the entire time. This was the haunted him in his sleep. He saw it every night, replaying Dana's death in his head.

The Reaper continued his assault as a crater flesh blood and sliced flesh formed in the center of Dannie's chest. The Reaper had pierced organs and struck bone, but that did not stop him. He kept striking. In some way, Dana's presence was still in that room and The Reaper wanted to show her that her death would truly be avenged. Blood splattered everywhere. Not only was the attacker covered in it, but it was also on the floor, walls, and ceiling. Fatigue began setting in as the strikes became slower.

The Reaper's arms felt heavy and could barely lift them to continue his assault. With the last of his energy, The Reaper raise his weapon and drove it down, directly between his victim's eyes. He let out a loud shriek in the face of the corpse that he was straddling. He basked in the moment, as the bedroom door slowly opened. The Reaper looked back at the woman standing in the doorway.

"Now that I'm done with him, bring in the next one."

AVAILABLE NOW!!!

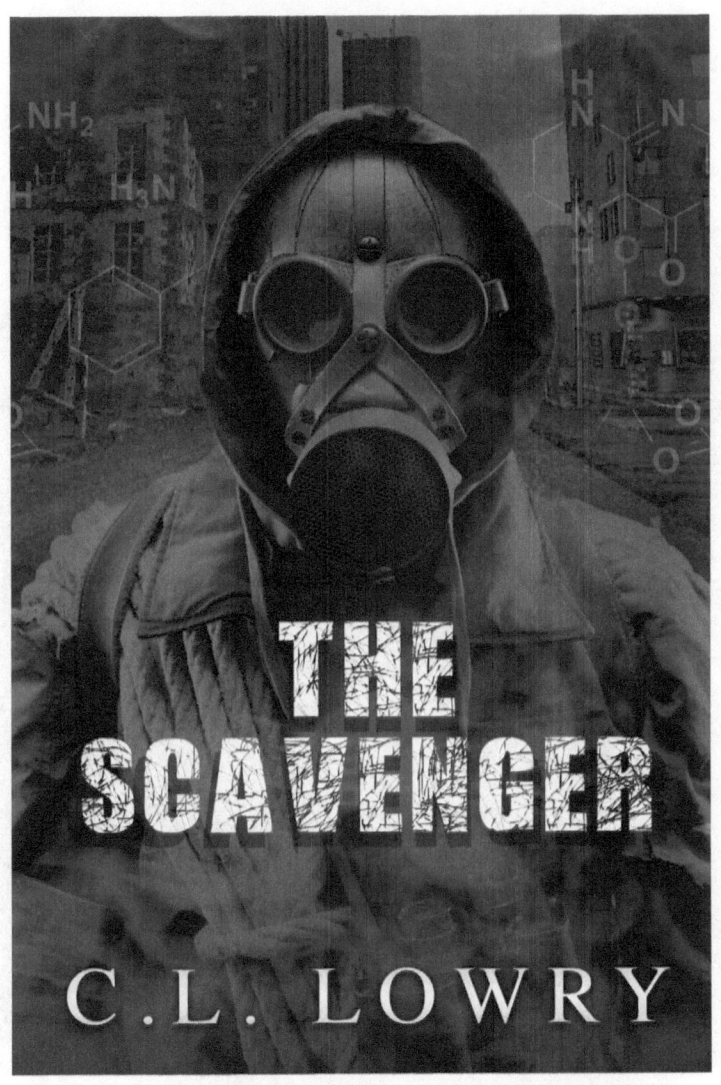

THE SCAVENGER

C.L. LOWRY

THE FIRST BOOK IN THE SERIES

AVAILABLE NOW!!!

Genre: Crime Anthology

AVAILABLE NOW!!!

Genre: Street Lit - Urban Fiction

COMING SOON...

C.L. LOWRY

THE
GUILTY
VERDICT

Genre: Crime Mystery

COMING SOON...

BULLET HOLES & *Broken* HEARTS!

CRIME SCENE DO NOT CROSS

C.L. LOWRY

Genre: Urban Fiction

COMING SOON...

DEAD GIRL

C. L. LOWRY

Genre: Crime Mystery

COMING SOON...

Hollywood

C.L. Lowry

Genre: Crime Mystery

BONUS

CHAPTER

Heavy rain poured on the roof of the gas station. Bolts of lightning lit up the night sky. Small beams of light shine into the abandoned business. Suddenly, the front door swung open and in walked two men, that wanted to escape the storm.

"I'm fuckin' soaked," one of the men announced as he shook off his soaked jacket. He was a heavy-set guy with a thick beard and a balding head. He was the typical hunting type that was draped in camo gear from head to toe. A hunting rifle was slung over his back. "Let's see what we can find in here."

"It probably won't be much. This place looks a mess."

His partner was almost as big as him, carrying around a little over 260 pounds on his six-foot frame. Their steps were heavy as they entered the store, checking their surroundings. Even though they were not in the woods on the hunt for deer or wild boar, their instincts never allowed them to put their guard down. The utilized small flashlight to illuminate the dark building. They were on a mission to find fuel and supplies.

"There has to be a way to cut on the gas out there."

"Cut on the gas? There's a tanker on top of the pumps. Even if we can turn the gas on, how the hell are we going to get to the pumps?"

"We'll find a way. If that doesn't work, we'll just see what we can get out of the tanker. Either way, we are going to leave here with something."

"I wish the keys were in the tanker. We could just bring the whole thing back to those idiots, and they'd be forced to give us all the food and guns they have stocked up in exchange for the fuel."

"I can't believe we drove all the way up here, from South Philly for this bullshit. Why the hell did they need us to come to the Northeast anyway? We could have gone over to Southwest or even downtown to get fuel."

"Hell no. Going over to Southwest would have been a suicide mission. I heard that the people over there will kill you on the spot. They don't let anyone go into that part of the city."

"That's every part of the city these days."

"Not up here. It seems to be nice and safe up these parts. We have yet to see another soul out here."

"Whatever. Let's just get what we need and get out of here."

"Go check the back for some more gas cans, and I'll see if I can work my magic behind the counter and get the pumps turned on."

The large man walked toward the counter as his partner headed to the back. "What the hell is this?" he asked himself, spotting the tarp that was spread across the counter. He immediately noticed what appeared to be hair and blood on the tarp. "Hey, Jimmy. There's something weird out here," he yelled.

"What is it?" his partner responded from a distance.

The man picked up a chunk of the hair that was covered in blood and examined it. "I think it's blood."

"What's weird about that?" The voice seemed to be getting further into the back office. Loud crashes of items hitting the floor could also be heard as the man continued his search for gas cans.

"The blood isn't red, it's black." He continued examining the hair, trying to piece it all together in his head. In all of his years of hunting, he had not seen an animal that had black blood. On top of that, the hair seemed to be human hair. "Ain't that a little weird, Jimmy?" he yelled out. He put the hair back on the tarp and walked behind the counter, looking for the control panel to activate the gas pumps. The gas station's interior had a rancid odor coming from it, which made the man frown his face. The odor fell somewhere in between rotten food and a decaying corpse. Behind the counter, the smell seemed to become more pungent. The register screens behind the counter were all deactivated. There was no power to the building, so another obstacle was placed in front of the men, making it more challenging to complete their mission.

Besides the inability to power to control modules, the smell was still getting to him. He looked down and found the source of the horrible odor. A puddle of black blood had pooled behind the counter, from the tarp. Black blood was still on his fingers, which he raised to his nose. The man took one whiff and stepped back. He quickly wiped his fingers on his pants after confirming the horrid smell was coming from the blood. "Jimmy, this blood smells like shit." He continued wiping off his fingers. "Jimmy?!" He yelled out his partner's name again after no response. "Jimmy, you okay?"

The man slowly walked over toward the door to the back office. There was still silence coming from the area. It was odd. A few minutes prior, Jimmy was just back there making all the noise in the world, and now there was nothing.

"Jimmy, you back there?"

Still, with no response, he became concerned. The rain picked up and viciously beat on the roof of the gas station. The strong winds blew off the broken signs that dangled in the front parking lot. He grabbed his rifle from the sling and aimed it into the darkness. "Jimmy, you got five seconds to let me know that you're okay or I'm going to start shooting." He took another step forward and rested his finger on the trigger. "Five..four...three...two...o – "

Just as he began pressing on the trigger, an empty can rolled toward him. More movement came from the darkness, followed up a low groan. "Jimmy, is that you?"

The man spotted the feet first as Jimmy emerged from the back room. He continued groaning and had his right hand pressed against the side of his neck. "What the hell is wrong with you?" the man asked as he watched Jimmy stumble into one of the shelves.

"Help me," Jimmy whispered, barely able to get the words out. His head bounced off the hard surface as he passed out and struck the floor.

"Jimmy, get up." His partner kneeled and rolled Jimmy over. His mouth dropped when he spotted a deep bite mark on the side of Jimmy's neck. The wound was deep, but it was something else that shocked the man. It was the blood that dripped from the wound. The blood was black. He raised his rifle and aimed it into the back room. *Whatever attacked Jimmy is still back there*, he thought. The growl that came from the room confirmed his thought.

A face slowly emerged from the darkness of the back room. The hefty man turned pale and began shaking. He fired a shot from his hunting rifle, but the creature swiftly dipped back into the darkness. The man blindly fired a flurry of shots, not knowing if his first shot had struck the creature. "I gotta get the fuck out of here," he mumbled under his breath before grabbing Jimmy by the collar and pulling him toward the door.

Another growl came from the back room. The man let go of his grip on Jimmy's collar and lifted his rifle. Another shot exited the long gun. "Come on out, motherfucker. I'm going to blow your brains out," he yelled, sending another shot into the dark abyss.

A deep growl caught the man's attention. However, the growl came from behind him and not from the back room. The man slowly turned around. His eyes locked onto Jimmy, who was now standing and blocking the front doorway. Black blood still dripped from the bite wound. Jimmy's eyes began turning colors. The whites of his eyes had now turned black. "Jimmy, you okay?"

Jimmy continued growling. The man looked at his friend, who was mutating right before his eyes. He never saw anything like this. He hunted the original beasts when the mutations first occurred, but this was a completely different experience. "Jimmy, don't let this shit take over your mind. If you're still in there, fight it."

The man's pleas fell on deaf ears. Jimmy growled at him and began advancing. The man raised his hunting rifle and took a shot, quickly dropping the mutation. Just as quickly as the fear set in, it was gone. Once again, his instincts took over, allowing him to pull the trigger on the only man he ever trusted. "Rest well, my friend," he whispered before stepping over the body and making a run for the older model Dodge 2500 that was parked in front of the gas station.

The rain seemed to be coming down even harder. He jumped into the truck and placed the rifle on the passenger seat. "Fuck," he blurted out, remembering that Jimmy was the one that drove to the gas station. Pulling down the sun visor and opening the center console, the man searched for the keys to the truck. He looked over at the gas station, but the beating rain made it difficult to see. *The keys are probably in his fuckin pockets.* "Damn you, Jimmy."

The driver's door of the truck opened, and the occupant stepped out into a puddle. He darted back into the store and headed straight to Jimmy. *These keys have to be in here*, he thought, as he dug through each of Jimmy's pants pockets. As he was looking through the pockets, the pungent odor returned. This time, the odor was more robust than before.

A growl traveled in his ears. It was a familiar sound. It was the same growl that came from the creature in the darkness. A thick, black liquid began to drip onto Jimmy's pants. He still could not locate the keys but looked up once he spotted the thick liquid running down Jimmy's pants. He gradually lifted his head as the warm and smelly air hit his face. He was now staring into the eyes of the creature from the darkness. Once a disabled young man named Tyler was now a hideous creature that was thirsty for blood.

Before the man could move, the creature pounced on him. It sunk its teeth into the man's neck, causing him to scream out in pain. His neck felt like it was on fire as the beast remained locked on his bite. It felt like fire was flowing through his veins. Finally, the creature pulled away, taking a chunk of the man's neck with him. The man tried crawling back toward the truck, but his body was too heavy. He could not pull the weight. Getting to the truck was the only thing on his mind but he would not be able to make it to the vehicle. The fire inside of his veins took over. It felt like he was going to burn alive. The cool breeze that was blowing through the broken windows did nothing to bring his temperature down.

The man felt his chest began to tighten, and his head began to pound. The pain was agonizing. A violent cough escaped the man's mouth, along with another one. He held his hand up to his mouth. He coughed again. A mixture of blood and saliva had escaped during the coughs. The man's eyes drifted onto the blood that he coughed up. His stomach turned. The blood was not red; it was black.

He crawled toward the counter, climbing over the debris that blocked his path. His body still felt like an inferno. Inch by inch, he continued crawling as pain shot through his entire body. The cluttered path in front of him began to blur, and everything around him began spinning. Even through all of the suffering, he continued crawling until the top of his head bumped the counter. With his last bit of strength, he reached to pull himself up. The nails of his claw dug into the counter.

ABOUT THE AUTHOR

C.L. Lowry is an award-winning author and filmmaker. Although he prides himself as being a prolific crime novelist, his pen game is versatile and allows him to navigate through multiple genres. Lowry was born and raised in Philadelphia, Pennsylvania but his family roots trace back to the beautiful island of Barbados, West Indies. Lowry uses his life experiences and creativity to demand his readers' attention with realistic scenarios throughout his stories.

When he isn't penning a page-turning novel, Lowry is behind the camera creating high-quality films under his production company, Black Lens Cinema. Lowry is also the host of the Fiction Addiction Podcast, where he interviews authors, filmmakers, and other creatives. Sign up for Lowry's spam-free newsletter to learn more about future releases, sneak peeks, special offers, and bonus content. Subscribers will also receive access to exclusive giveaways. To sign up, visit his website at **www.authorcllowry.com**.

CREEDOM PUBLISHING COMPANY

Creedom Publishing is a fully incorporated publishing company. Much like our slogan "The Home of Creative Freedom," we are committed to providing new and upcoming authors with the resources and opportunity to share their creativity with the world.

Creedom Book Services is the parent company to Creedom Publishing Company. Under our publishing company, we provide quality books for readers of all ages. Whether it's the eye-catching childrens book series for young readers or the page-turning crime thrillers by award-winning author C.L. Lowry, every book under Creedom Publishing Company is worthy of being added to your library.

Our books are available for purchase on our site and eBooks are available through Amazon Kindle.

CONTACT THE CREEDOM PUBLISHING COMPANY AT:

CREEDOMPUBLISHING@OUTLOOK.COM